The Illumination of
Emma Peters

The Illumination of Emma Peters

Brian Metcalfe

Inglewood
PRESS

Copyright © Brian Metcalfe, 2020

Cover design by Samantha Chin
Book design by Alex Bolduc

ISBN 978-1-9992597-3-0

This is a work of fiction.
Names, characters, places and incidents either are the product of the author's imagination or are used fictionally, and any resemblance to actual persons, living or dead, business establishments, events or locales is entirely coincidental.

All rights reserved. No part of this book may be reproduced,
stored in a retrieval system or transmitted in any form or by any means
without the prior written permission of the copyright owner.

INGLEWOOD PRESS
180 Bloor Street West, Suite 1200
Toronto M5S 2V6, Canada
www.inglewoodpress.ca

Prologue

After days of wavering between yes and no, Emma Peters decided that she would attend the opening night of *Romeo and Juliet*. She did not tell any of her friends that she was coming. She found a seat much higher than her usual subscription seat, on an aisle. She wanted to be away from people she knew, on the aisle so she could leave any time during the performance if she had to. She arrived five minutes before the curtain rose, wearing a simple black dress.

She sat and watched the men and women taking their seats below. The orchestra players were tuning and practising their riffs. She could barely see, she was so fearful of what she was about to watch. She felt a sudden urge to leave before the curtain rose — there was still time — but she could not. She reached into her handbag for painkillers; her head was already throbbing. The conductor entered the pit and bowed to the applause. The lights dimmed and Prokofiev's overture began; the rich, sweeping chords sounded harsh in her ears. The curtain rose and her fists tightened.

Romeo appeared in the first scene, leading the young Montagues in a fight against the Capulets in the town square. Stefan was superb. He took her breath away — his strength and virility dominated the stage. Juliet appeared in the second scene, chatting playfully with her nurse. Emma trained her opera glasses on Tatyana and was amazed; the dancer looked like a pretty teenage girl. Makeup, she muttered to herself, and lowered her glasses. In the third scene, when the masked Romeo slipped into the Capulet ball, saw Juliet and fell in love, Emma took another painkiller. The last scene of the first act began. Juliet re-emerged on her balcony and gazed at the moon, dreaming of Romeo. Emma studied her face and saw, through her glasses, the rapture of first love. Look at her, she thought. She really is a little girl.

Romeo entered. He leapt around the stage in delirious joy and then stared up at Juliet in wonder. Look at him, she thought. Foolish for her.

Emma sat transfixed as Juliet descended the balcony stairs to Romeo, who waited for her, his arm outstretched. And, as Juliet drew nearer, Emma saw the elegant curve of her body, and the beauty of her features.

She is young and beautiful, she admitted to herself. She *is* Juliet.

As Juliet approached Romeo, her steps and movements at one with the music and the love in her eyes, Emma was riveted. She leaned forward in her seat, her gaze on the stage, where Romeo — not Stefan, but Romeo — was waiting for Juliet. And when Romeo threw his body into a magnificent male mating dance, circling the stage with stunning leaps and spins at one with the music, she watched his legs, his buttocks, his arms and his noble face in awe. The music entered Emma; it sang in her bloodstream. She was both male and female, she was in the dance and the dance was in her — in her muscles, in her nerves and in her heart. And when they embraced and kissed, Emma knew that it was right, and felt joy. When Juliet, committed in love, ascended to her balcony, leaving Romeo below, also committed in love, his arm outstretched, Emma sat in her seat, enchanted.

By the end of the ballet she understood, as the applause mounted, that what she had seen was a perfection that could never exist except on the stage. Although its beauty had overwhelmed her, she understood it had nothing to do with her. By the time the scene ended, her anger and hatred had been washed away.

She left the auditorium barely able to find her way. Her head was spinning and her eyes were dim with tears. Emma had found in the brief hours of the ballet a place of music, beauty and love that would never leave her. She hurried through the lobby and into the night, avoiding her friends. She stood on the sidewalk, waving for a cab, feeling whole and purified.

BOOK ONE

Chapter 1

Emma Peters first became aware of the dancer, Stefan Grigoriev, when he was twenty-one. The very good-looking young man seemed to dance well, but she had no experience with ballet and a limited and mixed history with men. At the time she could not foresee that the impression he made would change her life.

She had grown up on her parents' farm near Isherton, a small town in the tobacco-and-corn-farm belt several hundred kilometers to the southwest. The couple were hard-working Presbyterians, committed to their crops and Knox Presbyterian Church on Main Street, Isherton. Emma worked on the farm as soon as she was old enough, feeding the chickens, weeding the vegetable garden and eventually milking the cows. She came to find pleasure in this work, and by the time she was sixteen she understood the value of things, the going price for their wheat and canola and the cost of their farm's seed, fertilizer and so on.

Isherton society at that time was imbued with a strict puritanism. Emma received instruction in sexual ethics at the age of twelve during her confirmation class in the basement of Knox Presbyterian. "The body is the temple of the Lord," the pastor would say, as he urged his young charges to avoid touching, to always remember that sex was God's gift for reproduction only and not for their pleasure, and that sexual relations outside Christian marriage was a sin. Her parents expected that she would find a young man in the community to marry, and settle down to farming.

However, at the age of fifteen Emma became aware of a boy in her class: Neil, a farmer's son, was tall and a good athlete. He played hockey for the school and was a miler on the track team. He had sandy hair and blue eyes and he carried himself with a mixture of strength and gentleness that she liked. She contrived ways to talk to him whenever she could. She could tell he liked her, but they both understood that a more serious friendship was not possible. For the first time, Emma began to evaluate Isherton's fundamental puritanism.

Later on, when she considered her adolescence, Emma understood that she had been formed primarily by the work ethic of her farming family and the strict Presbyterian values of her small town. She developed a passion for reading at this time. She loved to read histories and particularly historical biographies. She devoured descriptions of wars, revolutions, assassinations and love affairs, absorbing the richness and complexity of life in the world beyond her town. Although her parents were not aware of this aspect of Emma's development, they did understand that she had abilities beyond what were needed for farming. This became obvious in her final years at high school when she stood first in her class each year and was chosen to be valedictorian for her graduation. They decided that she could go to university provided she win a scholarship, which she did.

And she did well academically in her undergraduate years at the University of Toronto, obtaining first-class honours each year. She was popular with girls and her beauty attracted the attention of the boys. She was tall — perhaps five foot ten — and her figure was elegant. Copper-coloured hair fell over her shoulders, her eyes were blue-grey and her nose thin and delicate over full lips. She dated, but carefully. She was still influenced by Knox Presbyterian. Neil became a memory; he had gone to agricultural college and planned eventually to take over his family's farm.

During her fourth year she met George Peters, a young lawyer with Eberhart Williams, a prominent Toronto firm. George wooed her with dinners and theatre tickets, and she was flattered. In his late thirties, with family money behind him, he seemed the right man for the dutiful wife Emma intended to become. She graduated on the honour list, and in the same year, married George. The birth of her first daughter, Carolyn, came soon after, followed by Anne two years later. By this time, George had been promoted to junior partner in his firm, and Emma had committed herself happily to the roles of supportive wife and loving mother.

George left both his marriage and his firm shortly after Anne's first birthday. The birth of his second child precipitated a change in him. He began to come home late, to drink heavily and to take little interest in the children. He started to mock Emma's fidelity and modesty. She was shocked, but didn't know how to respond to him, so she soldiered on. George filed for divorce and shortly afterwards resigned his partnership and moved to Jamaica where he set up housekeeping with a local eighteen-year-old. Mystified and confused by the divorce, which was outside anything she had experienced, Emma was deflated and passively accepted her new isutation. George had offered her generous support, including enough money to buy a smaller house for herself and the two girls.

At this point, totally at a loss, Emma fell back on the only remedy she could think of: she got down to work. She applied and was accepted into law school and, with the help of a nanny that her support afforded her, she spent four difficult years studying and raising her girls. Carolyn was seven and Anne, five.

The collapse of her marriage shattered her idea of herself as the faithful Presbyterian wife. The demands of raising her daughters and her career meant that Emma had no time or energy to develop other interests. Moreover, she had no room in her life for a relationship while her daughters were young.

Soon after Anne left home for university, however, Emma began an affair with Ryan Connell, a married partner, and her boss at Eberhart Williams. She liked sex and no longer believed that she had to be married to enjoy it or worried about the commandment against adultery. Her work ethic remained, as well as her respect for money and a reluctance to spend it casually. At the time she encountered Stefan Grigoriev, Carolyn was twenty-four, married to Frank Thomas, and had a three-year-old son, Joshua; Anne was twenty-two, beginning a PhD program in the economics of urban planning at the Dalhousie

University. Emma believed she had now completed her job with the girls.

Her friends rarely saw her with a male companion. Other than her best friend, Julie Fredericks, they knew nothing of Ryan Connell. Her dates with Connell often turned into overnights at her house, a Victorian, red-brick semi in the nineteenth-century heart of the city. She knew that he was married and that he saw other women. She didn't mind the promiscuity and she ignored the strictures against intimacy within Eberhart Williams, an absolute in the currently-accepted corporate culture. The adultery, she thought, was his problem. For Emma, these nights were as necessary for her psychic well-being as her workouts at the gym and were similarly contractual. She believed that love was out of the question at this stage in her life and that sex was a commodity, a question of supply and demand. She worked seven days a week, from early in the morning for at least twelve hours, for most of the year. There would be occasional weekends off and two weeks in July at her cottage on Bear Lake, a three-hour drive north from the city. Once a year she would leave her girls with their nanny and fly to London or Paris for a week of theatre, galleries and shopping.

Chapter 2

Emma's entry into the world of ballet happened gradually, almost by accident. Her friend, Julie, was a member of Ballet Toronto's board of directors and had been trying for years to get Emma involved with the company. An extroverted, cheerful, forty-five-year-old mother of a teenage boy, Julie's connections in the financial world — her husband, Vernon, was a successful stockbroker — and her bubbly, outgoing style made her a natural choice to be the board's leader in its fundraising program. Although Julie was a close friend, she could annoy Emma. She liked to advise her in the style of a slightly smug older sister. She would mention her concern for Emma's love life, and she made it clear that Vernon was doing very well in the markets and would be happy to advise her. Julie kept mentioning what a perfect fit the ballet would be for her; Emma would make an ideal member of the board of directors, Julie kept saying.

Every year the pitch began the same way. Julie would invite Emma to a demonstration class of student dancers at the company's ballet school, followed by a lunch in the school's boardroom. "When I say you belong on our board, I know you think we're after your money," she would say. "Of course, you're not wrong, but that doesn't mean you're right. You work too hard. You need something like ballet in your life. This is what money is for, and ballet would give you more than a trip to Paris. Start with the ballet school lunch. There will only be fifteen or so women, the kids are fabulous, and the lunch is always good." And every year Emma refused.

She had no intention of sitting on anyone's board and she had no interest in becoming a donor. She was a value-for-money woman, used to fending off approaches from worthy causes. In her mind there was a market value for ballet and the other arts just as there was for vacant land or iron ore. Show me results, she would say, and I might show you some money. Financial statements were important to her in evaluating applicants. The ballet lunch was a first step the cautious Emma would not take.

Then came the crash of 2012. The collapse of numerous banks in South America and Eastern Europe set off a panic in world markets, which created legal problems for a certain number of Emma's corporate clients. Their brokers had not executed all the sell orders, they had over-anticipated recoveries with inappropriate trades, and so on. There were accusations of incompetence and even fraud. Her boss and occasional date, Ryan Connell, was tense and demanding during this period, overseeing her work needlessly, terrified of losing a client. Connell was the head of the corporate commercial section of her firm, a good-looking man with a quick temper. She became frustrated with Connell and refused to see him after hours, which increased his tension. For several weeks she worked almost around the clock, consoling, explaining and, in some cases, filing lawsuits. She slept very little, often on a couch in her office, and lived on deli sandwiches and diet pop; she became bitchy to her staff.

One day she fled her office for lunch with Julie. Emma requested that they meet in a bistro near the lake, away from the financial core.

"It feels like I'm shovelling shit in a chicken coop," she confessed, after her first sip of chardonnay. "And there is an endless number of chickens. Ryan has become impossible. I guess he's the rooster."

Julie laughed. Emma went on describing the pressures she was under. Julie listened, nodding, and then extended once again an invitation to the ballet school, for the last time, she said. Emma asked questions, hummed and hawed, and finally said she'd think about it. When they left, Emma had already put the invitation out of her mind.

*

"We need you, Emma."

Julie phoned her one Monday morning a week later in early May, she said on ballet business. It would not be her usual sales pitch but a request for a favour on behalf of Ballet Toronto. They needed an objective third party, probably a lawyer, to deal with a problematic director on the company's behalf. Would she consider helping out on a volunteer basis? Emma complained about the volunteer aspect. She had little interest in pro bono work — you get what you pay for, she had always believed. But Julie waited her out. Emma agreed.

I'm doing this for Julie, she thought. And it will be sweet to get out of the office.

"Fabulous," exclaimed Julie. "You'll be discussing this with Alec Runciman, our artistic director. I know he's free at two tomorrow."

*

Alexander Runciman, now in his fifties, had danced successfully as a young man with European ballet companies in London, Hamburg and Paris. At five to two the next day, May 12th, Emma's cab dropped her at the company's administrative offices in a converted factory on Lake Street near the harbour. The receptionist escorted her to the director's office, along halls with hung photos of dancers from the company's past. In the office, the director's assistant, Dora Lassinger, a comfortable-looking, middle-aged woman with a warm smile, ushered her into Runciman's office without a wait. The punctuality pleased Emma; she believed in operating on schedule. Runciman rose and walked from behind his desk to shake her hand.

"So good of you to help us, Emma. We are all enormously grateful."

His voice was a soft, mid-Atlantic drawl and his smile was warm. He had the slender, fit build of a dancer. His grey hair was tied in a ponytail, his eyes were blue, his face slim with bushy eyebrows and a firm, thin-lipped mouth. He was unlike the lawyers and accountants she usually dealt with; his quiet elegance pleased her. As he escorted her to an armchair facing his desk, she surveyed the office quickly: portraits of dancers — male and female — on the walls, a potted palm in one corner and a small bronze statue of a male dancer lifting his ballerina in the other corner. Behind his desk was a television screen with the necessary disc player and other equipment, and shelves of discs and books.

This is incredibly good, she thought. Civilized.

They exchanged introductions and brief summaries. She explained her commercial work and her familiarity with boards of directors and confessed to her ignorance of ballet. He sympathized and briefly outlined his five years as artistic director. He told her that the company had built a good repertory with a talented body of dancers and was gaining a reputation internationally. He then paused, touched the fingertips of each hand together, and frowned.

"And now to business. Julie tells me that I may rely on your absolute discretion in this matter. Of course, that goes without saying. And your reputation for competence is known to some of our directors, I am happy to say. I have contacted several lawyers myself, with no success. They either had conflicts or they knew nothing about our company and did not want to get involved, so thank you. And your inexperience with our ballet world may be an asset. Our problem is not an artistic one, it is a situation in which one of our directors who is a substantial donor is pressuring us to hire his sister, who is a dancer."

"He has a conflict of interest, obviously," she said.

"Yes, he does. However, the sordid reality is complicated. The man is a thirty-five-year-old, high-tech billionaire. His name is Bill Shrubb and his company is Algorhythmics, Inc. Have you heard of them?" She shook her head. "Good. No conflict there. Last year he donated one million in cash and some shares in his company. And further, he allowed us to recruit Tatyana Vasilievskaya last year when she decided to leave Russia. She was the Bolshoi's prima ballerina, a fine dancer, and everybody wanted her: New York, Paris, everybody. But Bill enabled us to make her an offer she couldn't refuse, and we got her. So, you may understand why I haven't done what I probably should have done."

"I do. You need his support."

He sighed. "Emma, I sometimes long for my dancing days. The only support I worried about then was keeping my ballerina in the air. But now, we need his money. We could survive without it, but our dreams and ambitions would have to be cut back drastically. So, here is where you can help. I am prepared to tell him no if I have to, and accept the consequences. But I would far rather have someone else explain my position first and see if there is any way we can resolve the problem without a rupture."

"Do you want me to negotiate if I sense an opening?"

"Possibly, if it means we can forget about his sister. You would of course check with me about anything like that. Remember, you'll will be dealing with a brilliant man. He tells me that he intends to create a software program — if you can believe it — that will produce hologram ballets. The dancers would be holograms that would perform complete ballets. No humans, only technology."

"Is that possible?"

"I have no idea. There's one other difficulty in the situation." He looked at her with a world-weary smile. "There are rumours that Bill and Tatyana are an item."

"That doesn't alter his conflict. In fact, it might even help you in the end, if the relationship strengthens his bond with the company."

"You may be right. I hadn't thought of that." He threw up his arms. "God, Emma, there is nothing more insane than leading a group of talented dancers with the usual human frailties but with very few ties to common sense."

"I sympathize. Let me see what I can do."

"Wonderful. And by the way, call him Bill, never William. For some reason he dislikes William; he has Bill on his birth certificate."

"Okay."

Chapter 3

She returned to her office on the fiftieth floor of the Empire Insurance building. Her window looked east to a pleasantly green area of the city. She sat staring at the green and musing over her meeting with Runciman. The director had been straightforward; but, given his career in ballet, he had also instinctively put on a performance for her. The elegance of his dress and person and the soft lilt of his voice were all part of his presentation. And his confession about the burdens of running a ballet company was genuine, but also part of the performance. It was designed to attract her sympathy, and it succeeded. She looked forward to working with him.

An hour or so later Ryan Connell stormed into her office to tell her that her assistant, Beverley, had sent him a file with many errors in the brief, and there were missing support documents; he had wasted several hours working with Beverley to put the file right. As he ranted, Emma looked him over appraisingly. Connell was an Irishman with dark hair, blue eyes and the lilt of the Black Gaels in his speech. He was attractive and had a sense of humour when he was not upset. Although his promiscuity didn't bother Emma, his temper did. And on this day panic had set in. When she explained that Beverley had been behaving erratically recently but was seven months pregnant and needed sympathy, Connell yelled something about not running a support group for pregnant women. He called her incompetent and left, slamming the door. Emma sat still, outraged, and then smiled.

"Goodbye Mr. Connell, hello Mr. Shrubb," she muttered.

She called the number Runciman had given her.

"Yeah? Bill Shrubb here." The voice was rushed and youthful. She explained her call. "No shit, a lawyer. What d'you want, lawyer?" She mentioned his intervention for his sister. "Yeah, yeah, so they needed a lawyer. You suing me, or are we just talking?"

"We need to understand…"

"Yeah, just talk. We're at 220 Colby Lane. Got it? Three tomorrow."

Chapter 4

Colby Lane was a narrow street with warehouses and small factories on both sides that had been converted to residential and small-business uses. Emma noticed a Che Guevara banner hanging out a window with a broken pane. The cab let her off at 220, a two-storey cinder-block building with a sign reading "Irving's Kosher Chickens" over the door. She stood wondering, then pressed the button on the intercom screen. When she identified herself and confirmed that she was standing at the door of Algorhythmics, Inc., the door clicked and she entered. She stood in a lobby that reached two storeys high. The second storey-level windows on two sides let in the natural light. To the left and right on the first level were halls that seemed to be storage areas and small offices.

"Emma, come up the stairs in front of you to the second floor, turn right and walk to the first window you see on your left, and smile."

The voice was a woman's, soft and welcoming. It seemed to come out of the walls. On the second floor she walked to the first window and stood still. "You're not smiling," said the voice. Emma smiled.

A person wearing jeans and a tee-shirt in a garish, abstract design, his shampoo-shiny hair falling to his shoulders, rose from a red velvet-covered chair. He shook her hand. His face was scarred from teenage acne, his eyes were dark and shining and his grin was a mixture of amusement and defiance.

"Hey, Emma the lawyer, how you doin'?"

"Fine, thank you."

"You realize that was me giving instructions to you in that sexy woman's voice."

"No, I didn't."

"I could have given you the same words with any accent you want, or in any of the world's major languages. And I could have had a hologram in the lobby — male, female or whatever — lip-syncing the words. Did Runciman tell you about the hologram ballet?"

"He did mention it, yes."

"I'm just teasing him for now. We're not there yet. Anyone can do a static hologram, but we want to create holograms in motion. You see that group over there?" He pointed to two men and a woman hunched in front of a television screen. She nodded. "That's what they're working on. Imagine *Swan Lake* danced by holograms, with movements executed more perfectly than Nureyev, Baryshnikov or anyone you name could do, created by programmers."

"All this for ballet?"

"Hey, you understand. They don't have the money. We're looking at all kinds of markets: combat simulation in military training, stuff like that. Ballet's just fun." His eyes gleamed.

She turned and looked around the room. Everywhere young men and women were hunched over their keyboards and staring at their screens or standing beside their desks, scribbling numbers on chalkboards. Above each desk was a larger screen that showed the activity on the desktop screen; the large screens were visible from all over the room. The floor-to-ceiling windows extended around the room, which was the full second storey. The room was silent, except for the occasional murmuring or coughing.

"Pretty impressive, huh? You see some of the smartest people in the business in this room. They come from California, India, Russia, wherever, because they want to work here. Come sit."

He motioned her to a chair beside his.

"So, you're the lawyer," he said. "Not what I expected. Nice legs."

He was trying to rattle her. She refused to pull down her skirt.

"I know I have nice legs," she said without a smile. "What I don't know is why a bright young man like you would try to pressure the company into hiring your sister to dance with them against their judgement."

"Very good," he said. "You aren't going to take any shit from me. I like that. And you know you have nice legs. I like that too. If you got it, flaunt it, right?"

She stared at him, poker-faced.

"Listen, why don't you come and work for me. I could use a good legal mind who tells me things straight up. You'd make more in a month with me than you'd get in a year with your law firm. And you'd have more fun."

His smile was teasing.

"I couldn't possibly work here. I can't stand tee-shirts."

He laughed out loud. "Then you're not for me, Emma. I live in my tee-shirt."

"And it suits you, I'm sure," she retorted. "Mr. Shrubb, shall we get down to business?"

He nodded. There was no business to discuss, he said. When he saw that this disturbed her, he threw up his hands.

"It's not what you think. I'm not going to insist that they hire my sister. She can dance, but she doesn't have a ballerina's body. Too curvy and sexy. I had to make the pitch for her, cuz she's my sis. She's a tough sell in ballet, but she's gonna try Broadway. She's got a shot at it there."

Emma frowned. "Then why didn't you tell Alec that? Why did I have to come here?"

"Because I couldn't cave that easily. There had to be a fight. And I was bored and thought it would be fun to cross swords with Alec or somebody on the board with some brains. Then they send you and I get more than I bargained for, brains and beauty." Again, the teasing smile. "I wish you could get to like my tee-shirt."

On her way out, Emma opened the door to the street and jostled a woman who was pressing the intercom button. The woman jumped back and yelled at her in a language she took to be Russian. When Emma tried to apologize, the woman brushed past her into the lobby with a dismissive wave of her hand. Emma glimpsed a severe ballerina's coiffure, a violet scarf, tight jeans and shiny cavalry boots, traipsing up the stairs.

*

At four-thirty she reported to Runciman in his office. He escorted her to a chair and sat watching her with a curious smile, his eyes twinkling. She told him that Bill Shrubb had given up his attempt to have his sister join the company.

"Bravo," he said, beaming and clapping his hands. "I couldn't be more pleased. Aren't you wonderful."

His praise bothered her. She had decided not to tell him that Shrubb had never intended to press his sister's hire beyond a ritual ruffling of feathers. She told him of her encounter as she left Shrubb's building.

"Did the woman have her hair henna-red in a ballerina's coif, with shiny boots and a bitchy attitude?" he asked. When she nodded, he continued. "Then it was Vasilievskaya. She doesn't like people who get in her way." His expression softened. "I've been thinking that you would make a good board member, Emma. We don't have a lawyer on the board since Allan Richardson retired. But I don't think I'd be doing you a favour. Many long meetings and lots of opinions, and you're a busy person."

When she demurred, he added, "Nevertheless, you have given me great relief and done our company a splendid favour. I would like to have you around when I need someone to consult informally. Perhaps we could establish a way of doing that. Julie Fredericks tells me that you have resisted her attempts to get you involved, that you don't consider yourself a ballet person. Have you ever seen a ballet?"

"My mother brought me to see *The Nutcracker* at Christmas in Detroit when I was eight."

"Right. Well, let's see if we can change your relationship with the world of ballet. Next Wednesday we have invited a group of women who support us, including Julie, to watch a student rehearsal at our school, and then join us for lunch. I know you have refused Julie's invitations previously, but this time you really must accept. For one thing, it is our inadequate token of thanks for the service you have done us, and it would be churlish of you to refuse. Moreover, I will be at the lunch table and would take great pleasure in your company."

She felt her face blush scarlet as she accepted. He had made his invitation personal, even emotional, without a hint of flirtation.

He charmed me almost without me knowing it, she thought. He's good.

Chapter 5

Emma Peters joined twelve women in the board room of the ballet school at eleven on Wednesday morning. Julie greeted her with a hug and began to introduce her to the other women. Emma noticed the respect the other women showed Julie; she was clearly a person who mattered. Emma was introduced to two wives of clients whom she knew, and the others shook her hand and smiled. One woman was a kindergarten teacher, besides Emma the only employed person in the group. Emma circulated as they waited to be led to the ballet class, listening to chatter about children and grandchildren, renovations of houses, recent trips to various parts of the world, and shopping. This was a world she understood and could tolerate when her business required it. Soon she was wishing she was back in the office staring at her computer screen.

They were led to a balcony overlooking a dance rehearsal room with its polished hardwood floor, mirrors and practice barres along the sides. Windows near the ceiling on three sides flooded the space with natural light. There were groups of both boys and girls on the floor below. One group appeared to be as young as fourteen and another was made up of older students, seventeen to twenty-one. The ballet master, a man in his forties with slightly greying hair, was watching the junior girls perform; a woman with red hair accompanied them on a piano in a corner of the room. Emma smiled as the little girls, not yet women, danced en pointe, leaping, turning and pirouetting across the floor, under the scrutiny of the master. At one point he clapped his hands: the music stopped, and the girls turned attentively. He explained briefly, then nodded to the accompanist and demonstrated what he wanted from them in a series of leaps, turns and pirouettes.

"He's so graceful," Emma whispered to Julie. "How can a man his age move like that?"

"That's Brent Sokolovski. I saw him dance years ago, James in *La Sylphide* with the New York City Ballet. He must be over forty."

Emma nodded, unsure of what it meant to dance James in *La Sylphide*. The juniors retired and the senior girls began a more complicated series of steps. The ballet master stopped them, and demonstrated once again. "He's amazing," murmured Emma.

The girls retired and the senior boys stood in a group while Sokolovski explained what he wanted and demonstrated a series of leaps, landings and spins with which the boys would circle the room. The piano started and the boys danced. One boy fell. Emma noticed one dancer, a tall, dark-haired boy, circle the room with leaps that seemed to pause, high in the air, land softly and turn effortlessly into a spin, his arms over his head. He circled the room twice in a performance that seemed excellent to Emma. The ballet master came to the student after his second tour, put his arm around the boy's shoulder and spoke to him. The boy nodded and executed a series of the same leaps and spins, but this time with his head more erect and his arms in different positions. Sokolovski smiled and moved on to another boy.

"That young man looks fabulous, don't you think?" Emma asked.

"He's young, of course, but he is promising." Julie spoke with the in-the-know confidence of the ballet insider; her blasé drawl irritated Emma. "His name is Stefan Grigoriev," Julie continued. "I hear the company may hire him directly next year, rather than put him through the normal two-year apprentice program."

"What does that mean?"

"Usually each year they accept several students as apprentice dancers in the company. For two years they train with the company's dancers and they perform in the corps de ballet for productions when extras are needed. If they do well they may be hired full time. But Stefan is sensational, and they're afraid they'll lose him if they don't hire him directly."

"Where's he from?"

"He's Bulgarian."

Intrigued, Emma watched the boy as he stood by the piano, observing some of the girls working on their leaps in front of the ballet master. Stefan Grigoriev was six feet tall with slim hips, broad shoulders and the legs of a long-distance runner. He was dramatically handsome; his eyes and brows were dark, and his chin firm. His black hair hung to his shoulders. She saw him wave with a warm smile to one of the girls as she danced past.

"He's gorgeous," said Emma.

"Aren't you glad you came?"

Emma smiled as their guide motioned them to leave the balcony for their lunch. The director joined them in the boardroom, shaking hands and kissing cheeks; Emma noticed with admiration that Runciman left each woman smiling.

When he reached her, he paused. "Emma dear, I'm so glad you could come." He turned to the group. "Ladies, Emma Peters has done some good work for us on the legal side and made my life much easier. Thank you, Emma."

He applauded her, and the others joined in. Emma noticed the women looking at her with interest. God, he's good, she thought. The director sat and lunch was served — poached salmon with hollandaise, asparagus, wine, fruit salad and coffee. The conversation turned to comments on the rehearsal class, then to gossip and chatter. Emma felt exhilarated, flattered by Runciman, and inspired by the young dancers.

"I am impressed," she said to Julie, sitting beside her. "The hard work and discipline required of those kids, especially the young ones. That will stay with them for the rest of their lives."

"Yes, and they are learning a craft that is both physical and transformative." Julie smiled fondly at Emma. "I'm so glad you liked it. Why don't you subscribe next year? We'll get seats together."

Emma hesitated. "Listen, Jules, it's very sudden, so I want to go back to my day-to-day grind and think about it. But I am impressed, more than I expected."

"That's my Emma, one step at a time. But trust me, this will be good for you. There are things you can't put a price on."

"Perhaps. Just give me a while."

*

Emma had only been back at her desk a half an hour when Ryan Connell entered without knocking.

"Emma, I've been looking for you all morning. You turned your cell off. Where've you been?"

"Out," she said, resting her head on her clenched fist, her elbow on the table. "Was there anything special?"

He hesitated. He was trying to be sweet again.

"No ... er ... well, yes. We're having dinner tonight. That's special."

"Look, Ryan, I can't tonight. Things have happened and I'm just not up to it. I'm sorry. Rain cheque?"

His face flushed.

"What's come over you, Emma? This isn't like you."

"Nothing's come over me. I'm the same hardworking girl as ever, with clients to contact, so if you don't mind...."

Connell turned and left, slamming the door. She turned off her computer.

Another of his little tantrums, she thought. He bores me.

Her mood soon changed, reverting to the high spirits her morning at the ballet school had given her. She felt liberated. There was the charm of Alec Runciman, certainly, but there was more to it than that. She wondered about the two men who had caught her eye on the floor, the ballet master, Sokolovski, and the young Bulgarian dancer, whose name she could not remember. All the young dancers had moved her with their passion, discipline and the rhythm and harmony of their movements.

It's like farming: hard work and passion, she thought, and then laughed at the comparison.

She let her mind drift for several minutes, recalling her half hour on the school's balcony. Transformative was the word Julie had used to describe what she had seen. The concept of pricelessness had come to Emma and given her a new way of seeing and feeling.

Chapter 6

The next morning Emma arrived at her office close to ten. She had slept in, something she had not done for years. She strolled past reception with a relaxed smile and entered her office. She would phone Julie and tell her that she had decided to subscribe to the ballet for the coming season. However, her door opened without a knock and Don Elton, the firm's managing partner, walked in. Elton was a tall man, well over six feet, with greying blond hair and a ruddy complexion; he had a booming laugh and usually a twinkle in his eye. But this morning he stood looking at Emma with concern. She put the phone down.

"Sorry for startling you, but you need to know right away that Ryan Connell is no longer with the firm as of six o'clock last night."

She stared, dumbfounded.

"May I sit down?"

She nodded.

"The cause is sexual harassment. He kept asking one of his articling students for coffee and she kept refusing. He'd already crossed the line, but she didn't report it until yesterday when she walked into his office to submit a report she'd done for him. She found him watching porn on his laptop. That was it."

"What did he say?"

"He didn't deny anything, but he lost it with Archer Brown and me and started to rant. The firm is a puritanical oligarchy that denies its lawyers basic human rights, according to him. Every human being has the right to freedom of sexual expression, crap like that. Ryan has been brilliant for us, but last night he was silly, pathetic even. He turned sixty-seven last month. Maybe that's it." He looked at Emma. "Am I right in thinking you're not surprised?"

"I'm not."

"Did you have issues with him?"

"Nothing serious. I can take care of myself."

"Glad to hear it. At least you're not sorry to see him go."

She said nothing.

"Okay then, upward and onward. We have to replace Ryan as head of corporate commercial. The two obvious candidates were you and Donna di Carlo. Archer and I polled the partners and the consensus is Donna. Not that you're not as competent as she is. The decision was a purely business one. Her family owns mines all over the country: gold, nickel and diamonds, mostly. Some are already our clients and she can bring in more of them. You do understand?"

Emma smiled and nodded.

"I'm glad. Now Donna wants to talk to you. I'm leaving and I'll tell her to drop in."

Donna di Carlo entered and stood unsmiling and nervous in front of Emma's desk. Emma motioned her to sit. She started with an apology for her selection as head of their division. She emphasized Emma's length of experience, her administrative skills and reputation in the firm. Donna was in her thirties, not a superb lawyer but a hard worker. Her modesty and honesty had always impressed Emma.

"It's the mines," Donna said. "They want more of our family's business. And I can get if for them. I guess that's the way of the world."

"It is," said Emma. "And don't worry about me. We'll work well together. I'll enjoy not reporting to Ryan."

As soon as she heard the name mentioned, Donna put her hand to her mouth. "Isn't that awful. Chasing students, and now the porn. The man is married, and he behaves like that! And something else," Donna paused, frowning. "Now he's gone I can say this. He tried to get me to go out for a drink one night. He's very good looking and he knows how to charm you. I said no, of course."

"Good girl," said Emma. "He's hit on me once or twice."

"Wow, you too. Unbelievable. And get this, he phoned me this morning, all upset. He says his wife is going to divorce him. He told me he was a mess and needed someone to talk to. Someone with a heart, he said. I said no. Of all the nerve." She smiled. "D'you think he's a sex addict?"

"Could be. Or he's just an asshole."

Donna laughed, hugged Emma, and left. Five minutes later, Emma's cell buzzed. She saw on the screen the name Ryan Connell.

She hesitated, then answered.

"Good morning, Ryan. What can I do for you? I've heard your bad news."

He thanked her for taking his call. The arrogance, the Irish bluster, was gone from his voice. He assured her that what the partners were saying was highly exaggerated. He had been treated unfairly, without a chance to give his side of the story. He was ruined. His wife was going to divorce him. He was a mess, couldn't sleep. He needed someone to talk to, someone with a heart. Would she please...

She cut him off.

"Sorry, Ryan, I can't help you."

She hung up. He really is an asshole, she muttered.

She couldn't concentrate for the rest of the day; waves of emotion kept her head aching and her mind reeling. She played with her cellphone and stared out the window. Finally, she took the elevator to the café in the basement of the building, where she sat, sipping her coffee, watching the girls on break chatting and laughing. She wondered what she was doing, sitting there. What had happened that was so awful? Suddenly she pulled her phone from her purse and called. She told Julie she needed to talk. Julie asked only when and where. Emma never phoned her in the middle of the day.

The Conference Room was a bar at the top of her building, full of light from large windows surveying the city to the west, south and east. Julie was waiting when she entered. She rose, held her arms open and gave Emma a hug. Julie was like that, spontaneous and emotional, with a wide smile, her blue eyes shining and her blond hair curling in a modified afro.

"I've ordered your gin and tonic," she said. "Or is this a martini moment?"

"Martini, please," said Emma.

Julie signalled the waiter and changed the order. She then reached across the table and took Emma's hand.

"Okay, tell me," she said. "I knew from the tone of your voice that something was wrong. What happened?"

Emma described Don Elton's account of the firing of Ryan Connell. Her friend watched her carefully. The drinks arrived and they paused.

"This is better than television," Julie said. "No, scratch that. Bad joke."

As Emma described Connell's pursuit of the articling student, tears formed in her eyes, and when she mentioned the porn incident she began to sob. Julie reached again and held her hand. She snatched it back.

"Fuck, fuck, fuck. Why am I crying!" she exclaimed. "How pathetic can I get?"

"Why *are* you crying? I thought he was just entertainment for you. And a pain in the ass at work."

"True, true," said Emma. "Look, Jules, it's not that I'm sorry to see him go. It's just that I look at myself and wonder why I spent my time with such a total creep. What's wrong with me? What is it with me and men? Let's not forget George, the father of my children, now lying on a beach in Jamaica with his bimbo." She shook her head. "When George left me with the girls, I vowed I would never shed a tear, and I never did. I wanted the three of us to be happy and we mostly were, but look at me now."

She wiped her eyes. Julie's hand took hers again and held it.

"You're not pathetic. Choosing men is not a straightforward business these days. So, you messed up on the first two. You're a warm, brilliant and gorgeous woman. If you want a man, you'll get one."

"But do I want one? Carolyn thinks that I don't. She tells me I'm too independent to make the compromises you need to make in a relationship." She shrugged. "Maybe she's right. Although I think I could, if men weren't so difficult. The thing is, Carolyn found the right guy for her and it makes her a little smug. She enjoys judging her mum."

"Right. I'm glad I don't have girls. Boys are so simple." Her blue eyes sparkled as Emma's composure returned. "Emma, Alec thinks the world of you. He's so impressed with whatever you did for him. I bet he'll want you on the board."

"No, I don't think so. First of all, I didn't do that much, really. I just discovered that the problem he thought he had wasn't really a problem, and I told him that. He was relieved and grateful. Then he told me that he had thought of the board but decided that he would rather have me available as a kind of ad hoc consultant, someone he could discuss problems and ideas with informally. Over a drink."

"There, you see!" Julie signalled the waiter for a refill. "He wants you one-on-one, whatever that means. There aren't many women who impress Alec Runciman."

"If you're hinting that he may be gay, stop right there. I think we get on well, but the chemistry is not romantic. We'll be friends, I think, and at this stage I've come to believe that a good friend is more important than a lover."

Emma continued with her account of her meeting with Donna di Carlo and Ryan Connell's two phone calls appealing for help. Julie burst out laughing.

"The moron," she roared. "Even when his life is falling apart, he can't resist conning the girls. Part of his problem is that he is very good looking. Handsome men stop thinking, they're so sure the world will adore them." She grinned at Emma. "You're smiling again, Em. That makes me happy."

Chapter 7

That summer was different for Emma. The loss of Ryan Connell as a boss and a lover was a good thing, she was sure. As far as the sexual relationship was concerned, she was relieved that it was over, and appalled that she had put up with him for as long as she had. And Donna di Carlo was certainly easier to work for. However, the real evidence of change was the easing of her work ethic. She had always been a slave to her career, out of necessity after George left, but this summer the urgency seemed to have passed. She began to delegate tasks to assistants and even to students, whom she would never have trusted before even with unimportant work. She slept in when she felt like it, arrived at the office as late as ten and rarely stayed late. She spent more weekends at the cottage on Bear Lake, several times with Julie and her husband. She and Julie met one afternoon each week at Café Vert in Eastern Park. She would leave work at three and they would spend an hour or two drinking and chatting.

But the most surprising development for Emma during those months was her growing friendship with Alec Runciman. It had started as the consulting arrangement they had discussed. He would arrange a meeting in his office. He would tell her what was on his mind, she would respond with comments and suggestions that usually pleased him. Then after one such meeting, he mentioned that he was uneasy meeting her so often in his office. People would notice and make all sorts of inappropriate assumptions, he thought. When she suggested a café, he worried that it would also be too public.

"I wonder," he said, with an awkward smile, "if we could meet once in a while at my place. You understand, Emma, why I hesitate in suggesting this."

"I do understand," she said. "No need to worry, your place or mine if you like. My yard is very nice in the summer."

The next time he called her he suggested they meet at his condo. She took a cab to his low-rise building near Eastern Park. When she followed him into his flat, she chuckled as she looked around. The room and its décor were mostly as she had imagined. There was a fine view east over the park: green trees and sky. There were a few pictures of dancers on the walls, but none of him. The paintings he had hung were elegant, semi-abstract landscapes in limited palettes of only three or four colours. They reminded her of the way he dressed. She could see no evidence of anything personal, no pictures of family or friends. In one corner of the room was a baby grand piano with sheet music open above the keyboard. It's monastic, but in perfect taste, she thought. Like him.

He asked her to sit while he made them tea. She leafed through a book on his coffee table called *The Primitive Dance* and saw pictures representing wedding dances or military dances in ancient cultures. He returned, poured the tea and offered her digestive biscuits.

"I'm glad we can meet here," he said. "I knew you wouldn't … misinterpret the suggestion."

"We're beyond that, aren't we?" she said.

"Yes, dear Emma." He sighed and patted her hand. "We're beyond that now."

They chatted for a while. Then Alec said he wanted to hire a ballerina under contract with the Paris Opera Ballet. He had talked with her in Paris a month before and she had mentioned that her contract was coming up for renewal. He assumed that in mentioning this she was letting him know she was open to proposals. He wanted to hire her. Tatyana Vasilievskaya was so dominant, he wanted another superb ballerina in the company to balance her. He wanted to know how to proceed, given that the Paris Opera Ballet would be negotiating in good faith to keep her. What was his liability if he interfered with their negotiations? What would constitute interference? What would cause the dancer liability if she negotiated in bad faith? Emma told him that she knew the Canadian law in commercial situations, but hesitated to comment on French law, covering artists in opera, ballet and orchestras. She outlined Canadian law, assumed that French law would not be very different and offered to see if one of her firm's partners could give her better information. He declined. He planned to consult the company's lawyers, and he wanted from his discussion with her the lay of the land in general terms, so he would be better able to be discuss the situation.

"Is poaching a common problem in ballet?" she asked. "Julie told me that you worry that someone might steal Stefan Grigoriev away from you."

"Yes, indeed. That boy is very good and he knows it. If we make him apprentice for two years, he'll be gone. I know it. It's a jungle out there. So, I'm giving him a contract for the coming season." He rose to his feet. "Now, my dear, I'm going to be very rude, but I have no choice. I have a piano lesson in an hour and a half, and I absolutely must practise now. Would you mind terribly if I called a cab?"

She didn't mind. He gave her cheek a peck as she left, smiling. The meeting had been easy, and he soon phoned her for another. This time he would come to her house.

*

Emma was setting out an ice bucket, with a bottle of mineral water for him, a half-empty bottle of California chardonnay for her and a plate of biscuits on a table under a sun umbrella, when she heard a car pull into her driveway. Runciman was usually punctual to the minute and this car was ten minutes early. She paused to survey the yard with satisfaction. The blossoms were perfect. She walked through her house to greet him but before she reached her front door Carolyn walked in with three-year-old Joshua. She kissed Carolyn and picked Joshua up for a hug.

"We won't be long," said Carolyn. "Joshua had an appointment at the Children's Hospital regarding a lung problem. They're driving me crazy. Tests after tests and they don't give me an answer."

"That's a worry, darling," said Emma. "I've got a meeting in a few minutes, but it's casual. We'll talk later. Come outside; I'll get Josh some apple juice."

She sat the two of them at the patio table. Carolyn was tanned and looked beautiful, she thought. She had inherited Emma's copper hair but George's slight hawk-nose and dark eyes, masked this day by blue-reflecting, wrap-around shades. Carolyn sipped wine and Joshua drank his apple juice while Emma listened for a ring from the doorbell.

"You look tense, Mum," said Carolyn. "Who are you meeting?"

"Josh and his lung problem make me tense, not the meeting. The artistic director of the ballet, Alec Runciman, is coming. I consult to him from time to time."

The doorbell rang. Emma left the table and walked through the house. She opened the door and Runciman stood smiling, holding a bouquet of daisies.

"I couldn't resist these, Emma," he said. "A girl was selling them on the street outside my building and they looked the essence of summer. I hope you don't mind."

"Of course not. Why would I mind?"

She led him to the patio and introduced him. Immediately she noticed the question and the calculation in her daughter's eyes. Alec

Runciman admired the puppy dog image on Joshua's tee-shirt. He smiled at Carolyn, telling her he had been trying to find shades like hers. He's charmed Carolyn, Emma thought. She went to the kitchen, put the daisies in a vase with water, returned and set them on the table.

"Flowers, how thoughtful," said Carolyn with an ironic edge to her tone. "They make a business meeting so personal. Come Josh, we need to leave Grandma and Mr. Runciman to get down to business."

When Emma returned from seeing her family off to their car, Runciman was strolling around the cobblestoned yard examining the garden.

"The only thing I regret about living in my condo is that I can't garden. I used to live in a house on River Street and I had a fine garden there." He returned to the table. "I believe your daughter was making an assumption about our relationship. It seems the daisies got her thinking."

"That's Carolyn. She is married to a good man, a helicopter pilot would you believe, and thinks everyone should be happily married. She's been on my case for years."

"It never once occurred to me that you weren't single. You have a daughter?"

"Two daughters," Emma replied.

"Two daughters and a grandson. So, you must have had a man, or a husband, even."

She laughed and then explained her history with George. He shook his head.

"What was he thinking?"

"Sex, alcohol and poker mostly," she shrugged. "None of it with me."

He leaned back and stared at the house. After a minute he turned to her.

"It seems I know more about you now than you do about me. Generally, I like it that way, but I trust you. A few details. I was an only child and I loved it. I never understand when people pity an only child. I was by no means the centre of my parents' lives, but I had a nanny who adored me and it was wonderful. We moved around when I was young — New York, Paris, London — which was exciting. My father was a banker and mother was a dancer. These moves were part of their attempt to harmonize two very different careers. I'm not sure how well they got on. I didn't see them much, but I had my nanny. Mother did make sure I was trained in dance, first in Paris, then in London. I adored it, and dance became my life." He looked at her, pausing as if he were unsure. "I am not a romantic person, Emma. My parents' marriage did not inspire me. I had several relationships early on — with women, in case that matters — but they didn't work. Dance mattered more to me than those very nice girls. I found over the years that I didn't need what most people search for; I am comfortable on my own. So, here I am."

He sipped his mineral water and watched for her reaction.

"So here you are." She raised her wine glass to him. "Alec, look, I have come to believe that friends, in the long run, are more important than lovers."

"My dear, how perfect you are," he said. He reached across the table and squeezed her hand. "So, I don't have a legal problem this time. I want to talk about my decision to promote Stefan Grigoriev from school directly to the company's employ and let him skip the usual two-year apprenticeship. It's not a question of whether I do it or not. I'm doing it. It's more how I handle it within the company, managing the politics, minimizing bruised egos and, most importantly, making sure that Stefan himself behaves properly to those around him, given the mark of favour he will receive. I do have ideas of what to do but it helps me finalize them when I hear what they sound like. And I need your thoughts as well."

She nodded and he continued. He had considered the other graduating students who were being accepted as apprentices and also the current apprentices. They might feel they were being passed over as Stefan leapt by them. He had considered the company's dancers as a whole, and how they would receive Stefan as an equal. Then there was the question of Stefan himself. Was he mature enough at twenty-one to avoid developing an oversized ego? To each of these problems Alec had ideas, based on personal interviews in his office with various people and on social events involving Stefan in various ways. He particularly planned to have a serious talk with Stefan. Having been a young male dancer himself, he thought he knew how to approach the boy. Emma contributed suggestions occasionally, but mostly listened.

"I am being very careful about all of this," he said as he finished. "I believe that if people are upset in a situation like this, they don't dance well. That, I cannot have."

She reached to refill his mineral water, but he pushed the bottle away.

"Emma, I am sitting here with you on this glorious summer afternoon in your beautiful garden, and I am relieved after our talk. I do drink wine on occasion and this is an occasion. Pour me your chardonnay, if you please."

She poured him her chardonnay and they sat in the garden and chatted for at least an hour. He kissed her lightly on her cheek as he left the house.

*

Before bed she checked her email and found a message from Carolyn: Mum, way to go, he's perfect for you. A little artsy, but still he's nice. Even Josh was impressed. Not gay, I assume. I don't know why it took you so long, you still look great. Yeah! Love, C.

Chapter 8

Emma met Julie at one-forty-five on a Saturday in July, in the lobby of the university's music theatre, the city's venue for smaller opera and ballet performances. They had tickets for the matinée performance of *The Last Supper*, a ballet created by a twenty-year-old Danish choreographer to music composed by a twenty-three-year-old

Danish electronic composer and performed by students from a Copenhagen ballet school. A Danish invasion, Julie called it. Emma googled the piece. It was described as a powerful dance of destruction, a presentation of mechanized, technology-driven creatures consuming the bounty of the earth necessary for their survival. She immediately phoned Julie to say that she didn't think the piece was for her, especially since it would be the first ballet she had seen since *The Nutcracker* at age eight. Julie, however, prevailed; the ballet had been her idea. They needed to expose themselves to new art forms and new ideas. These young artists were the coming generation and they needed to understand what the kids were thinking if they were going to avoid petrification. Emma gave in, even as she doubted that her Carolyn, close in age to the composer, would want to be in the audience for *The Last Supper*.

The curtain opened to a dark stage with a pale yellow back-screen. On it were projected images of wilted trees and half-ruined urban skylines. The music began as a low, electronic hum. As it morphed into a series of beeps, dancers appeared dressed in black, without identifiable gender, their movements in spasmodic time to the beeps. Battery-driven devices were attached to their black costumes that flashed to create the impression of computer screens, or neon lights or burning fires. They twisted and turned chaotically until they formed a line facing the audience and mimed with hands and mouths the act of eating. Then a series of dancers crossed in front of them, their motions imitating the acts of crawling, creeping, swimming and galloping. Each electronic dancer grabbed a creature and consumed it in a ritualized duet, casting the victim corpse-like on the stage. The sound system blared out a screaming, cacophonic wail. When all the creatures had been consumed, the electronic dancers turned on one another. As they devoured each other, their flashing lights went dark. Eventually there were only two dancers left standing, and their costumes had been torn away to reveal that they were male and female. They approached one another and tried to dance, but their pas de deux disintegrated. They slowly, lethargically sank to the floor, to join the mass of lifeless dancers and their victims, as the electric beeps grew fainter and further apart, until the stage was silent.

The audience response was divided. Some jumped to their feet, clapping, stamping their feet and whooping. Others remained seated, did not clap, and left quickly. Emma and Julie remained seated, but they did clap politely.

"I couldn't get into it," said Emma as they left the theatre.

"I need a drink," said Julie. "Let's go to Café Vert."

They got a table by a stream that meandered through Eastern Park and formed a small pond as it approached the café. The afternoon was sunny, orange lilies grew on the farther shore of the pond and boys were tossing a frisbee on the grass to their south. They both ordered gin and tonics. By the time they took their first sips, Julie was smiling.

"My God, Julie, I was so glad when it ended," said Emma. "I should have stayed home."

"I don't think you should judge," said Julie in her authoritative tone. "We're seeing a new generation dance with a new world view. We have to be open."

"Come on, Julie. It was crap."

Julie frowned, sipped her drink, and broke into a belly laugh.

"Okay, honey, you win. It was terrible. It was juvenile and ugly. But you shouldn't have stayed home. You can't expect to like everything you see."

"I understand that, but I'm not sure I have a ballet gene. I don't really dance."

"So, the ballet was a bomb. Big deal. We're here, the park is beautiful, the gin is cold and there's no such thing as a ballet gene. What's the matter?"

Emma sighed. A dream two nights before had confused her, she told Julie. She was standing alone on a stage and she knew somehow that she was in a ballet. The audience was expecting her to dance, but she couldn't move. She wanted to run, but her legs were rigid. Suddenly a male dancer came to her from the side and took her in his arms. She began to dance. She looked at him and saw that it was

Ryan Connell. She woke up with a start, sweating and shaking. Since then she had been in a sour mood.

"So, don't tell me there's no ballet gene," she concluded. "I'm not cut out for it. But apparently I am cut out for the arms of Mr. Connell."

"That is a totally weird dream, my dear. I'm guessing it has more to do with your love life. You say you're happy that Ryan is gone, but you probably miss the sex and you don't know where you are any more. But don't for God's sake blame it on the ballet. You can't judge ballet by this *Last Supper* nonsense, nor by anything so bizarre as your dream. You've subscribed for the coming season. Wait 'til it's over and see what you think."

Emma nodded.

"You're right. I am looking forward to the season." She paused. "But I have more on my mind. Carolyn has emailed me twice and phoned three times. She has an excuse each time, but what she really wants to know is how the relationship she thinks I have with Alec is going. She can be so annoying."

"She wants something wonderful for you, that's all. She's still young enough to be romantic."

"I understand that, but think what it means. She feels sorry for me. To her I'm a loveless workaholic having no fun and getting old."

"You were never loveless, Emma. You gave everything you had for your girls, and that was love. You didn't have time for romance, so you settled for Ryan. When you knew you couldn't handle a serious relationship, Ryan filled in. Now you have made a friend in Alec, which is no small feat. He lets very few get close, so value him. And you're smart enough not to look to him for an affair. Which reminds me," she paused. "Alec is throwing a reception in the second week of September to welcome this season's new dancers. He does it every year. They will be Stefan Grigoriev and Shirley McIsaac who are skipping apprenticeship to join the company, the new apprentices and also the imports, Jeanne Masset from Paris and Eckhardt Bremner from one of the German companies, maybe Hamburg. The board members will be there and some donors. I know Alec will invite you."

"And I'll go, Jules," said Emma. "Don't worry about me. You've given me a gift and I know it. When I think of the coming season it's like I remember the feel of returning to school in September." She smiled warmly. "Another gin?"

Chapter 9

Emma arrived at the company's administrative building shortly after six in the late afternoon on the last Friday of September, a misty, golden, early autumn day. Her mood was cautious. Would she know anybody other than Julie and Alec? They had pulled and pushed her into something new and seductive, but essentially alien. Would she fit in? She had lived, raised her family and built a career knowing what she was doing, always in control. She knew nothing about ballet.

She made her way to the reception for the company's new dancers in the small dance rehearsal room at the rear of the second floor. There was already a hum of conversation and clinking glasses. She entered a room decorated by the set people with modulated blue lighting, the room's mirrors and practice barres masked by enlarged photographs of the company's performances in years past. Emma paused at the entrance, surveying the room. Aside from the new dancers, the guests included the company's premier dancers and donors whose annual contribution was twenty-five thousand dollars or more. Emma Peters, by invitation of the artistic director, was the exception. She entered the room looking nervously for Julie. Her friend was standing in a group of donors — substantial people in business suits and cocktail dresses, hair grey or streaked blond — and dancers in stylish earth-fibre tops and tight jeans or leggings.

Emma was relieved to find a donor she knew, the chief executive officer of an electronics company she had represented in a successful lawsuit. He shook hands with a friendly smile, and Emma began to relax. Julie came over and introduced the two new dancers, Jeanne Masset from the Paris company and Eckhardt Bremner from Hamburg, and finally Shirley McIsaac. The two senior dancers shook hands gracefully; Shirley McIsaac beamed, but was barely able to say hello.

Emma took a glass of prosecco from a waiter's tray and stood surveying the crowd. She noticed Alec, chatting with a group of donors across the hall. They broke into laughter; someone had told a successful joke. The director turned, caught her eye and waved; she waved back. Farther back in the room she saw a group of dancers standing in front of a television screen. She could see ballet dancers on the screen and hear the lush orchestration. Julie came to stand beside her.

"It's the balcony scene's pas de deux from Prokofiev's *Romeo and Juliet*. Rudolf Nureyev and Margot Fonteyn."

"Oh," said Emma, aware of her ignorance.

Julie smiled sympathetically, "Don't worry, my dear. You have to start somewhere. We all do."

Emma noticed Bill Shrubb among the watchers. He was standing beside the woman who had brushed past her as she left his building. Her hair was no longer dark, it was turquoise and hung to her shoulders. Her lips and eye shadow were turquoise as was the silk top that showed her shoulders and the curve of her breasts. The miniskirt was metallic, with an aluminum sheen. Shrubb had his arm around her.

"That must be the Russian dancer with Bill Shrubb," Emma said.

"Yes. Tatyana Vasilievskaya, a difficult woman, they say, but a superb dancer," said Julie. "They're an item, you know. And you do see who's standing opposite her, talking to the two girls?" She waved towards Stefan Grigoriev.

"That's the dancer we saw at the school exhibition," said Emma. "The one who's been given a contract without apprenticing?"

"Yes, Stefan Grigoriev. Would you like me to introduce you?"

Emma hesitated, unsure.

Julie urged, "Of course you would. Let's go."

Julie introduced her first to Shrubb and then Vasilievskaya.

"We met already," said Shrubb. "The lawyer with the legs who doesn't like tee-shirts."

Vasilievskaya shook hands with a cold stare.

"I think we met outside Bill's building last week," said Emma. "You were in a hurry."

"I don't remember you," said the Russian, looking down her nose, indifference in her blue eyes.

"This is not good dancing," said Vasilievskaya, looking at the apprentices who were murmuring with admiration for Nureyev and Fonteyn. "You see better any season in Petrograd. This old lady is not Russian. How Rudi could dance with her, who knows."

The pas de deux ended and the television screen went blank. The apprentices drifted away. Shrubb took his dancer by the hand and, winking at Emma, led her over to the group around Runciman. Julie pushed Emma in front of Stefan Grigoriev, introducing her as a new supporter of the company. He bowed, smiled and shook her hand.

The memory of this encounter would remain with Emma forever. His smile was simple and friendly, without any overtones. He was handsome; she remembered the dark eyes over the slightly hooked nose and the high cheekbones. He spoke softly, with a Slavic lilt in his speech. These aspects of the man were attractive, but did not account for his impact on her.

He is not coming on to me or flirting or even posing, she thought. He is just saying hello normally, the way anyone would to someone they have just met. His smile is unaffected and reassuring. It makes you feel that everything will be okay. He looks at the young dancers, boys or girls, in the same way he looks at me. And they smile back at him and pass on. But I.... She smiled back at him, in an everyday, friendly sort of way.

"I am very pleased to meet you, Stefan," she said evenly. I saw you dance at the school last spring. You danced beautifully, I thought. Congratulations on being signed to a contract by the company."

He blushed. My God, he's modest too, Emma thought.

"Thank you, madam. It is a great honour for me."

"So, you will be given roles this season, not merely dancing in the corps de ballet."

"Is true." he said, and she saw a sudden fierce pride in his look. "I will dance the Bluebird in *Sleeping Beauty* and Chevalier in *Nutcracker*. This will be good for me, I think."

When she told him how much she was looking forward to seeing him dance, he bowed again. She moved on, determined not to linger. Julie took her by the arm and led her to Alec Runciman's group. She stood quietly as the director welcomed the new members of the company from abroad and then Stefan and Shirley McIsaac. Emma only half listened. The words seemed a faraway monotone as she gazed at the figure of Stefan Grigoriev standing near Alec. When the director finished, the assembly broke into casual groups and Emma moved among them, introducing herself to the apprentice dancers or to members of the donor group. Wherever she went, she positioned herself so that her peripheral vision located Grigoriev. Eventually she found herself standing beside Julie, away from the crowd.

"That boy is something else, Jules," she said. "Not only is he gorgeous and a gifted dancer, he's nice."

"It can happen," said Julie. "But in this world, they can't be too nice. The competition is fierce."

"Surely with his talent...."

She hugged Julie and walked from the room. The thought of this charming young man at the beginning of probably a fine career gave her pleasure.

Chapter 10

During the following weekend, thoughts of the reception and the young dancers faded as she prepared for her trip to New York.

Donna di Carlo was sending her to start a conversation with a company interested in buying one of their clients, Digital Connections,

Inc. The company designed switching mechanisms for highly-integrated electronic communication systems. Her job was to present documents the New York lawyers needed — financial statements and projections, organizational charts, product descriptions and customer lists — and answer preliminary questions. She spent Saturday and Sunday collecting files and organizing documents, and the professional Emma reasserted itself. As she delved into five-year projections and issues of share values, the world of ballet became barely a memory.

She arrived in New York on a day when the autumn sun was warming the sidewalks and canyons of Manhattan. Her meetings were productive. They opened with a rapid series of questions on issues concerning the valuation of her company, mostly from Miranda, a lawyer with piercing dark eyes and a voice that was both soft and aggressive. Emma realized she was being tested and gave accurate answers without hesitation in a relaxed tone. Soon the questions eased, the smiles became genuine. By the end of the day she understood that the lawyers and executives she met with were receptive to exploring the purchase further.

On Monday evening the lawyers took her to Chez Ma Tante, on East 82nd near Lexington. Miranda sat beside her. She began to chat. She kept Emma's glass full and asked sisterly questions about Emma's children. The conversation flowed: jokes, political anecdotes and memories of legal battles past. Emma ate, drank good red wine and returned to her hotel giggling and happy. The next night the chairman of the board and his wife took her to see a revival of *Brigadoon*, which was new to her, and she enjoyed the lush, Broadway-Scottish romanticism. She returned to Toronto with good memories of the meetings, of intelligent questions and thoughtful answers, and of the songs from *Brigadoon*. She thought everything about the dinner had been superb, from the sparkle on the rims of the wine glasses and the efficient courtesy of her waiter to the rich bourbon glaze on her duck breast. She knew that she had performed well, and the prospects for the sale looked good.

She arrived home from the airport at five-thirty and found a message from Carolyn marked urgent. Joshua had been taken to the Children's Hospital to see if the mild fever he had developed was caused by a flare-up of his lung problem. They had given him a battery of tests and were keeping him overnight. Could Carolyn sleep over? She phoned her daughter, still at the hospital with Josh, and arranged for Carolyn to come at seven for dinner.

"I hate leaving him there," said Carolyn. "He's so small and so…."

"Adorable?"

"Oh, he is so cute! I can't believe how he charms me. But the doctor insists they want to monitor him overnight." Emma stared at her daughter. The grandmother pictured Josh lying alone in his hospital bed and suppressed her tears. Carolyn looked annoyed.

"Mum, stop glaring at me. I know you think I was too young to have Josh, the same mistake you made with me."

"Darling, I made no mistake with you. It's just that he's so little."

"Enough! It is what it is."

Emma fell silent.

"I want to know about your friend we met last time, the cool dude with the ponytail."

"I work for him, Alec Runciman. What about him?"

"What about him? Please don't pull that bullshit with me, Mum."

"So, you've assumed that we are an item?"

"If you're not, you should be. You need someone in your life."

Emma tried to explain that her life was full and she wasn't looking. Amidst the bantering she thought briefly of Stefan, but the memory was inconvenient and she dismissed it. She was a mother, a grandmother and a good lawyer, not a lover, despite Ryan Connell. She smiled affectionately at her daughter.

*

Emma was of two minds as she contemplated the world of ballet. It was seductive, but its seduction aroused resistance from her cautious, conservative core. Sometimes she felt she might lose herself in this enchanting world. It was a relief to return to the familiar balance of work and family. She could not have known, however, that the phone call she made to Julie the morning after Carolyn left her would interrupt this sense of well-being. She had phoned to arrange a session at Café Vert; she wanted to describe her days in New York and Josh's time in hospital, and she wanted to catch up on news and events at Ballet Toronto from Julie. They planned to meet at the café at four on Friday.

"By the way," said Julie. "Here's ballet news that will interest you. The gorgeous Stefan Grigoriev has lost his sponsorship."

Emma sat confused for several seconds.

"What does that mean, lost his sponsorship?"

"Telling the public someone is sponsored gives the dancer prestige. In Stefan's case, since he will be dancing solos and maybe a principal role in his first season, sponsorship helps the company give him a higher rank and thus a better salary. An unsponsored dancer seems unappreciated."

"And Stefan had a sponsor?"

"Yes, Rhoda Marks. You met her at the reception. A skinny woman, close to eighty, with her hair dyed orange and purple, with purple lipstick. She has a gallery in the east end. She had agreed to sponsor our boy but changed her mind. Runciman isn't saying why."

"Right, I do remember her. Interesting. What does this mean for Stefan?"

"Perhaps fewer roles. It was mean of Rhoda to dump him the way she did."

As she put her phone down, Emma sat back in her seat and stared at the ceiling. She thought it wrong that this fine young dancer would have the development of his career hindered by Rhoda Marks's whim. Surely someone else could sponsor Stefan Grigoriev, she thought. She pictured him dancing at the ballet school and began to smile. She remembered the way he had responded to the comments of the ballet master. Was he not unusually gifted? Obviously, the company thought so, promoting him without requiring an apprenticeship.

I could sponsor him, she thought.

The thought startled her. But why would I?

She remained sitting and began to sort through the pros and cons. It would cost money, of course, but she had money, most of the cash portion of George's settlement, augmented by her years of saving. However, she would be committing herself to ballet, more than she thought she wanted. On the other hand, she would be helping Stefan on his way to a brilliant career. The thought pleased her. He was not only gifted; he was a likeable young man. And ballet had attracted her; she remembered Julie's adjective 'priceless'. She wanted to experience a life beyond the values of work and reward. She wanted to experience pricelessness.

Without thinking further, she picked up her phone and called Alec Runciman. Dora Lassinger answered; the director was out. With more urgency in her voice, Emma asked for a meeting as soon as possible, and Dora found time for her at two-thirty on Friday afternoon. Immediately after the call she grabbed a file from her in-basket and began to read furiously, blotting everything else from her mind. She arrived home at seven, finished a half-open bottle of Pinot Noir and found *Breakfast at Tiffany's* on television. She ate no supper. By eleven she was in bed. She slept fitfully during the night, awakened periodically by a recurring dream that she was falling from where she was into some dark place where she wasn't.

Chapter 11

On Friday morning she arrived at the office at seven and began to assemble a second batch of documentation in support of the Digital Connections sale for Donna di Carlo. The initial batch, a summary of the New York meetings and the paper the US firm had provided to advance the negotiation, had gone to Donna the day after she returned. She worked steadily, fuelled by coffee, thinking only of the task at hand, relieved to be distracted from her meeting with Runciman. Shortly after ten, Donna knocked and entered. Emma put aside her file and smiled.

"How are you, Emma?" asked Donna. "You look like you aren't getting any sleep. Anything wrong?"

"Not really. Josh, my grandson, has been in hospital for a recurrent lung problem — tests and such. It's very disturbing. It does keep me awake."

"Poor you. Children are so vulnerable. Look, Emma, the reason I'm asking is that the New York stuff for Digital Connections you sent me is all messed up. Somehow documents for Digital Polishes got in with your batch. I assume New York is not interested in nail polish."

"Dammit, Donna, I'm so sorry. Look, send it over and I'll sort it out right away."

"No need. Suzy's done it already. She'll send you the nail-file stuff this morning. Look at me, Emma."

Emma gave her a weak smile.

"This isn't like you. You're usually more organized than God. And you look a mess. Are you sure you can get me the new stuff this morning? It can wait till Monday if you want to go home and rest."

"I'll get it to you this morning. Give me another hour."

"Okay, Emma. You take care now."

Emma spent an hour reviewing the material she was assembling to make sure it was correct and then sent the package to Donna's office. She signed out for the rest of the day and went to her fitness club, where she spent an hour lifting weights and jogging. By the time she had showered and grabbed a quick lunch in the food court — an eggplant, red pepper and kale sandwich and cranberry juice — it was two-fifteen and time to meet Runciman.

*

"Come in, dear Emma, come in." Runciman shook her hand fondly and ushered her to a chair by the window. "How lovely to see you.

But my goodness, have you been sleeping? You look exhausted."

She mentioned Josh and his problem and the pressure of preparing material for her client's sale. Runciman shook his head disapprovingly.

"You must take care of yourself, my dear. Now, what can I do for you?"

"I would like to sponsor Stefan Grigoriev."

She noticed that the only sign of surprise in his response was a twitching of his left eye. His smile remained casual, his voice calm.

"So, you've heard that Rhoda has changed her mind." Emma nodded. "And here you are. How very convenient. May I ask why you want to sponsor Stefan Grigoriev?"

"I saw him dance at the school in the spring and I was most impressed." She strove to keep her tone of voice businesslike. "And he is so young and so far from home."

"So, he needs a mother," said the director, chuckling.

"That's one way of putting it."

"And he is a very handsome young man. I don't suppose that has anything to do with it."

She paused. "He is attractive," she said with a smile. "But Alec, you know I'm a grandmother."

"If only it were that simple," he said. "Look, I'm delighted that you want to be involved in supporting us. You realize that Rhoda had committed thirty thousand dollars for three years."

"I'll give thirty-five."

Runciman's jaw dropped.

"Emma, really, thirty thousand will do." He shook his head. "What am I saying, turning down an extra five thousand a year?" He stared at her inquiringly. "Do you know what you're doing, and more importantly, why you're doing it?"

"Yes, I do."

"Very well," he said with enthusiasm. "You're on and I'm delighted. You've saved me from going around begging for another sponsor." He paused. "Look, let me phone Rhoda to make sure she hasn't changed her mind again. She'll be at her gallery now."

He called and waited. After the preliminaries he explained that Emma Peters had offered to take over the sponsorship of Stefan Grigoriev. Emma heard loud chatter from the other end. Runciman started to laugh as he hung up the phone.

"Well, you're in. She hasn't changed her mind. She remembers you from the reception and asked me to tell you to beware those dark Bulgarian eyes."

"No problem. Tell me, Alec, why did she withdraw her offer?"

He sighed. "You might as well know; she's been bragging about it to everyone else." He paused. "She's found a young man in Florida who has become her 'companion', for want of a better term. Her attention and, I suspect, a good amount of her money will be needed there."

"God, that's a bit shoddy, don't you think?"

"Do I ever," he said. "But it relieves me, actually. Rhoda is a horny old girl with a history of this kind of thing and I was concerned for Stefan."

"Obviously," she said. "That's the last thing he needs."

"Well said. I assume I don't have to caution you against doing anything silly?"

"Of course not, Alec. I'm not only a grandmother, I'm a lawyer."

"Fair enough," he said. "I think the next thing to do is have the three of us — you, Stefan and me — meet here next week. I'll talk to him and arrange a time late in the day. Okay?"

"Okay." Her smile was suddenly nervous.

"Now we'd better talk money."

*

The afternoon was warm, but the blossoms in Eastern Park were mostly gone except for the yellow and mauve asters. Emma reached Café Vert shortly after four and found Julie sitting in the sun on the patio. She pecked her on the cheek and sat, apologizing for being late.

"No problem," said Julie. "I'm loving the sunshine. The usual?" Emma nodded and Julie motioned to the waiter. Then she stared at Emma, surprised.

"Emma, is something wrong? You look exhausted."

Emma repeated her explanation: the pressure of the New York project and Joshua's lung problem. Julie shrugged.

"I've seen you stressed before, but you look different now. Your eyes are weird. And for God's sake, stop drumming your fingers on the table."

Emma pulled her hand back onto her lap as the waiter brought their drinks.

"Something's on your mind," Julie continued.

Emma took a long sip of her gin and tonic, and tried to make her expression everyday casual.

"There is something?" she said. "Good news, I think."

"Tell me."

Emma sipped again. "I have agreed to sponsor Stefan Grigoriev."

Julie said nothing for half a minute. When at last she spoke, her voice was soft and flat, with no expression.

"You're going to sponsor Stefan Grigoriev."

Emma described the meeting with Alec Runciman.

Julie shook her head. "So, as soon as I told you about Rhoda dropping out you rushed to Alec and convinced him to let you take over." Emma nodded. "What are you thinking, sweetheart? I assume you have the money?"

"Of course I do. I got a lump-sum settlement from George years ago and I haven't touched it."

"How much?"

"Thirty thousand a year for three years."

"My God. So why are you doing this? And why Stefan?"

She focussed on Julie's eyes. "He is a beautiful dancer. I want to support his career and see him achieve the perfection that I think he has in him. Just that, nothing more. People do invest in beauty, and that's what I'm doing."

"But you're not buying a painting, you're investing in a human, a talented and gorgeous young man. So, your story is you're not attracted to him?"

"Of course he's attractive, but that doesn't mean I'm infatuated. Give me some credit. I'm a grandmother and I know it." She emptied her glass. "In fact, Alec thinks that I'm relieving him from worrying about Rhoda having designs on Stefan."

"Disgusting thought," said Julie. "My dear, you will do what you want. I thought the ballet would give another dimension to your life, and I see that it has, but this is not what I expected." She smiled at Emma. "I know you're not a Rhoda, but you are moving into uncharted waters. Just remember that Stefan will not be interested in you as a person. You will simply be a source of money, a generous older woman furthering his career. If you develop feelings for him, you may find yourself alone in a prison of your own making."

Emma got to her feet.

"You're too gloomy, Jules. I know what I'm doing."

Julie shrugged, then motioned to the waiter.

Chapter 12

Emma approached the director's office just before five on Tuesday afternoon. She went into the washroom in the hall, rather than use Runciman's ensuite facility. She applied new lipstick nervously, at the same time examining her lips and her throat in the mirror for wrinkles. At reception, Dora told her to go directly in. She saw no sign of Stefan — it was slightly past five — and her nerves were twitching. Why was he not there? She walked through the open door and was blinded by direct sunlight slanting through the office's west window; she couldn't see Alec sitting at his desk, or anywhere else in the room.

"Emma, hello."

She turned toward the voice and saw Runciman re-arranging books in a corner bookshelf. He walked to her, kissed her on the cheek and showed her to a chair facing his desk. He noticed the sun in her eyes, went to the window and pulled a venetian blind. She remained tense.

Was the sponsorship arrangement off or was Stefan just late?

"As you see, Emma, our young friend is not here. I asked him to come at five-fifteen so you and I could have a quick chat. You have been a friend and supporter, and a fine addition to our family, if I may call it that. Therefore, I want to make sure that the arrangement with Stefan works well for everybody."

She nodded. Stefan was coming. She tried to picture him entering the office, but she couldn't remember what he looked like.

"I am, of course, concerned that the sponsorship goes well for you. How could it not, you may ask. Let me tell you, as someone who was also at one time a twenty-one-year-old dancer beginning his career. Nothing else mattered to me in those days but my next role, my reviews and my next season. I would have killed for a lead, even when it was premature for me. I mean that metaphorically, of course." He chuckled; she smiled. "And I assure you, my dear, that the Stefan I have hired seems to me now more or less as I was then, hungry and determined. And so, it means that any feelings you develop for him will not be reciprocated. He may well be affectionate, but only as an expression of pleasure that you are helping his career. I hope you understand that. I don't want you to get hurt, my dear friend, but that is not my main concern. You are old enough to look out for yourself and if you don't, I cannot help you. I suppose I might pick up the pieces, but that's all."

"Please, Alec," she said. "I don't intend to become a dotty old fool for this boy."

"Glad to hear it. So, my main concern is Stefan. He is a tremendous talent. I have advanced him directly into the company, and it is important to me that he fulfill the promise I see in him. And why am I telling you this? What is my concern? I should think it is obvious. If you were to become a dotty old fool, obsessed with Stefan, I fear it might impede his maturing as a man and as a dancer."

Emma twisted suddenly in her chair.

Alec continued: "He already receives adulation from his fellows and from our patrons. There has even been some initial flattery from reviewers. My worry is that if you fall for him, his teenage ego will swell more than is healthy and he will become a conceited little prick, difficult to handle. Should that happen, his dancing would suffer. Dancing is an expression of one's heart and soul, and it falters if the soul is degraded."

"That is the last thing I want," she said. "I understand your concern for the investment you have made in him. I want to support him in the limited way money can, to achieve the success you hope for him. And let me repeat myself, I want only to assist his career. I want nothing more."

Her voice was defiant. Runciman smiled as the intercom buzzed. He flicked on the switch and listened. "Send him in," he said and turned to Emma. "He does not know why we are meeting or that you are here."

Emma froze. The door opened and Stefan Grigoriev entered. She stared at him. His dark hair was in a ponytail; he wore a green linen shirt over black sweatpants. He looked at her in surprise, and she felt once again the power of his eyes.

"Stefan, I believe you met Emma Peters at our reception. She is a devoted supporter of our company."

Stefan smiled at her. "Of course, yes, I remember you, madam. We had a good conversation." He hesitated, uncertain, before he extended his hand.

"So good to see you again," she said quietly, without a smile. She shook his hand.

"The reason we are meeting today, Stefan, is to introduce you to your patron. Emma has agreed to sponsor you for the next three years."

He blushed, then turned to her with a delighted smile.

"Oh madam, what a beautiful thing you do for me."

She marvelled at the unaffected joy in his expression.

He pulled out his cellphone. "I must tell my mother; she will be so happy." He shook his head. "No, is middle of night in Bulgaria. Tomorrow." He put away his phone. "Madam, I thank you so much. I don't know what I can say to you. Only maybe this. I will dance for you as good as I can dance, with all my heart. I want to make you feel good that you help me. You will see."

"I believe you will, Stefan," she said, careful to keep her voice steady. "One other thing. I would like us to get to know each other better. Would you come to dinner with me next week, perhaps on Tuesday or Wednesday?"

Emma kept her eyes away from Runciman. She had not mentioned the invitation to him. Stefan looked surprised.

"Madam, that will be nice." Stefan checked his phone. "Tuesday, I have late rehearsal. Maybe Wednesday."

"That's fine. Give me your cell number and I will phone you with the time and place."

The director rose from his chair, smiling benevolently.

"Very nice, Emma, very nice. Now would you mind leaving us? Stefan and I have some things to go over."

She rose, turned, and walked from the office without looking at either man. Immediately, she realized she had been rude and half-turned to re-enter and say her goodbyes, but she changed her mind and walked quickly away. She wondered, briefly, what the two men would be saying about her and her dinner invitation. Would Runciman be warning him about her? Men are impossible, she thought. But then, everything had gone perfectly in the office. The conversation had been businesslike and Stefan had been charming and grateful. How could she not have remembered his face?

Chapter 13

Runciman waited until the door had closed before he turned his attention to Stefan.

"This is good news for you, Stefan," he said with an avuncular smile. "You have already established yourself as a gifted dancer, which makes it easy to attract sponsorship money for you. Congratulations."

"Thank you, sir. Thank you, Mr. Runciman. I know this is honour for me. Mrs. Peters is kind and generous woman. I thank her from the bottom of my heart. And I am happy that I dance so good it makes money for you."

Runciman paused to scrutinize his young dancer. That he could dance was obvious, and his elegant figure and dark good looks suggested a successful career. The director would have preferred less self-confidence, however. The boy knew his worth and had almost suggested that he had earned the sponsorship for the company, which in a sense he had. Sitting across the desk smiling at him in a direct, confident way, he reminded Runciman of himself at that age.

It's probably good that he is full of himself at twenty-one, he thought. Humility comes to most of us soon enough.

"Yes. Now I want to talk to you a bit about Mrs. Peters."

"Of course, Mr. Runciman."

"You may call me Alec. I even prefer it. Mrs. Peters is a warm and generous person who admires your dancing very much. Now, we have had problems in this company with generous older men and women becoming romantically involved with young dancers."

Stefan looked upset.

"No, Mr. Runciman, Alec, I won't do that. I am not that boy."

Stefan's sincerity and innocence did not reduce the director's concern. The boy had no idea of the pressures of performance and the temptations that would surround him. His looks would be a magnet to women.

"I'm glad to hear it. Your personal life is none of my business, of course, unless it affects your dancing. And I have seen young dancers lose promising careers through too much partying, which means alcohol or love affairs or both. Do you understand me?"

"Of course, sir, but you should not worry about me. I don't drink wine much, except maybe at Christmas. And I had no girlfriend in Bulgaria since I was fifteen. I was only dancing. And Mrs. Peters is older woman, no? Does she have family, husband? She doesn't need me."

"She has no husband, but she does have two daughters and a grandson."

"That's good. She looks like a good mother. Too beautiful for grandmother, I think."

The director smiled fondly.

"Okay, Stefan. That's all I wanted to say. I believe you understand me."

"I do, sir. Alec."

After Stefan left, the director summoned Dora Lassinger.

"Dora, you know Emma Peters, I believe?"

"I know of her. She comes from Isherton, which is just down the road from where I grew up in Erie County."

"I thought so. Now, what do you think of her sponsoring Stefan Grigoriev?"

Dora was in her forties, a plain-spoken woman with a good mind and a rough sense of humour.

"I think he's gorgeous and she's got the bucks. I wouldn't mind having a run at him myself." She roared with laughter. Dora weighed over two hundred pounds, had three kids, and a husband who managed a mechanics' garage.

Runciman smiled.

"I'm afraid Mrs. Peters is new to this world of ours, Dora. She claims she is sponsoring Grigoriev for the best of reasons, and I know she means it. But she is an innocent here, with no idea how easily normal affection can switch to something else with just a glance or a smile."

"I know what you mean, boss," she said. "At least she's no Rhoda Marks."

"Thank God for that," he said. "Keep an eye on them, Dora. I don't like the vibes."

"Got it, boss."

Chapter 14

Emma sat on the patio of Mary Jo's, a restaurant on Pear Street near the harbour, waiting for Stefan. It was eight o'clock and the harbour lights were shining on the water. She had phoned Anne in Halifax for advice on the restaurant she should choose to entertain a young ballet dancer. She could almost hear the questions arising in Anne's mind.

"You mean a restaurant different from the ones you and your friends like?" said Anne.

"Of course," said Emma.

"So, who is this dancer? Is it a guy? And why are you taking him to dinner?"

"He's from Bulgaria, he's twenty-one and I am sponsoring his entry into the ballet company. Yes, he is good looking, probably not gay and no, it is not a date. We need to get to know each other if we're going to do business together."

"Sounds very interesting," said Anne, her voice nuanced. "Anyway, try Mary Jo's. It's on Pear Street near the harbour — seafood, Asian fusion and reasonable. Some clients are painters whose abstract stuff is for sale on the walls. The female waiters wear sarongs and the men wear silk Mao jackets. Nice patio, very cool."

Just as she began to worry that he had forgotten their dinner, Stefan appeared in the street, coasting to a stop on his bicycle in front of the restaurant. Of course he would arrive on a bicycle, she thought. He locked it to a post and approached the patio. A waiter pointed him to Emma, who waved. She noticed his white shirt, creased black slacks, the ponytail and his dark eyes. When the waiter came, he asked for mineral water; she ordered a gin and tonic. She could see that he was self-conscious, unsure of what he should say. Emma herself, moreover, felt a tightness in her stomach.

Why does he make me tense, she asked herself.

"I am delighted you could join me, Stefan," she said in her warmest voice. "I think it's better if we get to know each other. You should know, for example, that I am new to the world of ballet. I have only seen *The Nutcracker* as a child and have a lot to learn."

"Then I teach you, madam," he said with a smile. "I am happy to do this, you help me so much."

"I would like that," she said. "Now Stefan, you must call me by my name. I am not 'madam', I am Emma."

"I will do that, Emma. It's Canadian way to be direct and friendly. You can teach me Canadian way of doing, and then I teach you ballet."

Already his nervousness was gone. She marvelled at how direct and open he was. Suddenly, for some reason, she remembered when she and George were first dating, how charming and kind he was. Then there was Ryan Connell, with his Irish good looks and malarkey and the cold, impersonal sex.

Those have been my men, she thought. My only men.

She looked at Stefan, the lustrous dark eyes and the unrestrained smile, and wondered.

"You are from Bulgaria," she said, in her most cheerful and positive tone.

"Yes, my city is Varna. Do you know it?" She shook her head. "Is our port on the Black Sea. Bulgarian navy has their main base there."

"Bulgaria has a navy?"

"Of course, but does not matter. Russian navy controls the Black Sea. And Turkey. Is good, because in Bulgarian navy you never have to fight, never get killed."

She laughed nervously.

"And your parents are still there, in Varna?"

"Only mother. Father is dead. He was commander in navy, but he died. Not on the sea, but in automobile. Was drunk."

"How sad."

"Not so much." He shrugged. "I was only seven. But not good for Mama. She was a dance teacher, and she made not much money. Her pension was small. So, she became a dressmaker to get money."

"I see. So, she started to teach you to dance."

"Yes, when I'm five. But was problem with my father. He didn't want me to dance. He thinks is not good for a man to be a dancer. So, when he dies, there's no more problem."

There was no hint of regret for the father's death.

"Mama teach me until age ten," he continued. "Then she says she has no more to teach me. She sends me to teacher in Sofia. You know Sofia? Is capital of my country. Bulgarian national ballet company is there, and good teachers. I stay there with my uncle, go to school, come home on holidays. Soon, my teacher, name Lyudmila, says I dance good, should leave Bulgaria. She has contact here. They sent someone to see me dance, they offered me a scholarship to ballet school. Lyudmila talked to Mama, they agreed." His face broke into a broad smile. "So, here I am."

"So, here you are," she said. "Do you miss your mother?"

"At first, yes. Still a little. I phone her every week. I tell her that you sponsor me and she is very happy. She says thank you."

"What is her name?"

"Elena."

"Lovely name."

A waiter arrived with menus. Emma ordered sea bass with rice and spinach. She noticed Stefan's frustration with the menu.

"Bring me fish with white flesh and many vegetables," he said, setting the menu aside.

"We have sea bass, bream or pickerel," said the waiter.

"I don't know these," he said, turning to Emma.

"Bring him pickerel," she said. "Cook it simply, in butter, no fancy sauce."

The waiter bowed.

"So, Stefan, I am a lawyer."

He nodded. She began to describe the kind of work she did as simply as she could, but she noticed that his attention soon began to drift, so she gave him an account of her marriage, the birth of her two girls and her divorce.

"So, he leaves you with two babies," he said, the dark eyes angry. "What man do that? Is man without honour, I think."

She continued, describing her daughters' lives and Joshua, with his lung problem. She noticed that she held his attention with the story of her family. When she paused, he asked her daughters' ages and grimaced when she told them.

"But that means you are maybe forty-five, madam, I mean, Emma. Is true? You look like young woman. Beautiful young woman."

She wondered about the compliment. She couldn't decide if he was coming on to her or not. She scrutinized his expression; his eyes were twinkling, and his smile was warm. She wasn't sure what she wanted from him. She wasn't sure how she should be, sitting across from him. She restrained the natural warmth of her smile and waited, watching him. The dinner continued and the conversation turned to the coming ballet season and his schedule.

"I have three roles before Christmas," he said. "I will dance in *La Sylphide* first — Gurn, suitor to Effie, a good role but nothing special for me. Then I am the Bluebird in *Sleeping Beauty*, and in *Nutcracker* I will be the Mouse King and the Chevalier to Sugar Plum Fairy."

"Bluebird? You don't look like a bird."

"Is true," he laughed. "And I must be all blue: costume, skin, hair, everything. For this maybe I must cut my hair so they can dye."

"Oh no, your beautiful hair. Why do you accept such a role?"

"Is good for me. I dance with blue princess beautiful pas de deux and then a solo to finish. I show them what I can do."

"What about *Nutcracker*?"

"Also okay, but *Nutcracker* is a fun show, a Christmas party maybe. Good dancing for me. I like the Mouse King. He is fun in a fat suit and mask. The other guys laugh at me and is okay. I like to dance fun guy and make them laugh. But better for me is Chevalier to Sugar Plum Fairy. I dance the pas de deux with her, very romantic. This will be good for me."

Stefan's expression grew intense as he discussed his roles.

Naturally, he's thrilled, she thought. It's the beginning of his career.

Now there was no humour in his face, no lightness in his voice. He fell silent and began to look away at the lights shining on the water. He had eaten little; he left fish and vegetables on his plate and refused dessert.

How can he possibly dance, eating like that, she wondered. For the moment, maternal concern overcame uncertainty.

"I look forward to seeing you dance," she said very quietly.

"You will. But I must go soon, Emma. I have exercises to do before I sleep, and long day tomorrow."

They agreed to have lunch once a month. He touched her cheek, kissed her lightly and left the patio. She watched him unlock his bicycle and ride away, his white shirt fading into the night. She was left unsure and wondering.

Chapter 15

She had been looking forward to a wonderful autumn, rich with her newfound experience of the dance, but it never arrived. Donna di Carlo entered her office one morning shortly after the dinner with Stefan to tell her that they were proceeding with the sale of Digital Connections. Normally the Mergers and Acquisitions people would take over, but they were stretched thin and needed the two of them to fill in with the preliminary work in New York. When Emma checked the dates for the New York trip against her calendar, she found they conflicted with the date of her ticket for *La Sylphide*.

"Is there a problem? Emma, you don't look happy."

"No problem. I had a ballet ticket, but I can miss it."

"I can't wait," said Donna. "I need a break from Danny and the kids. The work on this deal isn't huge. Archer Brown will lay it all out for us and take over when the crunch comes. We'll do Broadway, Emma: shows, jazz clubs, good food."

"Sounds great," said Emma.

She would not see Stefan dance his first role. She resigned herself to the demands of law and worked over lunch, finishing the file she was working on and reviewing her notes on the upcoming Digital Connections meetings in New York. She took a break to buy some wine in the liquor store in the basement of her building and returned to find a message from Bill Shrubb asking her to call.

"Hey, Emma the lawyer. Thanks for callin' back. Listen, I think I got some work for ya."

"And what might that be?" She was not enthusiastic.

"I'm serious. We are about to launch a fabulous new product, bigger than anything we've ever done. We got to be protected on this one, copyright and all that shit, and the lawyer we got isn't up to the job. He does the annual legal stuff, does employment stuff, and helps the accountant manage the taxes. I thought of you right away. I know you are Corporate Commercial, right?"

"I am. We can provide you with all the protection you need for your project."

She was amused by the sound of her sales promotion mode.

"Great. Look, I need you to come over here and see a demo of this thing. It's unbelievable. You'll be amazed, then we'll have lunch. And I'll wear a clean tee-shirt."

"Good. Our fees double if the client's tee-shirt smells."

"I'll smell sweet, no worries."

They arranged a date after she returned from New York. As new business it pleased her only moderately. It was one more thing that interfered with her debut season of ballet.

*

New York was a mixed success. They had scheduled two meetings with their purchaser's lawyers and accountants, but a breakdown on the Amtrak commuter line from Connecticut meant that two lawyers and one accountant were delayed until shortly before noon. Furthermore, certain files relating to sales projections, which were to have been sent from Toronto, had not arrived. Donna got on the phone and discovered that they had been sent to the purchaser's plant in New Jersey. A phone call got them delivered in an hour. They chatted and drank coffee, discussed some preliminary issues, and eventually Miranda, the lawyer Emma knew from the first meeting, took the two to lunch in a nearby deli.

Emma and Donna compromised on their two nights on the town. Emma had found a performance by the New York City Ballet of works by George Balanchine for the first night, but Donna had no interest. She reluctantly agreed to go if Emma would come with her after the performance to a late-night jazz club in the village. Miranda discovered that they had no plans for their second night and offered them two tickets to a Mets game.

"We'll take them, thank you," said Donna. "Can we pay you for them?"

"They cost me nothing. My boyfriend plays for the Mets. He got them for me."

"How exciting," said Donna. "We'll look for him. What's his name? What position does he play?"

After lunch, the meetings proceeded smoothly for the next day and a half. The ballet evening, however, was difficult. The program featured Balanchine's *Stars and Stripes.* The show was very patriotic, celebrating the Fourth of July with dancing to march music. Emma sat silently through the performance, unmoved. She could see that the dancing was good, but her imagination was not engaged; something was missing. At the first break Donna rushed to the lobby and phoned Danny and her kids; this irritated Emma. Later, in a smokey, late-night club, Emma mildly enjoyed the jazz — a saxophone, piano and bass — for half an hour. Then she became bored. The room was dark, the drinks were very expensive, and Donna was snapping her fingers and shaking her body to the beat. Emma endured the club for another hour until Donna decided to leave.

"That was good jazz," said Donna. "We were lucky we got in."

*

"*La Sylphide* was good," said Julie. They were inside at Café Vert; the days were now too cool for the patio. "Ralph Lyndhurst danced James and he did well. Not as well as Emerson in London mind you. I saw him there last season, and he was superb." Emma noticed the hint of preening in her tone. "In our production, Stefan was Gurn, competing with James for Effie. Stefan looked good in his kilt, you'll be happy to hear."

"I'm sorry I had to miss it."

Julie fell silent and frowned. She began to talk, hesitantly, about her husband and the problems that had arisen with some of his investments. Emma sipped her drink and listened.

Chapter 16

The company's canteen was a functional space with tables and chairs where dancers could eat their kale and blueberry salads or drink their spinach and banana shakes. Stefan entered from an afternoon of exercise and practice in his grey workout suit, his black hair hanging over his shoulders When he appeared in the canteen, he attracted stares from the women and several men at their tables. As a new member of the company, he disliked the attention. He ordered a latte to take away and turned to leave.

"Hey, Bulgar boy."

He heard the words, a Russian woman's voice. He turned and saw a dancer sitting alone, beckoning him to join her. The woman's hair was black, and she wore a mauve workout ensemble. He recognized Tatyana Vasilievskaya from the reception for new dancers.

"Sit with me, I want to talk with you," she said in Russian.

"Don't speak to me in Russian," he said, looking down at her. "I don't like it."

"Okay." She shrugged and switched to English. "Sit and keep me company. They're all afraid of me."

She waved to the other tables; the occupants were watching them with interest.

"Why should they fear you?" he said.

"Because I come from Bolshoi. They know what that means."

He looked into a face that was lined under heavy make-up. There was an exotic quality to her features, the slant of her pale-blue eyes and the slope of her nose. Her lips seemed to be set in a perpetually sardonic smile. Stefan immediately felt the woman's charisma.

"And what does Bolshoi mean?"

"You don't know? Best in the world."

He laughed dismissively.

"Best in the world and you come here. Why?"

She scowled. "It's complicated. In Russia, everything is politics. Shrubb sponsored me and I am here. Good for them, good for me." She focussed her smile on him. "So, you are sponsored now also." He nodded. "What is her name, your sponsor?"

"Emma Peters is her name."

"Yes. I met her at the reception. Very beautiful, very sexy. You are sleeping with her?"

"No." He frowned, irritated. "She is an old woman with children and a grandson. She is very generous to me and I respect her."

Tatyana chuckled.

"How old are you?"

"Twenty-one."

"A baby!" she laughed. "And you come here to dance like a man, without apprenticing."

"I dance like a man. You have no idea."

"You are right, I have no idea. I have not seen you dance. I will look at you and decide."

"You decide nothing," he said angrily. "You have never seen a dancer like me."

"Oh-ho," she said. "I have danced all major roles, Juliet, everything, at Bolshoi with André Pleshnikov as partner. This is a world you don't know."

"I know me. I can dance here, I can dance for Bolshoi, no problem. Alec knows that about me. I dance Bluebird this fall."

"Alec is a nice man, but he does not…." She fell silent. He rose with his latte in his hand.

"I can dance anything, anywhere," he said and began to walk away.

"We will see, baby. We will see."

*

The next day, Stefan and Shirley McIsaac finished their stretching exercises and were listening to Brent Sokolovski explain a ballet he was asking them to learn.

"It's by an English choreographer, Anthony Pearson, and you will be dancing to the recorded songs of Elvis Presley. Are you two old enough to remember Elvis?"

Stefan shook his head.

"My mother loved him," said Shirley. "She still plays his records."

"Okay. I'm going to play two of his songs the ballet uses to give you an idea. First, 'Blue Suede Shoes'." He switched on the sound.

"It's rock and roll," exclaimed Shirley. "I can dance to that."

"Me too," said Stefan. "Is sort of boogie-woogie."

They grabbed hands and began to jitterbug. Stefan swung her full circle and tossed her in the air, catching her and landing her on her feet. They were both laughing.

"Okay, great," said Sokolovski. "No problem for you. Now listen to 'Love Me Tender'."

They listened quietly until the song finished.

"Is very romantic," said Stefan. "Can be a duet, Shirley and me."

"It makes me shiver," said Shirley.

"It's sexy, isn't it?" said Sokolovski. "Now let's dance it that way. I have Pearson's notes and he has sent me a video of a live performance in London."

They gathered in front of the screen at the end of the room to watch the video. Stefan glanced at the gallery to see if anyone was watching, and Tatyana Vasilievskaya waved with her fingers. He turned to the video without acknowledging her. When it finished, Sokolovski danced the opening male steps, describing what he wanted Stefan to do. When he was satisfied, he took Shirley through her opening steps. They continued in this way on the one song for half an hour until Sokolovski was satisfied that they understood the choreography. As they relaxed, Stefan looked up at the gallery. Tatyana was gone.

However, she was waiting in the canteen. Stefan and Shirley bought Gatorade and took a table. Tatyana came and stood over them.

"So, guys, you dance this rock music okay," she said with a patronizing smile. "I enjoyed what you did. But this is jungle music, not ballet. I will believe you can dance when I see you do the Bluebird."

She walked away without waiting for a response.

"Who does she think she is!" Shirley was annoyed.

"She is Russian bitch," said Stefan. "Don't worry about her."

Chapter 17

The demands of the practice of law at Eberhart Williams were becoming intense for Emma. She and Donna met with Archer Brown, their lead from Mergers and Acquisitions, a thin man in his sixties who wore three-piece, single-breasted suits and cleared his throat before every sentence. He was pleased with their report and the positive feedback from the potential buyer in New York, but wanted one of them to return to New York for a day with further documentation and replies to questions. Donna indicated that Emma would be going. On the Tuesday of the following week, she landed at JFK at eight-thirty, met with the purchaser from ten to twelve, had a deli lunch with Miranda, met again from two to three-thirty and ended up back in her Toronto office by eight o'clock. She prepared a report of her meetings for Archer Brown, copy to Donna di Carlo, and was home by ten-thirty. She checked her personal emails and found a message from Julie telling her she had their tickets for *Sleeping Beauty* for an evening performance on the last Thursday of the month. She warmed up some roast chicken and pasta with basil pesto, drank half a bottle of zinfandel and was in bed by midnight.

At nine the next morning she got to her office, more or less rested, but with a sore head from her zinfandel. She checked her calendar and cursed in frustration. She was due at Bill Shrubb's Algorhythmics for the presentation of his new product at eleven, and then lunch. She thought about postponing — she had to meet with Donna and Archer Brown at four — but decided to get it over with.

When she entered the lobby of Algorhythmics, the voice — this time a man's voice with a Brooklyn-Jewish accent — directed her to the second floor where Bill Shrubb stood waiting beside his red velvet chair. His tee-shirt showed a curvy image of Marilyn Monroe lounging on a sofa with the question, "Marilyn loved me, why can't you?" beneath.

"Nice try, but I could never love a man in a tee-shirt," she said before he spoke.

He smiled. "Whoa, lady, what makes you think the message is for you?"

"Because it looks new, doesn't smell, so I assume you wore it just for me."

As he escorted her to his office, she understood that dealing with the man would involve ongoing exchanges of jokes and wisecracks. However, his expression was serious as he asked her to sit in front of a television screen.

"I'm going to start this interactive job-interview software now, and it's programmed to interview you as a job prospect. Just respond to it naturally."

She nodded and began looking at the screen. After some preliminary product information, the face of Bill Shrubb himself appeared.

"Good morning, Ms. Peters. Thank you so much for coming to see us," it said.

"Good morning, and thank you for this interview," she replied.

"You're welcome. Now, first, would you tell me a little bit about yourself: where you come from, family details if you wish, education and so on, anything you think would help me understand who you are."

"Of course. I come from near Isherton, a small town in southwestern Ontario, near Chatham. My father was a farmer: corn, wheat, soya beans and some cattle."

"A farm background," said the voice. "Very interesting. I imagine you have to work hard and learn how to do things efficiently."

"That's true," she said. "I know how to milk a cow and wield a scythe."

The voice laughed. "Any siblings?"

"A sister and a brother, both younger."

As the interview continued, Emma was impressed at how effortlessly the Shrubb icon moved from question to question and managed to respond intelligently to her answers. The software adapted to her completely and maintained the logic of the interview throughout. The interview lasted thirty-five minutes.

"Wow," she said when the screen went blank. "Bill, that's fabulous. There was not a glitch in the whole piece that I could see."

"I'm ridiculously proud of it," he said, the pride showing in his smile. "We do artificial intelligence as well as anybody here, and you see what it can do."

"I do, indeed. And I can see the market possibilities."

"Sure. Large businesses get hundreds of responses when they advertise a job. They try to cut the list down to twenty or so by discarding anyone who doesn't fit their criteria. What they really want is a short list of maybe five. That's where we come in. They sit their twenty in front of the screen and give them the interview. An assistant thanks the candidates as they leave, tells them they'll hear in a week or so. Then the program makes a short-list selection, and the serious interviewing can take place."

Shrubb described the many thousands of hours of programming that had been necessary to produce software that was ready for market, and gave Emma an overview of how they tried to duplicate human intelligence in the interview. She marvelled.

"Now, there are limits. We have to keep the questions tight and control the responses totally. For example, if you started to explain that your family went on a trip to China when you were eight, we haven't programmed so as to be able to handle that. So we interrupt the interview quickly if that happens and get it back on track. Not bad, eh? Now, it's time for lunch. We'll look at what you can do for us then. There's a great gastropub around the corner."

Over lunch — her marinated crab salad and his rib steak — he gave her an indication of the kind of patent protection he wanted. Other people were working on similar software, he said, but nobody else would have their programming, which he described as some of the most sophisticated anywhere.

"The big risk is people being hired away from us by guys who want to learn our software. We can't allow that. And what if some smart guy makes a lucky guess about how we do it? We gotta stop him. So the patent has to be iron-clad, and our employee contracts, too. You think you guys have the talent I need?"

"No question. I'll talk to the patent lawyers in the office and set something up."

Shrubb sat back in his chair and sipped his soda water. She saw that he was appraising her. There was more on his mind than protection for his product. The corners of his mouth were creased in a half smile and his dark eyes were focussed.

"So," he said finally. "You gonna come and work for me?"

"No," she said. She was prepared for this. "I'm a lawyer, at the end of the day."

"At the end of the day." He smiled. "What a nice phrase. What do you do at the end of the day?"

She paused. "What has that to do with you, or your wonderful new product or the employment you offer, which I do not want?"

"Nothing," he said. "And that's unfortunate." He continued to stare at her with his cocky half-smile. "I understand that you're a lawyer, you want to continue to be a lawyer and you don't want to hang out during your day with thirty-year-old programmers, brilliant though they may be. So, I have to take it to another level."

What will this be, she wondered. Something crazy, something unexpected.

"What do you do at the end of the day? You put your files away, you go home and check your email to see if your daughters have phoned you, or anyone else, and when no one has, as usual, you eat something, then retire to the television with a bottle of wine and drink yourself to bed."

She sat still, her anger rising.

"And that's not good enough," he continued. "You see, I admire you. You are smart, with a good sense of humour and you are gorgeous. And most important, you don't take any shit from me." He hesitated. "Yes, Emma Peters, this is a come-on. I am attracted to you."

She felt the blood rush to her face.

"But you are in a relationship with Tatyana Vasilievskaya," she said uneasily. He snorted.

"Only because she thinks she owes me for getting her out of Russia. It's the only currency she has, but it's something. But she'll be gone in a flash as soon as she thinks she's paid her debt, sooner if she gets a better offer. And I won't mind because she is very, very stupid."

"Oh," said Emma. She could think of nothing else to say.

"So, hear me out," he continued. "You told me about your growing up in farm country — cows and all that. My father was a kosher butcher in the old Jewish market downtown. My parents were not observant Jews, nor am I. I am a contemporary citizen of the western world, and that is why I can do what I do. And that is why I am attracted to you."

She said nothing. She looked around the pub which had mostly emptied and watched a waiter clearing tables.

"This is sudden," he said. "I know, not what you expected. But in my world, you don't get if you don't ask. You don't have to say anything now, just think about it. I'm not offering eternal love, or great sex, or any of the big things. But we could have fun together, Emma.

I could make your end of the day something you would look forward to. I would respect you. I would be your friend."

She stared at him, dumbfounded.

"You don't know what to say." He turned and waved to the waiter. "Go back to work, go home and think about whether I can make the end of your day better."

"I'll do that," she said, as the waiter approached. "But right now, I have to use the loo."

She left the table as he was handing the waiter his credit card. When she returned, he was gone.

Chapter 18

"So, the plot is.... Let me get this straight," said Emma. "The princess is born, she is cursed by the wicked witch to prick her finger and die, but the good fairy changes the curse. She will prick her finger and fall asleep for a hundred years, when she will be awakened by a handsome prince kissing her. They will get married and live happily ever after."

"Right," said Julie. *Sleeping Beauty* in a nutshell. You have been using your internet."

"I like to be prepared."

Julie was wearing a skirt, blouse and sweater; Emma was wearing a green dress with scalloped neck and elbow length sleeves that complemented her red hair. It had been useful at business cocktail parties and weddings. Their seats were good. Julie was a director, and obviously seats mattered. The lights went down, the audience buzz hushed. Emma felt a nervous excitement despite herself. The conductor entered, bowed to the applause, and raised his baton. The overture began — lush, dramatic music with hints of the discord to come. Emma was entranced.

"This is Tchaikovsky?" she whispered. Julie nodded. "It's gorgeous."

The curtain rose. The court was assembled to witness the baptism of the new princess. Emma was delighted by the beauty of the set, the lighting, and the rich and subtle colours of the elaborate court costumes. She saw that every movement, even the walking movements of the courtiers, was in harmony with the music.

So, this is what it is, she thought. It's stunning.

She saw the good fairies enter and dance, and then the wicked witch with her grotesque supporters. Emma was relieved that she understood the opposition of good and evil — the fairies against the demons — in their contrasting music and dance movements. She understood the witch's curse of the baby: to prick her finger on a spindle at the age of sixteen and die. She was delighted when the beautiful Lilac Fairy floated onto the stage and overruled the witch. The princess would not die, but be put to sleep until the advent of the handsome prince.

Happiness in a kiss. Every feminist's dream, she thought, as she rolled her eyes.

In the second act, Prince Florimund was shown with his men hunting in the forest. Emma noticed how free and easy the men danced, compared to the formal dancing of the court. The Lilac Fairy arrived and conjured up a vision of Princess Aurora. The vision danced with the prince, and he was smitten.

"Where is Stefan?" she whispered to Julie. "Shouldn't he be in this?"

There were shushes from behind, and Julie shook her head.

"He comes in the final act," said Julie at intermission. "How are you liking it?"

"I like it," Emma said casually, hiding her excitement.

During the final act, she smiled at the graceful kiss, and the awakening of the princess and the entire court. As the celebratory entertainments began, Julie whispered, "Wait for it."

Stefan entered the stage, all in blue. She was glad to see they had not cut his hair; they had hidden it under an elegant blue cap. She saw through her glasses, however, that they had shaded his eyelids with blue; she was not sure about that. Princess Florine wore a lighter blue tutu; her eyes were shaded, her hair was black. Emma was enchanted as she watched them dance. They were often apart, miming as if they were singing together. He lifted her high, standing strong, as she turned in his arms, her arms and legs pointed and her face joyful. The audience applauded with enthusiasm.

The princess exited, and Stefan began circling the stage to the music, leaping high in the air, kicking his feet apart and together as he rose and fell. Emma thrilled to this display of masculine strength and courage. Finally, he landed a last leap and instantly began twirling completely around a number of times on one leg, then on the other as the applause became an uproar. His final twirl ended in a slow, controlled descent that ended in a perfect pose with one leg extended and his two arms arched over his head.

"My God, Julie, did you see that?" she exclaimed, her eyes riveted on Stefan as he bowed and strode off stage.

"Yes, I did. I gather you liked it."

"It was unbelievable."

Julie smiled, but fell silent as Princess Florine entered and began her solo. She twirled on pointe, arched gracefully and the audience applauded.

She is nothing without him, Emma thought. She is graceful but fragile. Is that what makes her feminine? The applause for her was affectionate. For him, it was ecstatic.

Florine exited, the music paused and then Stefan and his partner entered from opposite sides and danced together again.

They are happy to be together again, she thought. She smiles when he lifts and holds her. She is proud to be in his arms.

Emma could not follow the rest of the finale; the stage seemed empty without Stefan. The curtain fell and the curtain calls began; the audience rose to their feet, clapping and cheering. When Stefan and Shirley McIsaac took their bows, Emma restrained her applause; her emotion was overwhelming her. As they headed for the front exit and a taxi, Julie kept looking at her. Emma avoided her eyes.

"What did you think?" asked Julie once they were in the cab.

"I liked it," Emma said, still keeping her tone casual. "It was beautiful."

Even as she said the word, she knew that 'beautiful' was inadequate to describe what she had seen and felt.

"Jules, tell me something." Julie smiled. "When two dancers dance a pas de deux like Princess Florine and the Bluebird in *The Sleeping Beauty*, are they ever attracted physically? Do you think they sleep together? They are so close and intimate."

"If you're asking about Stefan and Shirley McIsaac, probably not. Why? Remember this is ballet, not life."

"I know. It's just that…. Never mind."

When the cab stopped first at Julie's house, she hugged Emma.

"Em, I hope it was more than beautiful for you," she said as she left the cab. "Let's have a drink soon and talk about your first time."

There were tears in Emma's eyes as the cab drove away. She was beyond any understanding of where she was. The rich, powerful music, the elegant, seductive movements of the dancers and the glorious colour of the production had bewitched her. It was as if in that evening a magnificent landscape had been presented to her — opened her eyes, her ears and her body itself — and urged her to enter. But she could not wholly embrace what was offered. Her life until that night had been lived in black and white, dominated by work and duty. There was a resistance in her that made her pleasure in the landscape of ballet an indulgence.

Chapter 19

Again, Tatyana Vasilievskaya was waiting for Stefan in the canteen. He noticed her out of the corner of his eye as he walked to the counter. She was smiling at him, her hair brilliant orange rather than black. She seemed to know intuitively when he would be coming into the canteen; she had, for him, a witchlike quality. He considered avoiding her, but he couldn't admit to himself that he feared her. He took a seat at her table and forced a smile.

"So, it seems my Bulgar boy can dance. I liked you as the Bluebird. Only problem was your partner. What is her name?"

"Shirley McIsaac."

"Strange name. Canadian?" He nodded. "She is too heavy for you. Farm girl."

"No one is too heavy for me. I lift her like feather. I think Alec will let me dance Romeo next year. Jeanne Masset should be my Juliet."

She held him in the focus of her ice-blue eyes, her lips twisted in a smirk. Everything about her — the arrogant posture, the flamboyant outfit and the dismissive tone of her voice — angered him.

"Alec has me as Juliet with Ralph Lyndhurst as Romeo."

"Bravo!" he exclaimed. "Then we see who can dance."

"No, Stefan! This cannot be." Her voice cracked like a whip. "I want you for my Romeo. You and I can dance."

He scowled as he searched for words. Her compliment did not overcome his dislike of her.

"But Ralph is good — senior male principal."

"But you are better and you are younger. I want you."

"But do I want you? You are old for Juliet."

He dismissed her with a wave, but her gaze never wavered.

"You don't know what I can do for you, Stefan. When I dance with you, I am Juliet, a young girl."

"I don't know," he said, looking away from her.

"Of course, you don't know. But I know. You will be my Romeo." She rose, winked at him and walked away.

Chapter 20

Over the next week and a half, images of the ballet faded in Emma's mind. Her memory blended the specific scenes of the performance into a collage of dancing, music and visual splendour. Somewhat to her relief, however, even this remembered pleasure was dispelled by the demands of her other life. On the Monday morning after the performance, Don Elton knocked gently on her door. He took a seat facing her and greeted her with his most enthusiastic smile. Immediately her nerves tensed.

"I bring what I hope will be good news," he said. "Archer Brown is not happy with Donna's work on the Digital Connections file. He would like you to replace her."

A feeling of hopelessness swept over Emma.

"But I've enjoyed working for Donna. I thought we did a fine job in New York. Archer gave no indication that he was dissatisfied with our work."

Elton sighed. "It's about her family's mines. She would not have been chosen if we hadn't expected that she could deliver some of the family mining business to us. This isn't going to happen. Her Uncle Joe doesn't want to change lawyers. You were the obvious choice, based on merit and experience. So, Emma, welcome to management." His smile became more affable.

She winced. "Donna must be upset. Don, give me a day to think about it."

The smile disappeared. "Donna's okay. She understands the problem with the mines and says she'll be happy to work under you. She admires you. Take a day if you must, but no longer. Otherwise we'll have to poach someone."

She didn't want the appointment. It would lock her into her professional world — a system of buying and selling, power plays and conflict, arbitrary rules and the power of money. This was a new attitude for her, the result, she was sure, of her vision of the ballet, a world apart. She sat for several minutes after Elton left, trying to think of how she could refuse the appointment. He had made it clear that he would replace her if she did. The threat angered her, but she knew reality was not always beautiful and she was a practical woman.

I'll suck it up, she muttered. I can do that.

Then there was Bill Shrubb. Ordinarily she might have been flattered by the interest of this brilliant and amusing young man. However, in her confusion she didn't want to put him off or encourage him. If he would only just disappear for a while. Every so often, usually in the middle of the night, she remembered she owed him an answer and felt guilty, but she did nothing. However, over the weekend, he texted her.

He understood from her lack of response that she was not interested in pursuing a relationship. She was making a big mistake. He assumed that her sponsoring Stefan Grigoriev had something to do with her lack of interest. Just because he never wore tee-shirts, Grigoriev was not for her. She laughed as she read. She could picture his grin and his sparkling eyes, but she did not reply.

And she owed Stefan a dinner. They had agreed to meet once a month and she had been unable to arrange anything for October. She would phone him and set it up. The prospect lifted her spirits. She decided that the anxiety she had felt in their first dinner was neurotic and unjustified. In sponsoring him, she told herself, she was ultimately supporting the art of ballet. She had forgotten her fear and his kiss. Their relationship was professional and proper. Moreover, Anne's birthday was on some day of the next week. The family would have a dinner — Anne, Carolyn, Frank and Joshua. Wonderful!

She remembered Joshua and felt a pang. Carolyn knew she would be desperate for news and had ignored her. She pictured the little boy and felt teary. She shook her head, pulled herself together and called Don Elton. She was pleased to take over as head of Corporate Commercial.

*

They agreed to have their second dinner Friday evening. Stefan did not want to return to Mary Jo's on the harbour. He wanted Italian; he loved pizza and pasta. She was amused by this. She could not imagine the Bluebird munching down a slice of pizza. She booked a table. She decided to invite Stefan to her house for a drink before they went to the restaurant. It was appropriate, she told herself, that they should get to know each other, and that he should understand how she lived.

He arrived on his bicycle at six-thirty, wearing a sweater over his white shirt and the same grey warm-up pants. They embraced briefly and she led him back to the sunroom, looking through a floor-to-ceiling window to her garden, grey and leafless in November.

"It's beautiful, your house, Emma. How long you live here?"

"I raised my girls here. What can I get you to drink?"

"Mineral water, please."

She had returned with the drinks — his mineral water and her gin and tonic — when she heard the front door open.

"Hi, Mum," came Anne's voice. "Where are you?"

"In the sitting room. With a friend."

She heard a bag thump in the hall. Then Anne appeared in the doorway, took one look at Stefan and looked back at her mother. Emma jumped to her feet, barely aware of the surprise and guilt in her expression.

"Sorry, Mum, I got a cheap flight a day early. I didn't know you'd be entertaining."

Anne smiled briefly at Stefan, then smiled sympathetically at her mother.

"No problem, darling," Emma said cheerfully. "Stefan, this is my daughter, Anne. Anne, this is Stefan...."

She couldn't remember his last name. She stood silent and blushing, unable to think of the name or find the right words.

"Grigoriev," he said, smiling at Anne.

"Pleased to meet you," said Anne, extending her hand.

"Delighted," said Stefan, who bent to kiss her hand.

She withdrew her hand quickly and turned to her mother.

"Stefan is a dancer with the ballet, whom I am sponsoring. We are having a drink before we go to eat at the Italian restaurant on Earl Street."

"Sure, terrific," said Anne. "You guys finish your drinks. I'll go up to my room, settle in and unpack."

"Anne, maybe you come with us for dinner," said Stefan.

Anne paused, obviously considering.

"No, thank you," said Anne. "I'm tired after the flight. Mum, I'll see you later."

The Ristorante da Maria was a cozy but typical Italian place with the standard pastas and pizzas on the menu, candles in wine bottles on the tables and waiters who called their patrons 'Signore' or 'Signora'. Emma had long suspected that the waiters were actually Filipinos.

They took their seats and their waiter bowed. Again, Emma was tense. They were two again, the intimacy as it had been before Anne arrived. She had bungled the introduction with her display of nerves. She wondered what Anne made of it. She surely found Stefan attractive and would make false assumptions. My mum, at her age, with this gorgeous young man. She put the memory out of her mind, determined to return to the present. She looked across the table and Stefan smiled, a friendly, easy smile, but when she took in once again the dark eyes and the broad lips, her fear returned.

"Emma, your daughter is charming. Beautiful, like her mother."

"Yes, she is lovely. And bright as a penny."

"What is this 'penny'?"

"Never mind. She's very intelligent, let's say."

"Yes, like you. Must be intelligent to be a lawyer. With dancers, not so much. Can't be stupid, but can't think too much. Can't dance if you think always."

His comment made her picture his graceful, effortless dancing. That's it, she thought. You cannot think. You must be free of your mind to dance like that. In that moment she wanted passionately to be part of the world of dance, but she knew, sadly, that her mind was not free.

Stefan ordered a pasta with a tomato and basil sauce. She ordered gnocchi in a gorgonzola sauce, a carafe of chianti for her and mineral water for him. She asked him about plans for his upcoming year. He mentioned his two roles in *The Nutcracker* — the Mouse King and the Sugar Plum Fairy's Chevalier.

"Last show is December 28. Then I fly back to Varna and my mama."

"How sad. You don't spend Christmas with your mother."

"Yah, I do. Bulgaria is Orthodox Christian. Orthodox Christmas is January 7. They follow old calendar; is different."

"I'm so glad."

They discussed his roles in the coming year. He explained that he had supporting roles in a Balanchine evening, a new ballet putting dance to the music of Elvis Presley and some new Canadian ballet about the arrival of the first French settlers, called *Maria Chapdelaine*.

"Is okay. I like Elvis. I think I will be dancing to 'Love Me Tender'. You know this song?"

"Of course. We all grew up with it."

"Good. You will like it. But next year, in November, will be very good for me. They will do *Romeo and Juliet*, and I think I will dance Romeo. My first lead."

"Fabulous. Does it make you nervous?"

"No way. I can do that really good, you will see. Why I be nervous?"

"I see. You believe in yourself."

"Must do. Otherwise, you will not succeed. And others believe in me. The Russian, Vasilievskaya, saw me dance the Bluebird in *Sleeping Beauty*. She liked me. She says she will dance Juliet next year and she want me for her Romeo. But director say I dance with the French one, Jeanne Masset. I don't know what will happen. The Russian can be difficult, I think. But for me, doesn't matter."

During the meal he talked more about his future. She was content to listen, charmed by his enthusiasm, privileged to be sharing his excitement as he contemplated the beginning of his career. As she finished her coffee, she was determined to avoid his parting kiss.

"Stefan, I will drive you," she said. "I must get back to Anne."

When she eventually reached home, she found Anne in the sunroom, leafing through a ballet magazine.

"Carolyn phoned," Anne said, laying aside her magazine. "She says she's coming for coffee at nine-thirty."

"But Anne, I have to be at work by nine-thirty,"

"Tomorrow's Saturday, Mum."

"Right," said Emma. "I'm beat."

"Did you have a nice dinner?" Anne asked.

"Good pasta, good wine," she said, and left quickly for bed.

*

Carolyn arrived precisely at nine-thirty, dramatic in blue-tinted shades, dark lipstick, blue jeans and boots.

"Croissants," she yelled and headed for the kitchen. "I'll make the coffee."

Emma and Anne looked at each other and shrugged. That was Carolyn, energy driven by a will to have you do, what you would soon learn, was good for you. They were sitting in the rear sunroom watching sparrows pecking at the seeds Emma had scattered on the patio. Ten minutes later, Carolyn wheeled in a server with the croissants and coffee. She handed the croissants around on plates, poured coffee for each: black for Emma, cream only for Anne and black for herself. She knew without asking. She then turned to Emma.

"Mum. What's this with you and this teenage dancer?" she asked, staring intently at her mother.

Emma turned a startled gaze to Anne, dismayed. Anne looked out the window at the sparrows.

"Nothing is with this teenage dancer, as you put it." Her tone was cross. "First of all, he is twenty-one. Secondly, he has been hired by the company; he joins the ranks of full-time dancers and he has a brilliant future. I have decided to sponsor him and invited him to dinner at da Maria's so we could get to know one another. We were having a drink here before dinner. What on earth is the problem?"

"Didn't you invite him to Mary Jo's a while ago?" asked Anne.

"I did. But girls, I don't want to be cross-examined this way. Stefan is my protégé, that is all."

There was a moment of silence. Anne was keeping her eyes on

the sparrows. Carolyn removed her blue shades and set them on the coffee table.

"Mum, we're afraid you are heading into a mid-life crisis or something. I came here in the summer and you were with that ponytailed dude. He was nice, and he looked right for you. Now Anne finds you with this dancer and she says he's a hunk."

Anne's face turned red; she continued to focus on the sparrows.

"Anne and I understand, and we care for you. We just don't want to see you miserable when some boy-toy jilts you."

Emma rose to her feet. "He is not a boy-toy, he is my protégé," she said tersely. "I sponsor him."

"You sponsor him." Carolyn's tone was tense. "How much does that cost?"

Carolyn understood that she had gone too far and got to her feet, wringing her hands. Emma turned to leave.

"Girls, I'm going to the office. Enjoy the coffee."

As her mother left, Carolyn threw her arms in the air. Anne turned from the sparrows and shrugged.

When Emma reached her desk she sat, furious. Her daughters provoked the anxiety she felt with Stefan and her hesitation to embrace the landscape that was the ballet.

Chapter 21

Anne's birthday dinner was scheduled for that Monday evening at Emma's. Emma had decided that the best way to overcome the tension from the weekend was to have a superb dinner, early so Josh could be there. Anne refused to eat red meat, so she chose poached sea bass, three bottles of unoaked chardonnay and a cake as the basic meal. Emma was intending to leave work early, set the table and cook.

However, events began to interfere.

There were two messages on her line at her office Monday morning.

The first was from Ryan Connell. He had been taken on by another firm, things were looking up and he wanted to meet for coffee or a drink. He regretted the way they had left things and hoped they could still be friends.

That, I don't need, she muttered as she erased the message.

The second was from Archer Brown. Would she have time to meet around eleven to chat about what he called "the new arrangements"? Reluctantly, she left him a phone message confirming the meeting. She did not like dealing with Archer Brown. He was shy but demanding and spoke in a rapid monotone, with a snort between sentences.

Then Donna di Carlo opened her door without knocking at about ten o'clock. She stood in the doorway, her face flushed. Emma smiled cheerfully despite a sense of foreboding. From Donna's expression, she judged that nothing good would result from the conversation.

"Emma," she said in a melancholy voice. "I hope I'm not disturbing you."

Emma repressed a sarcastic response. In her experience the people who hoped they weren't disturbing you knew they were disturbing you but had to pretend that they regretted it.

"What is it, Donna?"

"I just wanted to say that I have no problem with you taking over. You are smart, capable and more experienced than me. I only got the job because they thought I would bring some family business to the firm. I didn't, so now you're it."

"Donna, we always worked well together. No worries."

"Absolutely." Donna stepped into the office. "Do you mind if I sit for a minute?"

I fucking well do mind, Emma thought. And it won't be for only a minute.

"Have a seat," she said.

"Thanks." Donna sat, crossed her legs, and sighed. "I'm thinking of retiring. I mean quitting the legal profession."

"Are you?" said Emma, a sinking feeling in her gut. "That's a big decision."

"It is, but it's right, I'm pretty sure."

Donna launched into an account of how her father had put pressure on her to enter law school. She had done only moderately well in her bar exams and was just taken on by the firm because of her family's business. She had never felt she belonged at Eberhart Williams and could never relax there, feeling she wasn't up to the job. When she began to describe the attempts she had made to get help from therapy, Emma waited several minutes with an expression of feigned interest and then intervened. She told Donna of her eleven o'clock meeting with Archer Brown. Donna got to her feet, apologizing profusely.

She escorted Donna to the door and then locked it. She began to review the files she guessed Brown would want to discuss. Her Corporate Commercial unit provided services to Brown's more specialized Mergers and Acquisitions unit. After ten minutes of reading, her phone rang. The name on the screen was Roland de Witt, the partner in Intellectual Property to whom she had introduced Bill Shrubb. They were having trouble with Shrubb, he said. He was making unreasonable demands, asking for more protection than any legal device could provide. After their last meeting, which had been a shambles, the client had suggested that Emma Peters might be useful in smoothing out their communication problems. Would she join them for their next meeting, this coming Thursday at three? She checked her schedule and agreed.

After half an hour more of reading, she left her office for her meeting with Archer Brown in his office.

"Come in, Mrs. Peters," he said after clearing his throat with the usual hawk.

He pulled out a chair for her in gentlemanly fashion, waited until she was seated and took his seat behind his desk. He pressed his fingertips together, hawked again and began. He wanted to discuss with her the proper relationship between his Mergers and Acquisitions group and her Corporate Commercial. Hers was a service group from which he would summon assistance of various kinds in the middle of a deal. His words were formal and precise. She thought he looked like a fussy undertaker in his blue suit with its pocket handkerchief and his pince-nez glasses. She was sure he was over sixty-five.

Eventually he mentioned that he needed responses from his requests for service with the utmost speed. He had not been satisfied with Mrs. di Carlo's ability to produce the speedy turn-arounds he needed and explained that that was the reason for Emma's promotion. She used her sincerest tone to assure him that she would do her best to satisfy him. He smiled briefly, cleared his throat and began to list the main areas he would involve her in. She knew what they were and tried to mask her growing boredom. At noon he looked at his watch and rose quickly. He was chairman of the finance committee of his church, he explained, and had to rush to a twelve-thirty meeting. He ushered her to the hall, cleared his throat, thanked her and returned to his office.

Back in her own office she ordered a tuna sandwich and cranberry juice, and stared out the window. Mostly because of the nuisance values of Donna, Roland de Witt and Archer Brown, she had passed her morning without thinking of Ballet Toronto or Stefan Grigoriev.

She arrived home at four-thirty, having bought the food and the wine, full of enthusiasm. She wanted Anne's dinner to be a happy reunion of the family after the difficulty of Saturday morning. She believed it was her role as mother to do this; her energy was surging. Anne was there to help. Anne had always been at ease with her mother, happy to chat, willing to confide. Carolyn, by contrast, was distant, competitive even, with her mother. Anne set the table and ran out to the local grocery for olive oil and some spices as Emma set to work on the dinner. As she completed each task — slicing, mixing, oiling and seasoning — she felt increasingly satisfied. By six o'clock the fish was in the oven, the vegetables were cooked and warm, the cake with one candle was on a sideboard and glasses and hors d'oeuvres were set out. When the doorbell rang, Emma hugged Anne and went to the door.

Carolyn walked in, gave her mother a quick peck on the cheek and proceeded to take off Josh's jacket. Emma picked Josh up from the floor and squeezed him. He laughed and wriggled. Then came

Frank, a tall, good-looking man with dark hair and blue eyes who wore, as always, jeans tucked into tooled leather boots, and a black shirt under a rawhide jacket. He beamed at Emma and embraced her. Carolyn got Josh a carton of apple juice from the fridge and took him upstairs, set him in front of the television and inserted a disc for a space movie; he would join the adults for dinner. When Carolyn returned, Frank was pouring drinks. She stood in the doorway and stared at her mother with a tight smile.

"Expecting anyone else, are we?" she said, her voice tight with innuendo.

The room felt silent; Emma stiffened. "I forgot something," she said and walked quickly to the kitchen. She stood motionless, furious, unable to think of what to do. How can you hate someone you love, she fumed.

Anne's voice came to her from the sunroom.

"Carolyn, how could you do that? That was really shitty."

"Somebody's got to do something, and it won't be you, little sister. She doesn't know what she's doing with that pretty boy."

"You should leave her alone." Anne's voice was trembling. "You have no business interfering."

"I'm not interfering," yelled Carolyn.

"Ladies." Frank's voice was quiet, but both women fell silent. "Carolyn, isn't there something about the pot calling the kettle black? I'm sure we both remember the crush you had on Josh's play-camp director last summer."

"That wasn't a crush!" exclaimed Carolyn. "We both liked the same music...."

"Sure." Frank was smiling. "Now either you two shut up, or I go and get Josh and we go home. Which is it?" Neither spoke. "Right. I'm going to help Emma."

In the kitchen, Emma had managed to get the fish out of the oven and was unwrapping the baking foil. He hugged her and set to work carrying bowls of rice and puréed broccoli to the table. Emma filleted the fish and carried it on its platter to the table.

"Wine?" Frank asked, as he went around the table.

Emma smiled gratefully and pointed to the refrigerator. He opened the chardonnay and took it to the dining-room sideboard. He called the sisters for dinner. Anne, and then Carolyn with Josh, took their seats. Frank poured the wine as Emma filled the plates that were passed to her. There was a plate of macaroni and cheese for Josh. The awkward silence was broken by ritual praise for the fish, first from Anne, then Carolyn and then Frank. There were questions for Josh about how he liked his macaroni, how he liked his teacher, then silence. When the main course was finished Anne and Carolyn cleared the table. Emma then grabbed Josh by the hand and led him to the kitchen. They returned with Josh holding the cake with its one candle lit, his eyes shining. Frank led the singing of 'Happy Birthday'. Then there were presents for Anne: a leather attaché case from her mother, earrings from Frank and Carolyn and a birthday card from Josh. Anne went around the table kissing them all. Carolyn returned her embrace.

When the family left, Emma felt that the evening had gone as well as she might have expected. But as she stood at her door watching them head for the car, she heard Carolyn berating Frank for raising her connection with the camp director. She and Anne washed up and then sat in the sunroom sipping mineral water.

"Mum, you know Carolyn loves you," Anne began. "I think she's worried about Josh. It makes her bitchy."

"I know," Emma sighed. "I don't want to talk about it."

When she finally lay down, Emma was still tense, staring at the ceiling. This night, Carolyn's rudeness had stimulated the return of Stefan's image — his face and his black hair — to the forefront of her mind.

Chapter 22

The month of November ended in cool, dismal days, when the low clouds, mist and drizzle formed a grey depression over the city. Emma Peters barely noticed. During the period that had started with Anne's birthday and ended with the approach of Christmas, she seemed to be ricocheting from meetings to lunches to crises, from work to ballet to family. The turmoil reminded her of the bumper cars she used to ride at the fairground as a kid, screaming with laughter as she careened off walls and other cars. Except that she rarely laughed during these rainy days.

She agreed to meet Ryan Connell for a drink. Since they had been lovers and colleagues, she decided that it would be petty of her to cut him off completely. He had been taken on by a smaller firm to lead their corporate commercial work and his wife was speaking to him again. He wanted bygones to be bygones, he said, and just meet as friends and catch up.

They met in the Conference Room bar at the top of her building and as soon as she saw him, she knew she had made a mistake. His hair had turned dramatically white and he had sprouted a moustache and a goatee, all perfectly trimmed. His face and hands were bronzed, from either the West Indies or a tanning parlour. She noticed his dove-grey socks that matched his dove-grey tie, set in a mauve shirt and a blue suit of creaseless silk. His smile was too fond, his embrace too personal and his assurance that the drinks were on him too patronizing. He began to hint that it would be a mature and sophisticated thing to take up their affair again and forget what he called their 'unfortunate misunderstandings'. She was revolted by Connell. She excused herself to visit the loo and did not return.

Then came Thursday and her meeting with Roland de Witt and Bill Shrubb. She entered one of the firm's smaller meeting rooms to find Shrubb smiling at de Witt and Jack Stevens, one of their intellectual-property team members, both of whom appeared frustrated. She sat down and de Witt began to explain their differences. Shrubb wanted an impossibly detailed patent for his software, which any judge would think unreasonable.

Their client, now wearing a suit, a shirt and a multicoloured tie, leaned forward. "Guys, I've been thinking about the patent. You may be right. Give me a final version and I'll sign off on it."

De Witt and Stevens looked at each other, shrugged and smiled. De Witt started in on the employment contract, saying that the restrictions on right-to-compete were too severe. Shrubb waved his hand in the air. He had re-thought his position on employee contracts and would accept their draft. With each contentious issue that de Witt raised, Shrubb agreed and withdrew.

"We seem to have settled things," said de Witt, smiling at Shrubb. "Emma, thanks for stopping by. Bill, we'll walk you to the elevator."

"No need, my friend. I want to talk to Emma for a minute."

She stared at him. He smiled cheerfully.

"What was that all about?" she asked in a testy tone after they left. "They didn't need me."

"I wanted to see you again," he said. He had stopped smiling.

"Then why in hell didn't you phone me? Why all this play-acting nonsense?"

"Because if I had phoned and asked to see you, you would have turned me down. And we had to meet."

"And why is that, exactly?"

"So you could see what I'm like out of my tee-shirts." The impish smile returned. "I wanted you to know I own a suit."

She began to smile, then broke into a laugh.

"So, you wanted to look like a lawyer?"

"Please, don't push me too far."

She paused. She could see that for once he had nothing to say.

"Bill. You're brilliant and funny and awfully sweet. I'm flattered that you resorted to subterfuge to see me. But you and I are not on. Let's be friends."

"I was afraid you'd say that." He looked at his watch. "Jesus Christ, I've got a programmers' meeting at four. Gotta run."

He grabbed his satchel and rushed for the door, without a smile.

Too bad, she thought. I like him.

When she returned to her office, she picked up a message from

Archer Brown demanding a meeting as soon as possible. The tone was fussy. She walked to his office and found his door open. He was sorting through a pile of files on his desk and did not see her enter.

"Hello, Archer," she said.

He looked up, startled. His expression changed quickly from confusion to annoyance.

"Oh, there you are, Mrs. Peters." He cleared his throat loudly. "I must say I am extremely upset. Your report from the last meeting in New York regarding Digital Connections is not here. I expected it immediately after your return and I do not have it. I am extremely disappointed. I expected much more from you."

"But Archer, I gave it to you the day after I returned. You must have it."

"Impossible. It is not in my log of incoming mail and communications of all sorts, which I keep meticulously. It is not here."

"Is that what you are looking for?" She pointed to the mess of files on his desk.

A cloud of doubt appeared on his face.

"Er … no. Of course not. I was just…."

"Never mind. Archer, I will get you a copy now. Give me two minutes."

"No, Mrs. Peters, that will not do. That report might have been useful but time has passed, and the situation has changed. You have embarrassed me. The New York people must be wondering why they haven't heard from us." He started to clean his glasses with his breast pocket handkerchief. "I want you to return to New York as soon as possible, apologize and return with an updated report."

"But Archer…."

"That is all, Mrs. Peters. My instructions are clear. I expect an updated report within three days." He hawked. "And I hope I don't soon regret replacing Mrs. di Carlo with your good self."

She left his office, stunned; she walked immediately to Don Elton's office.

"Don," she began. "I think Archer is losing it."

Before she could continue, Elton sighed with a resigned look on his face and waved her to a chair.

"Tell me," he said.

She repeated the conversation she had had with Archer Brown, including his order that she make an unnecessary return to New York. Don Elton kept nodding and frowning.

"I was afraid of this," he said when she finished. "He has early Alzheimer's. I know I should have told you, but I thought he would be okay to handle the Digital purchase. Clearly, he is not. I'm sorry."

"But what do I do? I can't go to New York again."

"Obviously. What you do is disappear for a day, take a break, whatever. Then send him the original report the next day. I'll visit him and make sure he understands he has it. I suppose I'll have to take over the file, discreetly so as not to upset him. I'll phone Joe Hirsch in New York and explain what we're doing."

"But why...?"

"Why haven't we dealt with his problem?" She nodded. "It's complicated. We lose clients if he leaves in anger. There has to be a process that satisfies him. I was going to work it out with him, give him a paid leave in Italy — he calls Italy his spiritual home — whatever it takes. I don't want him exploding and going to another firm with his Alzheimer's and his business."

"Got it," she said. "Thanks, Don."

*

It had started to snow just after daybreak and continued until mid afternoon. Emma had been wondering how he would arrive; probably not on his bicycle given the snow. It was the night for their monthly dinner, and she had been checking her messages all day to see if he would cancel. When the doorbell rang at the appropriate time, she felt a tremor, which irritated her. She opened the door to Stefan. He stood there in a long sheepskin coat and sheepskin boots. Snow had blown over his black hair, and he was grinning at her.

He looks like Good King Wenceslas, she thought.

"Emma, where is…?" He waved at her snow-covered walk and made a shovelling motion.

"Shovel?" she said. "You want to shovel my walk?"

"Yah. Where is shovel?"

She pointed to her side alley. Although the snow had stopped earlier, she had put off shovelling. He returned and started shovelling her walk and sidewalk, heaving the snow onto her lawn or the street with what seemed to her almost no effort. He finished in ten minutes or so. She ushered him into her house; he stepped out of his boots and hung his coat over a bannister.

"Water?" she asked.

"No, Emma. Tonight, I shovel in cold night. You have Slivovitz, schnapps, something like that? Is good for the heart."

She poured a tumbler of brandy which he gulped in one swallow.

"I thought you never drank."

"Not after dancing. After dancing I sweat; booze is bad when sweating. Tonight, I shovel in cold and don't sweat. Booze warms heart and that is good."

After ten minutes of desultory chatting they put on their coats and boots and she drove them to da Maria's. Their waiter took their coats and they sat smiling uncomfortably at one another. It had been a while since they had last spoken.

"How is your mother?" she asked finally.

"Mama is good," he said. "When I am good, Mama is good."

"She is happy because she will see you for Christmas."

"Little bit. But really, she is happy because I dance Chevalier in *Nutcracker*."

"Naturally. She is proud of you."

"Yah. Is true."

He fell silent for a moment and she noticed a dreamy, speculative smile.

"Things go well for me, Emma. I am happy."

"Tell me."

He launched into a description of his rehearsals, mentioning how well he was dancing and the compliments he was getting from the ballet master. He complained about the dancer dancing the role of the Sugar Plum Fairy. She did not know the correct position for his final lift in their pas de deux and would not listen to the ballet master. He said that the practice pianist played too fast sometimes and too slow other times. His litany of boasts and complaints and the pride in the attention he was receiving continued through the meal, his expression rising to a beaming smile and then falling to a scowl. She was sympathetic at first, understanding the importance of these early months with the company for the rest of his career.

He paused for a moment.

"This Russian is problem for me, I think."

"Why?"

"She goes to Alec and tells him I must be her Romeo. She don't tell me she will do this. She don't ask me. She acts like she decides if I dance with her. Alec phones me, wants to talk with me about. I don't like this."

"They say she is difficult," said Emma.

"I know she is bitch, but I can deal with her."

He was still smiling but his eyes were fierce.

She looked at her watch.

*

That night, sleep did not come easily. She couldn't forget his appearance at her front door, a snowy mediaeval hunter in from the forest. The ease with which he had shovelled her walk reminded her of his dancing — rhythmic and strong. Eventually, however, she had become bored during the hour and a half she listened to his stories and watched the emotions flicker across his face. She was his audience. He was not interested in what her day had been like or what she thought about anything. She was there to listen, sympathize and admire, as she would do in the ballet hall. Her dilemma was bittersweet. She was merely his sponsor; there was no reason for him to have any other feeling for her than gratitude for her money.

Chapter 23

Dora Lassinger entered the director's office and found him staring out the window, muttering quietly. She paused to listen but could not make out the words.

"What's the matter, boss?"

He turned slowly.

"It looks like rain, and I wanted to bicycle home." He shrugged. "Where's Stefan? He was supposed to be here at two-thirty."

"He phoned. He twisted his ankle…"

"He what?" Runciman froze and his eyes began to blink rapidly.

"He's getting it taped. He'll be here in ten minutes."

"But can he dance? It's *Nutcracker* soon."

"I don't know. You'll have to ask him."

"God help me, who in the hell have we got if the boy can't dance *Nutcracker*? It will have to be one of the young guys. Dammit, I can't even remember their names. Dora, please get me a list, right away, please. Twisted ankle." He threw his hands in the air. "That's all I need."

"Okay, can do. But may I suggest we wait until you talk to Stefan?"

He exhaled and smiled at her gratefully.

"My dear Dora, how well you know me. Of course we wait, no need to panic. Yet." He sat down in his chair. "I have been tense, shall we say, about the Romeo issue. I talked to Ralph about dancing with Jeanne Masset. He was not happy."

"He has to be happy. You're the boss, boss."

"Right. Sometimes I wish I weren't. This job can feel like chaperoning a high-school dance." He reached into a desk drawer, drew out a package of peppermint lozenges and stuck one in his mouth. "Ralph's a man; he has a male ego. He will see this change as a threat to his status as our principal male dancer. He's looking at this talented, handsome, young man and wondering about the future. So, he wants Tatyana."

"But she doesn't want him."

"But you understand that I can't tell him that. I need him happy and eager to dance."

"And you need her happy and eager to dance."

"Right. Is it possible?" He sucked on his lozenge. "It just may be. Ralph is ultimately a reasonable guy, a good guy. I may be able to convince him it's for the good of the company, or at least bribe him. Inducements. I think I could get him a gig with The Manhattan Ballet next year, something like that. But Vasilievskaya is something else. She is not reasonable." He grimaced. "It all depends on Stefan. Will he do it? Can he do it?"

"You think he can, don't you?"

"Maybe. We'll see."

They heard the outer door open. Dora walked to the reception area and brought Stefan in, limping slightly.

"Hello, Stefan. Thanks for coming." He motioned Stefan to a chair as Dora left the office. "How is your ankle?"

"Is no problem. No ligament torn, no muscle. I can dance in three days."

"Thank God." Runciman sat down, smiling. "As I mentioned, Tatyana came to me two days ago and asked that you be her Romeo next November."

"She didn't ask me," said Stefan, scowling.

"She didn't mention any thing about this to you?"

"She told me she liked me as Bluebird, wants me for Romeo. Only that."

"At any rate, she asked me. Now tell me, what do you think of the idea?"

Stefan shrugged. "Doesn't matter to me. Only, Jeanne Masset is nice girl. I am okay dancing with her."

"And Tatyana is difficult. She didn't come to me and ask that you dance with her. She demanded."

Stefan laughed. "She would do that. She is Russian bitch. I always say so."

"I wouldn't put it quite that way, but I know what you mean," said Runciman. "On the other hand, she is a brilliant dancer. Her experience at the Bolshoi gives her a background none of our other dancers have. Did you know that she danced Juliet to André Pleshnikov's Romeo?"

Stefan nodded.

"So, let me tell you the upside of you dancing with her."

"Upside? What means upside?"

"I mean by that, the benefit to you. She has been, and is, a great dancer, and she likes you. That means there could be chemistry in your dancing that would make it sensational. If you feel it."

"Can be chemistry with the French girl, Jeanne." Stefan stared at the floor, then looked up with a shrewd expression on his face. "So, Alec, you think is a good idea."

"Maybe. If you commit to dancing with her, she can teach you,. She can expand your idea of what you can do with Romeo."

"So, will be good for me?"

"If you want it."

Stefan sat still for a minute. The director sensed the calculations behind the dark eyes.

"Yah, okay," said Stefan. "I will do it. I can handle her."

Runciman noticed the fierce, almost predatory glint in his dancer's eyes and felt encouraged. The boy would do it.

Chapter 24

The canteen was almost deserted. As soon as Stefan saw her, he knew she had tracked him down to gloat over her success with Runciman. Nevertheless, he decided he would sit with her. He wanted to get to know her since they would be dancing together. He had difficulties thinking of her as his Juliet.

"So, Stefan, you are Romeo and I am Juliet."

"You didn't tell me you were going to Alec. You didn't ask."

She annoyed him: her voice, her expression and even her posture were arrogant.

"Why should I tell you? You didn't know what should be. I knew, and Alec agreed with me."

"Is not true. He agreed with me, that you are Russian bitch."

Her laugh was bitter.

"Yes, I am Russian bitch. That is why I am still alive, sitting here and talking with you. That is why you will dance *Romeo and Juliet* with me." She glared at him. "I think, my baby boy, that if we are going to dance together, I need to explain some things to you."

She looked at him appraisingly, adopted a sad smile and began her account.

"In Russia, I come from a small city in Ural Mountains." Her speech was slow and quiet, a change from her usual banter. Stefan was fascinated. "I can dance, but there are not good teachers there, so they send me to ballet school in Moscow. After two years they notice me, and I am accepted in Bolshoi corps de ballet. I am good, but everyone accepted by Bolshoi is good. To rise in the company, being good is not enough. I do what I need to do, and I rise. Problem was, I attract big oil and gas billionaire, name Leonid. He sees me dance and wants me." She scrutinized his expression. "He buys me apartment, fur coats, Alfa Romeo, everything; but I am prisoner. Sex whenever he wants, and not nice sex. I can have no friends. I cannot leave apartment without his permission. I go to artistic director of Bolshoi but he can do nothing. Leonid is friend of Putin, so no hope."

She shook her head, a helpless victim, trying to calculate the impression she was making.

"So, one night I am going crazy, so I run from the apartment and find a hotel with room. Police find me in middle of night and take me back to Leonid. He hits me. He tells me if I run again, he will kill me. I believe him. I go to artistic director again and same thing, but he is my friend and he has idea for me. He will ask quietly if any company in the rest of the world will buy my contract. I am sick because of Leonid and can't dance so good, so Bolshoi will let me go. Leonid has new girlfriend and is happy to see me leave. My friend asks, but only this company will offer for me. Is because Billy saw me dance in Moscow and puts up money for contract and to buy off Leonid, who is still saying to friends he might kill me. So, I am here and free person."

Stefan's fascination was gone.

"A nice story you tell. Maybe true, maybe not. I think you take from your boyfriend, then go with other men. So, he wants to kill you. You are bitch, and I understand what is bitch."

She jumped to her feet, the innocent victim gone.

"You think you understand me?" she yelled. The few heads left in the canteen turned to look at her. "You understand nothing. I fight just to stay alive, with everything I have: I lie, I fuck, I run and I hide. Now I am here and I am safe, but I fight every day for me the way I learned. That is why you dance with me. I need you for me. And you need me for you, although you are baby boy and don't know anything."

She sat down and the cool mask returned, her lips twisted in a cynical smile. Stefan was speechless, amazed at her change from bitch to pathetic victim and back again.

"So, baby boy, enough of Tatyana. What about you? Are you sleeping with Emma?"

"Is not your business." He scowled. "I told you she is good woman, generous, with family. She don't need me. You don't understand woman like that."

Her laugh was harsh.

"Stefan, it is you who don't understand. This is a beautiful woman. She wants you to touch her. That is why she sponsored you."

"No," he exclaimed. "You use your body to rise in Bolshoi, you cheat your boyfriend and now you sleep with Bill Shrubb to pay him for helping you. You think all the world is like you but is not true. You are hooker."

She rose as if to leave but stood in front of him and mimicked a kiss.

"You call me hooker. Maybe it's true, I don't mind. I do what I have to do and it's honest. So, if I am a hooker you better pay me to dance with you."

Her smile mocked him.

"Don't be stupid," he said angrily.

"Then what will you give me for what you will get from me? One thing to know, Stefan. Men and women want each other. I sleep with Billy because he saved me and because he wants me. Even your sponsor with the grandson. She is a beautiful woman and she wants you to touch her. If you do, will that make you a hooker? Like me?"

It was Stefan who left the canteen first, fleeing her laughter.

Can I dance with her, he wondered. Is she bitch or witch or what?

Chapter 25

Early December passed, and the approach of the holidays did not bring the usual excitement for Emma. The weather depressed her; the snow and cold of late November warmed into mist, slush and dismal grey. Moreover, the combination of non-stop Christmas entertaining and frantic maneuvering to keep the Digital Connections deal alive without alienating Archer Brown, reduced her days to chaos.

"Hang in with Archer until January fifteenth," said Don Elton. "I've given him two months in Venice on his way out the door. He's ecstatic." Elton had stuck his head in her door to bring her up-to-date.

"Does he love painting and going to galleries? He doesn't seem like the type."

"He isn't. He has a fondness for handsome gondoliers." Elton rolled his blue eyes. "I discovered this when he got in trouble with the Venetian police two years ago. Underage gondolier."

"Unbelievable. Isn't he an elder in his church?"

"That's why he needs his trips to Venice, apparently."

Julie had purchased their *Nutcracker* tickets for a matinee the

Saturday before Christmas. She had invited Emma to come back to her house after the ballet for dinner. Emma accepted.

During that time, however, she refused to anticipate the ballet or Stefan's performance, and concentrated instead on her files. Then Carolyn announced that it was time for her to prepare the family Christmas dinner and hold it at her house. She claimed that Emma was too busy with all her activities, and that it was time she gave up her usual role. Frank would cook the turkey.

Emma agreed, reluctantly. She felt that she was being overthrown in a kind of generational coup. Last year Carolyn had been critical of her turkey; it was overdone, dried out, she said. It was true that Emma had cooked it too long. Moreover, the idea made sense; she really was too busy.

As they entered the lobby of the ballet theatre, she noticed in the crowd a number of mothers with young daughters in flowered dresses, white stockings and in what she used to call Mary Jane shoes. She doubted that her mother had dressed her that way when they had gone to Detroit to see *The Nutcracker*. She wouldn't have been able to buy the clothes in Isherton. As they took their seats, Emma was determined again to contain her excitement. The lush strains of the overture soothed her, and she sat back, hoping Stefan's entrance would come soon. When he finally appeared as the Mouse King, she was disappointed; this was not the Stefan she wanted. He led the mice in a battle against the gingerbread soldiers, who were led by the Nutcracker. When the girl, Clara, threw her shoe at the Mouse King he was distracted, and the Nutcracker was able to stab him.

Emma turned to Julie.

"What a stupid role," she whispered. "He's better than that."

"Wait 'til the second act," said Julie.

She waited. Sure enough, from the moment Stefan strode on stage, elegant and handsome as the Sugar Plum Fairy's Cavalier, she was entranced. And as they danced their pas de deux she held her breath. She felt his strength; she couldn't take her eyes off his glowing face. She was moved by his care for his partner — lifting her, twirling her, setting her gently down — all of it with grace, as if his fairy were a beautiful feather.

Emma watched with clasped hands, enthralled. Julie looked at her and smiled. By the end of the performance, Emma had returned to the world of ballet. Archer Brown, Carolyn and the host of pressures that had been pursuing her melted away like snow in April.

*

Entering Julie's house sometimes seemed to Emma as if she were entering a movie set. You were meant to notice first the impressive hallway with its black and white tiled floor and the two opposing stairways curving to the second floor. Then you would notice the nineteenth and early twentieth-century Canadian paintings on most walls and the formal dining room with mahogany and cut glass everywhere you looked. The house was Julie's realm and Emma usually took pleasure in her hospitality, but this evening their entry was different.

Usually Vern came quickly to the door. The large man, ruddy and blond with the body of an athlete who was living well, would exclaim, "By God, it's the gorgeous Emma," before enveloping her in a brief but enormous bear hug. This time when they entered Julie waited, then yelled, "Vernon, we're here," in an impatient tone. When he appeared after a minute or so, Emma was shocked. His smile was brief, the the bear hug perfunctory. He looked suddenly older — stooped somewhat and tentative. He took their coats. When he had served them their usual gin and tonics, he paused in the doorway.

"I have to phone Montreal, Julie. They may have a buyer."

Julie looked intently at Emma.

"We're trying to sell some of our rental properties in Montreal and Ottawa," she said. "I mentioned to you that he's lost a ton of money in the market this past month. I don't understand it; something to do with artificial intelligence." She took another swallow. "It's bad. We've put a mortgage on this house, but even with that we'll have to sell the properties."

"Jules, I'm so sorry. But you'll deal with this, I know you will;

you and Vern." She paused. "Why doesn't Vern talk to Bill Shrubb? Artificial intelligence is his business."

"He wouldn't. Vern thinks Bill Shrubb is a fly-by-night, a hustler."

"He's making good money."

"I know. But Vern can be … impossible." She wiped a tear from her eye. "And that's not all." She grimaced. "That stupid little brat of ours has been caught selling dope at school. Fortunately, only the guidance teacher knows. Another kid ratted Wilson out to him. Because he's the guidance teacher, he respects Wilson's confidence. Neither the principal nor the police know."

"Wow! If there's anything I can do…."

"Just be my friend, honey. We'll find the dough, somehow."

Despite her sympathy, Emma felt relief at this crack in the Fredricks' ramparts; it was reassuring that Julie had problems along with the rest of humanity. However, she put these thoughts quickly out of her mind. After hearing Julie's problems, the afternoon's performance seemed to Emma well in the past. They agreed that the ballet was light but Christmassy, and Stefan had been fabulous. The mention of Stefan brought no wry and knowing smiles from Julie.

Over dinner, Vern announced that no buyers had surfaced. Emma complimented him on her barbecued steak. He managed a vestige of his old smile; he had done her steak exactly as she liked it. He wanted very much to please her, so she gave him her warmest smile. Tension between Julie and her husband was obvious during the meal; Julie barely spoke. By common agreement, it seemed, there was no lingering after dinner. Vern called a taxi; Julie escorted her to the door. Without a word the two women had a long embrace.

*

By contrast, Christmas dinner at Carolyn's pleased Emma. She had gone with some resentment over the end of her reign at the family Christmas, but from the moment she entered the house the mood was jovial. Frank hugged everyone and made pathetic jokes as he poured their drinks. He assured her that although the turkey was smelling good, it would never measure up to the standard she had set over the years.

Why wasn't I able to find a man like that, Emma wondered.

Josh hugged her and begged her to read the book she had brought for him. The weight of his small body cuddling into her comforted Emma. But it was Carolyn who surprised her. From the warm hug at the door, to asking her questions about her work and the ballet, to serving her at the table, Carolyn's attention to her mother never wavered.

She's won what she wanted, thought Emma. Now she can afford sympathy for me, her old mum.

The conversation at the table was lively. The dinner, including a plum pudding, was excellent, everyone agreed. No one mentioned the turkey.

"Carolyn was a sweetheart," said Anne on the drive home. "She's happy we've moved to their house for Christmas and she wants you to feel okay. Do you?"

"My dear, if I cook even one more turkey in my life, it will be too many. Or something like that."

*

Emma was unsure about New Year's Eve. Every year the company threw a party in their rehearsal hall for their dancers and administrative staff. It was always magnificent, Julie claimed. The hall was transformed by the designers each year. Last year they had created a Caribbean island effect. The dancers dressed for the tropics, very sexy, and naturally they could all do the calypso. But no, she would not be going, Julie said. Vern had to be in Montreal for some reason to do with their real estate and she was going with him. The theme this year was to be Buenos Aires.

This means the tango, thought Emma. Never in my life.

But there was Stefan. This would be her last chance to see him before he returned to his mother. Would he dance with her? Did she want him to? She couldn't really dance. Perhaps she would dance with him, but not the tango. On the last day of December, she decided to go. She had a black cocktail dress with a slit up one leg; it would have to do. She decided to arrive late, ten-thirty or so, reconnoitre the scene and decide how to proceed. When she approached the hall, she heard not tango music but a soft song with a slow Latin rhythm, a love song.

Not so bad, she thought. Perhaps I can do this.

She entered and paused by the door, and a waiter offered her a glass of champagne from his tray. She stood sipping and surveying the room. Dancers everywhere were dancing Latin style, the women in tango dresses, the men as banditos, but she could not see Stefan.

"He is not here."

The voice was musical and deep. Emma turned to see Tatyana Vasilievskaya smiling at her. Her hair was black again and hung over her bare shoulders. Her lips were scarlet, and she had bright blue eyeshadow under false eyelashes. Her emerald-green dress was slit up one side and barely covered her bottom and her breasts.

Sexy, Emma thought. She looks like a hooker.

"He went to Bulgaria to see his mummy," she said.

Emma stopped breathing, blinked, then forced a nonchalant smile. He had left without telling her.

"That's nice for him," she said weakly. "And for her."

"You know the director is thinking that he will dance Romeo with me next year?"

"Yes, he told me. You are lucky."

"How would you know who is lucky?" Vasilievskaya's gaze was cool and appraising. "So, you are sponsoring him. Tell me, what do you want from him?"

Startled, Emma searched for words.

"You are nervous. That means you don't know what you want." She spoke with contempt. "Nothing here for you tonight, lady." She turned and strutted to the dance floor.

Emma wanted to leave. She set her glass on a table, but before she could turn for the door, Alec Runciman was standing beside her.

"I saw you talking to Tatyana. Now I see the look on your face and I see you leaving. I make some assumptions as to why you are leaving, but let's forget them. If you will stay long enough for a drink and a dance with me it will be my bedtime and we can both leave."

She smiled and nodded. He brought two glasses and they stood drinking while he commented on the couples on the floor. She began to relax.

"Okay, Emma, shall we dance?'

"No, Alec, it's a tango," she said. "I can't…"

"Yes, you can. Just hang loose, like a rag doll, wriggle your bottom to the beat and let me do the rest."

They danced. She followed instructions and discovered that no matter what she did, he moved to make it look as if she had moved well. She began to enjoy herself and with that began to move her bottom enthusiastically.

He laughed. "Look at you," he said. "Fabulous."

"It was you. I can't dance."

"Nonsense. I enjoyed it and so did you. We'll have one more, and then I must go."

They danced again and this time she laughed. When the music stopped, they embraced.

"Thanks, my dear," he said. "Best New Year's Eve in a long while."

During her taxi ride home, she was humming a tango tune they had danced. When she fell asleep, she was still smiling.

BOOK TWO

Chapter 26

Since Stefan's return from Bulgaria in January, Emma had seen him dance twice and had had dinner with him in February, their only contacts. No problem with that, she thought. Strictly business. Although he had been in her thoughts, she was unable to ask herself why. Carolyn assumed they were having an affair, that Stefan was her boy-toy. That was vulgar, she thought, and beneath the woman she believed she was. He was an attractive man, she would admit, and she told herself sometimes that he represented an element of the overall beauty of ballet, which was what intrigued her. She insisted to herself that she was merely sponsoring him. She did wonder, however, how she should interpret his obvious affection for her. She hoped it was merely friendship and told herself that she wanted nothing more from him. She floated through the weeks and began to feel passive and indecisive. Eventually she became furious with her confusion. Her anger demanded that she clarify her situation with Stefan and limit the relationship to strict sponsorship — no more dinners, just a cheque every month — but that thought was immediately unacceptable.

She arranged another dinner at da Maria, which had become their restaurant. She arrived before him and took a table. He arrived on his bicycle and approached her table, smiling warmly. He kissed her on the lips and sat across, staring directly at her.

He is different tonight, staring at me, she thought. What does he want?

"Emma," he said. "I must talk with you."

"Of course, Stefan." Her nerves quivered. "What can I do for you?"

"Maybe nothing, I don't know." His voice was soft. "Please, please don't be angry with me, I beg you."

"Angry?" She kept her voice calm. "Why would I be angry with you?"

"Because, you are so beautiful, so kind to me. I have feelings for you. Very strong."

Oh my God, she thought. This is it. He wants.... "That does not make me angry, Stefan." Fool, she said to herself. Is that all you can say?

"Then, you have feelings for me maybe?"

Oh yes, she thought. Here I go at last. "Yes," she said and smiled at him.

He rose and came around the table. She rose and they embraced. Then the waiter arrived and they sat down, smiling. Afterwards she remembered nothing of the dinner. She could remember only his eyes, his smile and her feeling of relief.

Why had she been lying to herself? This was the truth that she had been so fearful of.

They finished eating and she paid the bill. She knew what she wanted, but she didn't have to say it. He invited her to his flat. She remembered nothing of the flat except there was no elevator and they walked up the stairs to the second floor, holding hands. His lovemaking was tender and strong; they could feel the joy in each other. When they finished, they lay back on the bed, laughing.

Is this really happening, she wondered. Then why did I not know? What was I afraid of?

Chapter 26

It took them two hours from Toronto before they reached the lakes and pines of cottage country. Stefan remarked on the change in the landscape from the farm country to the south.

"Is wild and romantic, this land," he said. "I like so many lakes."

It was dark by the time they turned down the dirt road for Bear Lake. Her headlights picked out pink granite rocks and shiny pine trunks as they twisted and turned. A deer emerged from the forest and stood facing them on the road. He watched intently as Emma drove slowly forward; the deer turned and trotted back into the trees.

"Is bears here, Emma?" he asked.

"Sometimes," she said.

She turned at a sign that read 'Peters'. Her drive sloped down from the road towards the lake. Emma had used her remote to turn on the electric system. It would be warm inside; the electric fireplace would be glowing. They stepped out of the car into total silence.

"Look at stars," said Stefan. "So beautiful." They stood still for a moment, winding down from their drive. He was enchanted; she could feel it.

"Let's get inside and unpack," she said. "I need a drink."

He carried a cooler with food for the weekend and set it in the kitchen. She followed with their bags. The cottage consisted of a kitchen, dining area, two bedrooms and a large sitting area with a view of the lake. The walls were varnished pine, hung with landscapes she had bought over the years from local artists. The pine floors were covered with rugs in the colours of the country: autumn reds, golds or oranges, lake and sky blues, and forest greens. They sat with their drinks, staring out the picture window into the night.

"Thank you so much," he said. "Is beautiful. So kind you do this for me."

His gratitude amused her.

"I wanted you to be here with me. I wanted you to see more of the country. All you ever see is cities and ballet halls."

"Is true. And now I see. Thank you, again."

She looked at him, and admired his beauty. So here we are, she thought.

Their night was winding down. Tired after the drive, they talked for perhaps twenty minutes, mainly discussing what they would do the next day. She suggested they get out the canoe and she would paddle him around the shoreline. They could drive into town, visit some galleries showing local artists and have lunch. He was agreeable to anything. As she finished her drink, she became tense. She glanced at the bedroom door.

I'm tired, she thought. I'm getting old.

"Time for bed," she said, getting to her feet.

"Okay, Emma," he said. "Listen, this was long drive. Maybe we talk tonight."

"Thank you, my dear," she said.

She gathered their glasses. They changed, showered and lay down beside each other. They chatted quietly, kissed and he rolled over; she glanced at him and smiled. Her fears had been needless. Despite her age, her body delighted him. The warmth she had been unsure of was real; he loved her. She sighed and fell asleep picturing his face.

When she left her bedroom in the morning there was no sign of him. Although it was still too early in the year to swim, she had asked him if he could swim, and he had reassured her that his father had taught him before he died. She went to the window and saw him standing on the dock. She got out of her nightclothes, put on a housecoat, and left the cottage for the dock. Stefan was standing naked on the dock, soaking up the early morning sun and smiling at her. He reached for his towel and wrapped himself in it. She walked up to him, snatched the towel away, stepped out of her housecoat and embraced him. He looked down at her.

"You want?" He was smiling.

"What do you think?" she said.

They kissed for a minute, then walked hand-in-hand up to the cottage and entered their bedroom together. The lovemaking was slow and friendly; they smiled and whispered together. When they had finished, he looked down at her fondly, letting his breathing subside; he kissed her and rolled away. She stretched lazily.

"Aren't you wonderful!" she said.

"You think so? Is good. And you are so beautiful, my Emma. I am so happy this happened. I did not know if you wanted...."

"I didn't know either, but I figured it out."

A cloud passed over his face.

"Is this why you sponsored me?"

She sat upright. "Of course not. I sponsored you because I saw you dance. You were so beautiful." She giggled. "Stefan, think about it. If I wanted to buy a lover, I could probably do it cheaper."

He laughed.

"What's funny?" she asked.

"Life is funny," he said, and hugged her again.

From that beginning the rest of the day unfolded like a series of dance steps, like music in a dream. She paddled him up and down the shoreline in the canoe. She taught him the paddling strokes and he managed to propel the canoe zigzag for a quarter of a mile, with much laughter. They went to town, looked at paintings in several galleries and talked easily together about what they liked. They ate in a cozy café, drank some wine, chatted and laughed.

I'm in my forties and he has just turned twenty-two, she thought. So it won't be forever. Amazing, how good you can feel after sex.

When they drove back to the city the next afternoon, she felt that she was driving through a different country: the trees were greener, the road clearer and the miles sped by.

Chapter 27

Stefan began to sleep at her house, so her days at work were a struggle to focus on the practice of law. At her desk, she dreamed of Stefan walking in her front door, of eating together, of making love and waking in the morning beside him in her bed. She would laugh out loud as she thought of her lover leaving for a rehearsal, knowing he would be back sometime that day because he wanted to be with her. Her body felt wonderful as it grew accustomed to their relationship. She walked with an easy swing in a new rhythm. She found herself humming songs she had forgotten she knew. Problems and office politics seemed harmless, even amusing. She went to a retirement reception for Archer Brown in the firm's boardroom and greeted Archer with a hug and a kiss, laughing as the old man jumped away in alarm. Occasionally she was mindful of the person she had always been. She knew that the ecstasy she was experiencing would eventually subside. A calmer, everyday routine was inevitable, but she refused to consider when that might be. She was determined to exult in every moment without thinking.

The first shadow fell when Stefan insisted on sleeping over only occasionally. She was miserable when he left for his flat after they had made love. He also told her that he would move out from the flat he was sharing with one of the apprentice dancers and find one of his own, now that he could afford it. He needed to be free to come and go according to the demands of rehearsals and performances and would not be able to spend every night with her. When he noticed her disappointment, he hugged her and told her he loved her. That satisfied her. Keeping his own flat made sense, she decided. He had his career and, as for her, it had been years since she lived with a man.

Nevertheless, over the first few weeks he did spend most nights with her. However, as time passed, she became aware of his personality in a way that had not been possible before. This meant adjusting to compromises and the inevitable minor annoyances. He was obsessively tidy; a neat freak, she called him. He would tidy the kitchen after she left it, pick up newspapers and magazines that she left lying around and wipe dust off window ledges. He liked to watch television after dinner and his interests bewildered her. He found a channel that seemed to show nothing but tag-team wrestling. It was new to Stefan and he loved it. He would watch the costumed, overweight performers commit make-believe mayhem on each other and laugh. "Is ballet," he would say. "They are dancers, is ballet." He also liked cop dramas because they showed the struggle between the forces of good and evil, which he thought was the theme of great ballet. Emma was surprised at first, but accepted these qualities as part of the real person that was her beautiful dancer.

She also came to realize that the joy she felt just thinking about him, let alone the tremor that passed through her when he walked through the front door, was not shared. When he came home — could she use that word — he kissed her, asked what was for dinner and went to her sunroom to read the newspaper. He was trying to learn more English words by reading newspapers. After dinner he would look for one of his shows on television. She began to feel that they were heading towards an old-married rut. Although he made love to her passionately and said that he loved her, she wasn't sure what he meant by the words. One morning she sat at her desk worrying that Bulgarian was one of those languages that has different words for different kinds of love, as the Innuit have words for many kinds of snow. What if he meant a different kind of love from the kind she wanted when he said he loved her? Annoyed with herself, she picked up her phone and called Don Elton to ask if he had Archer Brown's new phone number.

Emma was in love. The reality of Stefan, with his peculiarities and foibles, was stunning. The effect on her became obvious one Saturday morning when she drove him to an exhibition that he and three other dancers were performing for interested students and some parents in a suburban high school. He had slept in and had not left himself enough time to reach the school with city transit. She offered to drive him, feeling responsible for his sleeping in, and decided to stay for the performance and drive him home, she hoped to her house. She sat in the auditorium watching the stage. The four dancers — Stefan, Shirley McIsaac and two apprentices — came out and did some stretching exercises. The kids clapped. Then they did a kind of peasant dance with twirling and tossing, and the kids clapped again. Then Stefan turned on a recording of the music of the Bluebird pas de deux, and he and Shirley McIsaac danced. Emma had never before seen him dance as she saw him now. When he lifted Shirley, Emma could feel his arms around her, and she understood the strength of his legs. Although they danced in workout gear, she could sense his sweat. When the dance ended, she rose to her feet and clapped.

Every so often the old Emma — the work-ethic, value-for-money Emma — emerged briefly and thought about what was really happening. The relationship was inherently unbalanced and could not last forever, she told herself; when he was thirty-five, she would be almost sixty. Marriage was obviously out of the question. Once as she dreamed, however, the idea of bearing his child came to her, apparently out of nowhere. Although it was still possible, the fact that she could even think of it appalled her. At the same time, she would imagine the beauty of the impossible child. She felt mad. She was in something she did not control, that swept her past the obstacles and anxieties of her real life to … she didn't know where. She called it her tsunami. She was insane. She phoned Julie.

*

They met on a sunny Saturday afternoon in late May at Café Vert and sat on the terrace. She hadn't mentioned the purpose of the meeting; she believed that so far no one knew about her and Stefan. Julie, after a brief update on their still-precarious financial situation, sat still and waited. Emma didn't hesitate and announced her affair in one short sentence. Julie shook her head.

"Emma, Emma, do you know what you're doing?"

"No," said Emma. "But I don't care."

"You do care. That's why are we having this conversation?"

Emma wiped a tear from her eye.

"You're right. I do care. The thing is, Jules, I don't really know what's happening to me."

She began an account of the first night in his flat, then the weekend at Bear Lake and the months since. She made Julie smile when she described the annoyances in the new domestic relationship. Her voice became quieter and tenser as she described her confusion and worries. When she confessed to her bearing-his-child fantasy, Julie frowned. At the end of her story, after perhaps twenty minutes, Emma fell silent.

"So, you're in love," said Julie. "After I warned you."

"And I don't want it to end," she said quietly.

"It will end. You know that."

Emma flared. "Please, Jules. I didn't ask you here to scold me. Of course it will end. But right now, I'm in it and I don't know how to think, what to do."

Julie's disapproving frown melted. She took Emma's hand. "I'm sorry, sweetheart. I don't mean to be negative. In fact, I'm a little jealous." Her smile was sympathetic. "You say you don't know how to think, but you do. You've just given me an insightful account of what happened between you and the gorgeous Stefan. And you do know what to do. You're going to go with it, come hell or high water. You understand the risks but you're in love." She paused. "Who knows about this?"

"Just you. But the word will get out soon enough. This is a ballet company."

Emma ran through the reactions she expected. Carolyn would be horrified and judge her as a silly old fool. Anne would be sympathetic but worried. Alec Runciman would be tolerant; he had already warned her of the dangers.

"And then there's me," said Julie affectionately. "Em, I hope you get everything you dream of from Stefan. And whatever happens, you know I love you."

Emma nodded and wiped away another tear.

Chapter 28

Although Emma knew she had to tell Anne and Carolyn about the relationship with Stefan, she agonized for days about how to go about it. The problem was Carolyn. She was sure that she could phone Anne in Halifax, explain the situation and Anne would be concerned but sympathetic. Carolyn's sympathy was unlikely, however, so Emma did not want to face a phone conversation with her oldest daughter. No matter how she did it, she felt she must treat the two girls in the same way. She decided that the solution was email. Usually Emma didn't believe in email as a way of dealing with personal and emotional issues, so she kept putting off writing it for several days. When, on a Saturday afternoon, she forced herself to get down to it, she sat at the computer for twenty minutes composing, erasing and re-composing. Finally, exhausted, she clicked on the send button. When the screen confirmed that her message was gone, she held her head in her hands. She looked up at the screen from time to time to see if there was an immediate response. There was none.

She had started to make herself some tea when her phone rang. It was Anne, reacting as Emma had known she would. Stefan seemed nice. Anne was happy for her. She knew Emma understood the risks for herself in this kind of relationship. She didn't mention the difference in age, but obviously it was on her mind. Anne sounded very emotional. She told her mother how much she loved her, how happy she was that her mother would not be alone any longer — Emma had never mentioned Ryan Connell to the girls — and wished her happiness. Then Emma asked Anne if Carolyn had contacted her about the email. Anne answered no and advised her not to take Carolyn too seriously; this confirmed Emma's concern. She sat teary-eyed after she put her phone down.

She checked the computer screen and saw Carolyn's email in the in-box. She took a deep breath and opened it. It was as bad as anything she could have imagined. Carolyn had read her email just after returning from the farmers' market. She thanked her mother for ruining a happy day. She was appalled that her mother would behave in such an irresponsible way, falling for some gigolo who was not even half her age and was obviously after money. She had disgraced herself and the entire family. As long as this tawdry relationship was going on, she did not want to communicate with her mother. She would not bring Josh to her house and expose him to the affair. It ended with the line, "This was the worst news ever."

Stunned, Emma sat breathless for several moments, but then her gorge began to rise. The email was more than disapproving, it was vicious. Cutting her off from Josh had nothing to do with the effect of the affair on the boy; it was meant to hurt her.

The bitch, she thought. The absolute bitch. She hates me.

She calmed herself. Carolyn probably didn't hate her, ultimately; but Stefan provoked her for reasons that Emma could only guess at. She decided to put the email completely out of her mind. Next she wondered if Stefan was mentioning their affair to anyone in the company. She hoped not; she couldn't imagine why he would.

*

On Monday morning she found a voice message on her office phone from Alec Runciman, wondering if she had any time late in the day to come to his office for a chat. Instinctively, she knew that he had been informed of the affair. For one thing the message had been left at eight-thirty when he knew she wouldn't be able to answer. And there had been no reason given for the meeting. Stefan must have told him.

It was five o'clock when Dora Lassinger waved her through to his office with a warm smile. Clearly, she hadn't heard the news. Emma entered prepared to do battle, refusing to feel guilty. Runciman, however, came around from behind his desk with his usual shy smile and hugged her.

"Sit down, dear. We have to talk."

"It's about Stefan and me, isn't it?" she said as she sat.

"I knew you'd guess."

"Fine. But before we begin, did he tell you?"

"Not at all. He wouldn't have the nerve. Julie Fredericks told me."

Runciman noticed distress in her face. "Emma, it's important that I know these things. You must see that. It doesn't matter how I know. Imagine how it would be if the board or the company knew before I did."

"I understand that," she said.

"Good." He paused. "So, against common sense and my warning, you fell for him. Emma, I am not going to lecture you. I don't even necessarily disapprove. The heart has its reasons, as I well know. And in a ballet company the reasons are many and complex. Think about my job for a minute, supervising up to a hundred young men and women in their physical prime, all gorgeous, all talented and mostly unaware of practical considerations of any kind. Sometimes I feel like I'm sitting in a hormonal pressure cooker."

She began to laugh.

"Still laughing, my dear. That's a very good sign." His smile faded quickly. "My job, as I'm sure you know, is to put the very best shows on stage, our best possible. I'm going to give Romeo to Stefan. Tatyana is demanding he be her Romeo and he is so incredibly talented that I believe we can pull it off. I have high hopes for them." He paused. "So, my only concern with your affair is its affect on Stefan. If the relationship makes him tense or disturbs him in any way it could affect his dancing and I cannot have that. My priority here must be the show, even above our friendship, which I value immensely. Do you understand?"

"Of course," she said. "The last thing I want to do is make problems for you. I want Stefan to be magnificent, as you do, and I intend to keep him healthy and happy."

"I'm sure you do." There was doubt in his voice. "The thing is, affairs have their own momentum, their own chemistry and are not subject to rational decision-making. Tell me, are you in love?"

She drew a deep breath. "Yes."

"And he loves you?"

"He says he does."

"Okay, on we go." The shy smile returned. "Emma, I wish good things for you. But remember what I said. He must be healthy and happy. We need him to be a spectacular Romeo."

*

"Julie, how could you tell Alec about Stefan and me without

letting me know? I can't believe you would do that."

She had phoned Julie immediately after returning home.

"What are you talking about? I'm a director, I sit on the board. How could I not tell him? What if the word spread, and he was the last to know?"

Emma calmed down. "Okay, I get that. You're forgiven."

"Thank you so much," said Julie sarcastically.

"I'm sorry, Jules, I've had a very rough weekend." She read Carolyn's email to Julie. "She's cutting me off from Josh. It's like she hates me."

"That is nasty," said Julie. "Hate? Who knows? I wonder if she is in competition with you. Maybe jealous of you and Stefan?"

"But she has a great husband. You've met Frank. Why would she be jealous?"

"You're talking as if your relationship with her is rational. She's become the family Christmas lady. Your job is to retire, be a granny. Taking up with the gorgeous Stefan is not in her script for you."

"Oh God," moaned Emma. "Families can be terrible."

"Tell me about it," said Julie.

*

When Stefan arrived around six o'clock, she intercepted him en route to his session with the newspaper. She asked him if he were telling people in the company about their affair.

"No," he said. "Why would I?"

"I don't know. Maybe you're proud of it and you want everyone to know."

"It's not their business," he said.

"Alec knows."

He stared at her.

"He knows how?"

"Julie Fredericks told him."

"Why?"

"He has to know. He's worried that our love affair might upset you, and your dancing might suffer."

115

"What you mean dancing suffer?"

"That your emotions might make you dance poorly."

"Is not possible," he said with a scowl.

*

Bill Shrubb showed up unannounced at her office at nine-fifteen the next morning, minutes after her arrival. It was obvious that he was part of the ripple effect the affair was generating. He breezed through her open door wearing a tee-shirt featuring Bugs Bunny eating a carrot.

"What are you doing here?" She made sure her voice had an edge.

"Just wanted to check out with you a few things de Witt is telling me. I don't understand…"

"Cut the crap, Shrubb. You're here because you've heard about Stefan and me."

He shrugged. "Well, yeah, more or less. Sorry I didn't get an appointment, but I move fast. It affects me."

"How does it affect you, given that you weren't ever on my wish list?"

"Ouch. You don't avoid the bitter truth. That's one reason I love you. No bullshit."

"You don't love me."

"True. But see what I mean? No bullshit." His smile faded. "Look, you know that he's going to be Romeo against Tatyana's Juliet." She nodded. "And you know Tatyana threatened to get suddenly very ill if Runciman didn't give her Stefan." Emma hesitated, then nodded. "So, then you know why it affects me. And you."

"What do you mean?"

"Hell, lawyer, read the signs. D'you need a flashlight?"

His expression was a mixture of anxiety and cunning and it made her furious.

She rose from her chair.

"Get out of here. Now. I'm sick of the sight of you and your dirty little mind."

"Of course dirty. It's a filthy world. I need the key to the john."

"No key. Turn right, last door on the left at the end of the hall."

She sat back in her chair, ignoring the implication of his visit.

Chapter 29

Driving north, Emma couldn't begin to relax until they turned off Highway 400, the multi-lane escape route from the city, onto the smaller country highways that would take them to Bear Lake. For several days she had been dealing with the reaction to her affair, unable to sleep, tearful at the least difficulty that arose and worried that the news would reach people at work. It was Stefan who suggested they spend a week at her cottage.

"You make yourself crazy, Emma, for no reason. You got to calm yourself. Take me again to your cottage, so beautiful. I'm not dancing for a week, maybe more."

The idea was perfect and the fact that he had suggested it delighted her. He cared for her. Things were reasonably quiet at work. Don Elton wished her a happy week.

They had left at seven on a Monday morning in late June. Stefan was watching the countryside, asking her questions about the farms and the towns. She was smiling happily when she turned down the drive to her cottage just after ten. The sun was shining, the lake was sparkling and the city was far behind. As they left the car, his phone rang. He walked away from her and began a conversation in Bulgarian. She carried her bag into the cottage. Five minutes later he entered without speaking. She put some coffee on and began to unpack.

Soon after they had unpacked, however, things began to go wrong. He emerged from their bedroom and removed a cushion from the sofa and tossed it on the floor in a corner.

"What are you doing?" she asked.

"I do not like this cushion," he said. "Is terrible colour. Does not belong."

"I've had it here for years and I like it." Her tone was terse. "You can't just throw it away without asking me."

"No big deal," he said, frowning. "If you like this horrible yellow so much I put it back."

He picked up the cushion and replaced it on the sofa. She could see that he was upset. She had been planning to replace the cushion for some time, but she would not tell him that.

"Let's figure out what to do after lunch," she said in her cheeriest voice. "Why don't I get the motorboat out and give you a tour of the lake?"

He shrugged.

"I don't think so. These motorboats are not so safe. I cannot have accident and hurt my body for dancing."

He was sulking. He knew nothing about motorboats.

"Okay. I'll go into town after lunch and pick up supplies. Do you want to come?"

"No. I stay here."

They ate lunch in silence. She drove into town, bought some groceries at Foodland, bought some pain-killing tablets for her headache and then sat on the patio of White Pine Café, drinking a latte. This was their first fight. Why did he make such a fuss over the cushion? He seemed petty and unable to get out of his funk. If he continued to sulk she might as well drive them back to the city. Yet she couldn't do that.

She arrived back from town around four o'clock. She saw him sitting on the dock, staring out at the lake. He must have heard the sound of her car, but didn't turn his head. Still moody, she thought. She made up her mind, stripped and put on her housecoat. She walked down to the dock — he didn't turn his head — walked over and snatched the newspaper from his hands. She dropped her house coat, sat on his lap and kissed him. He froze for a second or two, then kissed her back. Soon she felt his erection under her.

Men are so simple, she thought.

She pulled him up and led him to the cottage and their bedroom. He stripped, without speaking. When they came together his anger was evident. He penetrated her forcibly and began to screw her without a hint of tenderness.

"What are you doing?" she screamed as she rolled away. "Do you want to rape me?

He sat on the side of the bed and covered his face with his hands. She found her housecoat and put it on.

"So sorry, Emma," he said finally, his voice almost a whisper. "I behave bad, yes?"

"Yes," she said. "Why? And why me?"

"My mother, she phone me when we arrive here. She has blood when she pee. Doctor say maybe cancer. They test her."

"My God, why didn't you tell me?"

"Is my problem. I don't want to spoil your day."

"So, raping me was your way of giving me a good day?"

"No, Emma, was stupid." His voice was almost a sob. "I am not always smart. And my mama is no reason to be stupid and behave bad. Especially in the bed. I can be like this, when there is bad trouble, I know it. I am so sorry Emma, that I do this to you. I hope you know I am not like this. Especially with you. I love you."

He spoke sitting on the bed looking up at her. Like a naughty puppy, she thought.

The explanation was not an excuse, but it touched her. She looked at him with relief. "Put your clothes on," she said. "We need a drink. I'll get the scotch; you get two glasses and we'll head for the dock."

They sat without speaking. Stefan was clearly contrite. He kept looking at her, but she kept her gaze out on the water. The sun was starting to slant on the perfect summer afternoon. She could hear children several cottages down, screaming as they plunged down a waterslide off their dock into the water. A powerboat sped by, towing a blond boy of sixteen or so on skis, turning from side to side, creating jets of spray.

What a beautiful summer day, she thought. We'll forget about the bedroom.

"What you call, what that boy is doing?" he asked.

"Water-skiing," she said.

"Of course. Those are skis in the water. I would like to do water-skiing."

She raised her eyebrow as she looked at him.

"We can do that. I have the boat and the skis. But your body, Stefan. I don't want to hurt you and end your career."

He smiled sheepishly.

"That was old Stefan, behaving bad. If this boy can do it, I can do it. Will you permit me?"

"Yes, I will permit you. Leave your drink here. We'll finish them when we get back. Help me get the boat out."

The powerboat and the skis were in the small boathouse near the dock. They tugged the boat out and moored it to the dock. Emma attached the ski rope to its stanchion. Stefan got in, she cast off the mooring lines and hopped in. She revved the motor and headed out to the middle of the lake. She let the boat idle and explained to him what would happen. The skis would be thrown in the water and they would float. Stefan would jump in the water holding on to the bar on the tow rope. He would swim to the skis and slip them on his feet. He would then face the boat with his skis upright in front of him, gripping the tow bar. She would slowly accelerate and when the tow rope was taut, he would stand up and ski. She repeated the instructions slowly.

"Yah, Emma, I understand. Is like dancing. Don't worry."

She laughed and waited until he was in position, then slowly accelerated. She watched him rise and then slip sideways into the lake. She dragged him slowly through the water until he let go of the tow bar. She circled back to him.

"Good try," she called. "Try again?"

He nodded. She waited until he had grabbed the tow bar and got his skis in position. This time he made it to his feet and skied for several seconds until he fell. She circled back. He was smiling and eager to try again. This time, he made it. He rose, leaned back with his skis out front, and began to ski. She looked at him and was happy for him. She saw his dancer's body upright in the sun, his dark hair plastered to his neck and shoulders and a triumphant smile on his face.

He makes it look like dancing, she thought. What a beauty.

She circled several times, forcing him to go with her, first left and then right. He managed the turns easily, then let go of the bar and waved to her happily as she came around to pick him up.

"Thank you, my Emma," he said as they approached the dock. "I am so happy to water-ski and you permit me. Thank you."

Their evening went amicably. They ate on the dock and sat sipping wine as the sun set. Just before dark a loon called, and the echo reverberated around the lake.

"What is that bird?" he asked.

"It's called a loon," she said.

"Its sound is very romantic."

She was concerned with the word romantic, but as the night grew dark, he made no approach. He seemed to understand that this was not a night for lovemaking. They lay side-by-side in bed holding hands. She fell asleep picturing him upright and laughing in the sun.

Chapter 30

The hours of their week slipped by in midsummer perfection. Emma and Stefan were drugged into a lazy bliss each day by their lovemaking, by the sun on their bodies as they lay on the dock, by the sound of the wind in the pine trees and by the summer fragrance of the clear water in the granite-bottomed lake. This morning they went in for a swim, ate their granola, drank coffee on the dock and read, he his newspapers and she *The Economist* and a cottagers' magazine. She kept in the shade of an umbrella, but he lay in the sun and let it bake his olive skin.

Stefan was looking at her fondly. The prospect of dancing with Tatyana was fading from his thoughts.

"You look like cherries and ice cream, Emma," he said. "Pink and white."

"Then you'd better like cherries and ice cream," she said.

"Is my favourite."

Eventually he would say, "Water-ski, Emma. I want to water-ski." He became more sure each day, twisting, skiing one-handed and generally showing off. As she enjoyed his antics and his exuberance, she realized how little contact she had had with young males. When they returned to land he would ask, "What we do next, Emma?" making her feel like the mother of a boy on his school holidays.

As the days passed, her confidence grew, and she was able to think about the age difference without anxiety. When she looked at him on his skis, she saw a youthful body, elegant and strong, made to dance. The word was virile. He still needed his mother, however. She looked at herself and saw a softer, accommodating body, made to nurture. She recognized that he might be attracted to the maternal in her. The idea didn't bother her; in fact, it pleased her. Her sponsoring him was nurturing and naturally he loved her for that. But when she tried to figure how the sex fit this picture, she failed. He did not come to her bed for breast milk. The thought made her giggle.

Stefan looked up from his newspaper.

"What means 'proprietary', Emma?"

"It means belonging to the boss or the owner," she said. "Alec has the proprietary right to hire and fire dancers."

"He hire me but he never fire," he said. "Believe it."

She did her best to invent things to fill their days. They canoed up a stream that flowed into Bear Lake. They reached a point where beavers had built a dam that had created a pond behind it. They walked to the pond and saw a beaver with a branch in his mouth, swimming to the dam. Stefan was intrigued and told her the creature's Bulgarian name, *bobur*. The next day was rainy. They had lunch in town and toured galleries and studios. She noticed that he didn't seem interested in the paintings. When she mentioned this, he explained that the paintings were all about trees and lakes and rocks and cottages; they never showed people, which he preferred.

Every Friday night the Bear Lake Golf Club held a dinner dance for the cottagers — one hundred dollars a plate, roast beef or pickerel, with wine. Emma was debating with herself as to whether they should go; it would be a golfers' night. She knew how to handle the golfing scene, but she wasn't sure how Stefan would fit in. And the band would be local musicians playing big band and Broadway numbers for people with grey hair. Stefan would never want to dance to Glenn Miller. When she raised the idea with him, however, he surprised her.

"Yah, Emma, is great idea. We dance there, no?" She nodded. "They play boogie-woogie maybe. I like very much boogie-woogie. Can dance boogie-woogie in hotel in Sofia."

And so, at six-thirty Friday evening, the midsummer sun still high in the sky, Emma and Stefan cast off the boat and motored to the Golf Club dock at the far end of the lake. She wore a turquoise sleeveless dress that she kept at the cottage for these summer social events. Stefan had brought with him black slacks and a white, collarless silk shirt. She had taken him to town and found a black jacket. She was satisfied they looked smart enough for the occasion. The sun was slanting to the west, the water was gold where the sun struck, and the green forest took on a slightly mauve cast as night approached.

As they were escorted to their table, Emma noticed the gazes Stefan attracted as they passed — his dancer's posture, his flowing black hair, and his cheerful smile. They had been assigned a table with a golfing couple, Al and Marjorie, who had already arrived. Their cottage bordered on the ninth hole. Marjorie was freckled and sunburned with hair dyed bright orange; she was wearing a peasant blouse cut low to reveal the sunburn line on her breasts. Al had a drinker's red face and hoarse voice, wore a lemon-coloured jacket over a pink golf shirt and was looking for a waiter to refill his martini.

"How yuh doin'?" growled Al, without rising. Marjorie giggled and said nothing. Emma was about to introduce Stefan, but he walked around the table and shook Al's hand.

"I am delighted to meet you, sir," he said. "I am Stefan."

Al did a double take.

"Yeah, sure. Pleased to meet you, Steve. Have a seat."

Stefan circled around to Marjorie, bent over, took her hand and kissed it.

"Madam, I am Stefan. I hope you will dance with me tonight."

Marjorie's face flushed red as she drew her hand back. She glanced at her husband, who shrugged.

"I'd like to, Steve," she said with a warm smile.

Emma ordered a bottle of red wine.

"I'm not drinking more than a glass, and Stefan doesn't drink," she said to Al and Marjorie. "Feel free to help yourselves."

"I will drink wine tonight, Emma," said Stefan. "They have nothing for me until two weeks."

"On holidays are yuh, Steve?" said Al. "What do you do?"

"What I do when?" He looked at Emma.

"He's a dancer," said Emma.

"You're a dance instructor?" said Marjorie.

"No, he's a ballet dancer," said Emma.

"Interesting," said Marjorie.

Silence followed. The waiter brought the wine, uncorked it and poured for Emma and Stefan as the band began a waltz, 'Moon River'. Stefan rose and bowed to Emma.

"Please dance with me, Emma."

He danced slowly with her, holding her and guiding her, adjusting to her missteps. She began to relax. When the tune ended they went to return to their table, but the band began 'Chattanooga Choo Choo'.

"Emma, is boogie-woogie. We dance this."

Emma let him twirl her and catch her. She fell once and he picked her up with a twirl making it look as if her fall was part of the dance. By the end, she was breathing hard and laughing.

"Wonderful," said Marjorie. "You guys sure can dance. Al doesn't dance."

"I'm a golfer," said Al. "Do yuh golf, Steve?"

Stefan shook his head. The waiter arrived with their dinners, pickerel for Emma and Stefan and roast beef for Al and Marjorie. Emma was relieved by the silence as they ate their dinner. Stefan poured red wine for the two women and himself. Al was on his third martini. The band turned to Broadway hits. As they began 'There's a Place for Us' from *West Side Story*, Stefan rose and stood beside Marjorie.

"May I have this dance, madam?" he said as he bowed.

"Why sure."

She rose and her husband stared at her. Emma watched closely. Marjorie was a graceful dancer. Emma saw the pleasure in her smile and imagined the relief she must be feeling, away from Al as he worked his way through his martinis.

"How old's your boy, honey?" said Al.

She controlled her temper.

"He's twenty-two," she said. "How old are you?"

"Old enough to know better," said Al.

He rose from the table, walked to another table and joined two men whose wives had left to dance together.

Marjorie returned smiling.

"He can really dance," she said to Emma. "I'd love to see him do ballet."

"Why don't you? He's dancing Romeo in *Romeo and Juliet*."

"I'd love to. But Al wouldn't go."

"Then come on your own. Lots of women do."

"It wouldn't be worth it," she said, looking at her red-faced husband, engrossed with his golfing pals at the other table.

Stefan kept drinking wine as the evening wore on. Al returned to the table, announced to Marjorie that they were going home and turned away without a word. Marjorie rose, shook hands and followed Al, who was swaying as he went. Stefan took Emma to the dance floor again. After the number ended, he led her back to the table and walked to another. Emma watched him bow, ask an attractive older woman who was sitting alone to dance. She smiled and rose. This was the pattern for the next half hour; he would dance once or twice with her and then approach a woman who had not been dancing. One or two refused; he would bow and move on. The husbands were startled, some annoyed. Emma watched, intrigued. No matter how experienced a dancer the woman was or what her size and shape was, he made her feel she danced gracefully and that her dancing gave him pleasure.

It's too easy for him, she thought. Everything he does is graceful.

They went home on a calm lake under a full moon. She began to laugh at herself. She was proud of the elegance and generosity with which Stefan had danced with his partners, including her. The night had been pleasurable, the music and dancing mildly erotic. The moon, the warm breeze ruffling her hair, were seductive; she felt herself in a languid, sensual dream. He was beside her, staring into the darkness. She looked at him and wondered if he had any idea what she was feeling.

"You made a lot of women happy tonight," she said.

"Of course. In Bulgaria, a man must offer to dance with a woman who is without a dance partner. It is his duty to make her happy."

"Charming," she said. "We need more of that in the world. Stefan, I wish I were a better dancer for you."

"No, Emma, you are good dancer. Best one tonight."

"You flatter me."

"What means flatter?"

"Telling a lie to make me happy. You know very well that the tall dark-haired woman in the red dress was the best dancer, by far."

"Emma, no, no, no. She is sack of potatoes compared to you. When we get to dock, I will show you how good you are."

When he hopped onto the dock to tie up the boat, she saw him stumble. He's drunk, she thought.

When she stepped onto the dock, he grabbed her.

"Emma, you are my ballerina. We dance pas de deux."

"No, Stefan, don't be ridiculous. I am too heavy. And it's dark."

"No, you are not. I will lift you to my shoulder. Be quiet and stand in front of me, with your back to me."

He moved her to his desired position and put his hands around her waist.

"Stefan, don't do this. You are drunk."

"Quiet, Emma. Now raise right arm over head and bend to nice curve."

"I don't want to."

"Do it, Emma. For me. I want you to be my ballerina."

Against her better judgment she raised her arm to what she hoped was a graceful pose and shut her eyes. He began to hum, lifted her and set her on his shoulder. She felt elated for a moment but then shifted her weight. He wavered, then fell sideways and they both tumbled off the dock into the water. They surfaced together.

He looked embarrassed. "You moved, my ballerina."

"I haven't had any training," she said, and started to laugh.

"I am drunk, Emma," he said.

"Not too drunk, I hope."

"What is too drunk?"

"We'll see."

They climbed onto the dock and walked hand-in-hand and dripping wet to the cottage.

Chapter 31

When Emma woke before nine, Stefan was snoring gently beside her. She had never heard him snore before and it amused her. Maybe he still had water in his throat from the pas de deux, she thought, and giggled. She lay on her back with her eyes shut, wondering how to describe what had happened to her in these ecstatic days on Bear Lake. Her senses were stimulated to a level of intensity she had never before experienced. The colours of the lake, the sky, his hair or her dress, the sounds of the lake water striking the dock, the wind in the pines or the tunes the dance band played and the smells and tastes of food, wine or Stefan himself — all were vivid in her senses and her memory. These perceptions were constant and joyful. She was alert to everything that happened, everything that was said, every nuance of meaning that she could extract from every moment.

She tried to think of this blissful week as a journey. There were analogies: the drive from the city to the lake or the boat trip to the dance and back. But these trips were unlike her week; they had a starting point and a destination, a known distance and length of time. They were planned. This time with Stefan had flowed like water that arose from nowhere and whose destination could not be known. She was alive in each intense moment, ignoring any kind of analysis as she submitted to the journey's flow.

She rose quietly from the bed to avoid waking him and looked out the window. The sun was shining and the lake was smiling under a faint breeze. She heard a snort and then a moan; the snoring stopped. She looked and saw that he had shifted in his sleep and was now facing away from her, his hair, one shoulder and the beginning of his back exposed. The dark hair curving elegantly over the shoulder to his back delighted her. He began to snore again. Looking at him, listening to him, almost made her laugh. This perfect body that could dance with such beauty also snored, burped, farted and collapsed into the lake in a drunken stupor. He liked tag-team wrestling and police shows on television. As she stood watching over him, she felt tenderness for everything he was.

He will have a hangover. Where are the painkillers? She had become completely devoted to his needs. She had never wanted to care for anyone in that way before.

Is this love or slavery, she wondered.

She dressed and took her coffee down to the dock. She stretched out on a deck chair, sipped the coffee and smiled, remembering the dance and the dockside pas de deux. They would return to the city the next day, Sunday, but the trip seemed far away and hard to imagine. She lay there, adrift in the moment; even Carolyn remained a distant problem. She heard the screen door to the cottage slam and turned to see Stefan walking down to the dock in his swimsuit. He smiled briefly, ran and plunged into the lake. He swam a hundred yards or so and then returned to the dock.

"I have bad headache, Emma," he said, towelling himself off.

"You drank most of the wine, my dear."

"I know. Is hangover, yah?" She nodded. "No water-skiing today."

"Give me a minute; I'll get you something for your headache."

She ran from the dock to the cottage, got the bottle of painkillers and a bottle of water and began to run back to the dock. Wait, what am I doing, he's not dying, she told herself. She walked to the dock and gave him two pills and the water.

"What is this pill, Emma. I must know what goes into my body."

"They're painkillers. I take them myself. They're not addictive."

"Okay." He swallowed the pills and some water.

"Is my first hangover. Is not good."

"I should never have let you drink so much."

"Are you my mother? I drink what I like. Is not your problem."

"Of course. But I know that if you had been sober you would never have fallen in the lake."

He threw up his arms.

"So, you think it was me who put us in the lake. Emma, I put you on my shoulder and you moved. That makes me fall. You cannot move in pas de deux." He smiled. "Is okay. You are not ballerina."

He waved his hand dismissively and sat back in his chair, staring out at the lake. She took the pill bottle back to the cottage.

Of course I'm not a fucking ballerina, she muttered. He was drunk; end of story.

The rest of the day passed amicably. They had lunch on the dock: gazpacho and ham-and-cheese sandwiches. They swam and canoed during the afternoon; he did not want to water-ski. In the late afternoon she drove to town and bought their supper. When she returned, he was learning more words by reading an old copy of *The Ontario Fisherman*.

"Emma, what means fly-fishing?"

She explained the art of fly-fishing — the lures and the casting rods.

They ate on the dock as the sun was setting at the west end of the lake. The ripples on the surface of the water sparkled crimson gold; toward nightfall a loon's cry echoed around the shores. She had brought a bottle of wine for herself and apple juice for him.

"No, Emma, I want wine."

"My darling, you shouldn't, you are not used to it. I feel awful that I…"

"I will drink wine. Please remember, you are not my mother." He saw her face fall. "You are better than mother, Emma. You are lover." He leaned over and kissed her. "Is so beautiful here, my Emma."

"It's paradise. I don't want to leave."

He looked suddenly worried.

"But no, I cannot stay," he said. "I must have meeting with Alec, Tatyana and production team for ballet Tuesday in morning."

"We'll leave tomorrow. I have to work Monday, so don't worry. I only meant I wish I didn't have to leave."

"I understand; is good. And Emma, what means paradise?"

"It's a perfect place, like heaven."

"Is very nice here, but is not perfect. I don't believe there is heaven or this paradise."

"You are probably right. Unfortunately."

He ate her dinner happily and drank only one glass of wine. When night fell they walked together to the cottage. Sensing the end of their week, they made love and then talked for nearly an hour. Most of the conversation was about growing up in Bulgaria and his dreams for a great career. Eventually he turned over in the bed and fell asleep. She waited for the snoring, but none came. She looked at his head on his pillow, her love tinged with sadness. She knew that during the week, Stefan had not experienced the ecstasy that had overwhelmed her.

Chapter 32

By Monday, the flow that had carried her through the week seemed distant, a memory. She had begun to worry about Carolyn, half hoping to get an email from her, but by nine o'clock that morning there had been none. When she left for work, Stefan was still sleeping. She was alone again.

At the office there was a message from Don Elton asking for a quick meeting. Before she could leave for his office there was a knock on her door. When she yelled okay, Donna di Carlo entered and stood in the doorway. She didn't speak immediately; Emma could see from the red around her eyes that she had been crying.

"What is it, Donna?"

"My husband says he'll leave me if I resign from the firm."

Emma rose from her chair.

"Why?"

"He works out of the house. He doesn't want me there during the day."

"Have a seat."

Emma despaired as she surveyed Donna. The woman had put on weight in recent months and her attractive dark eyes were disappearing under pouches of flesh. The sadness in her face left her looking slightly bovine.

I understand the man's problem, thought Emma.

"What does your husband do?"

"He draws and writes comic books. He sells them all over the world."

"I see." Emma thought for a minute. "So, you have a choice. You keep your job and he stays with you, or you quit and he's gone."

"Yes."

Tears shone again on Donna's cheeks and this frustrated Emma. She thought of her happy week on Bear Lake, however, and determined to be generous.

"So, you don't know what to do?"

"No, I don't." Her voice was barely audible.

"Do you love him?"

"I guess so. He's cute and kind of funny. I like his comics."

No kidding, thought Emma.

"Does he love you?"

"How can I tell? He doesn't want me there."

"But he's okay with you nights and weekends. That doesn't sound so bad."

"Maybe, but Emma, I can't stay in the firm. I don't belong here; I have to go."

Emma paused and smiled.

"So, why don't you find another job? One that you like."

"I thought of that, working for the family businesses as corporate counsel."

"Good idea."

"Maybe. The trouble is, it would have to be approved by my Uncle Joe and he's a tough old bastard. He scares me."

"Nonsense. If you don't ask you don't get. Does he have anything against you?"

"No. I don't think so."

"Then go for it. He'll probably say yes. If he says no, deal with it then."

A cautious smile appeared on Donna's face. "You're right, you know. We don't need much money. I'll talk to Uncle Joe. Somebody said we've nothing to fear but fear itself. Thank you."

Donna left, trailing profuse thank-yous behind her. Emma shut her door with relief. She sat for several minutes thinking of Stefan and their week at Bear Lake. She left for Elton's, walking briskly with a confident smile on her face.

Don Elton offered her a chair and said he hoped her week had worked out. She assured him it had; he wouldn't know she had been with Stefan. He told her a two-line joke so bad he didn't bother looking to see if she was smiling. She groaned and they got down to business. It appeared that Archer Brown had not turned over some significant communications from the prospective purchasers of Digital Connections, both emails and faxes. He wanted her to go to Archer's condo and ask to check his papers, in the most diplomatic way possible. It was important not to ruffle Archer's feathers. She agreed pleasantly, hiding her displeasure. She wanted nothing to do with Archer Brown.

She phoned the man reluctantly, but when he understood who she was he responded warmly. Of course, she could come over and look for whatever she liked, perhaps tomorrow afternoon. His record-keeping hadn't been what it was in recent years. He would make some tea. She decided to review the Digital Communication file; from what Elton had said, it seemed they were not yet close to a deal.

After an hour or so she was interrupted by a call from Alec Runciman. It startled her and she decided not to pick up. His name and number on her screen brought Stefan and the ballet company back into her thoughts. After several minutes it occurred to her that there was no reason Stefan and the company should not be in her thoughts, and she phoned the director back. He greeted her warmly and hoped she had had a splendid week. She assumed that he would guess that she had been with Stefan. He explained there was still a possibility of legal problems from Germany over his hiring of Eckhardt Bremner. Could she drop by later the next day for a chat? She agreed to meet, at the same time wondering why he needed her rather than the employment lawyer she had found for him. She sighed. Archer Brown at three Tuesday, Alec Runciman at five. Bear Lake seemed far away.

She left the office at four-thirty, early for her, and took a cab home. She couldn't get rid of her feeling of distaste for the conversation with Donna. The image of the pudgy, passive and teary woman depressed her. Feeling a twinge of guilt, she tried to understand her lack of sympathy for the woman. She had never met Allan, the writer of comic books. He had never attended the firm's Christmas party or other social events. She imagined a slightly built, narrow-chested man, sitting at his computer all day and snickering as he drew his superheroes

133

and villains. But why must he be so unimpressive? She realized that she had imagined an anti-Stefan, someone who could never give poor Donna what Stefan had given her. Being with Stefan was physical; it drove logic, analysis, self-awareness and powerful restraints on human eroticism out of her mind. Being with him had held her in present moments of sensuality and laughter. This had been her flow, her life out of time.

When the cab let her out, she entered her house, anticipating the moment when Stefan would walk through her door and she would enter that flow again. She organized the dinner she would prepare for him — veal sautéed in white wine and garlic with jasmine rice and cauliflower — and put out a ballet magazine for him to read. She had been considering weeding her garden — a job she tended to put off — when the doorbell rang. She opened the door to Frank Thomas, holding Joshua in his arms. Emma screamed with pleasure.

"My God, Frank. And Joshua, my darling. Is Carolyn with you?"

"No, she played golf today. Now she's having dinner with her girlfriends."

"I brought a book, Grandma," said Joshua, holding out his book. "So you could read to me."

"I'd love to. But do you have time?" She looked at Frank, who nodded.

"They're stories about a boy who loves animals. Lots of pictures. I'll watch the news."

Frank went to the television room while Emma and her grandson sat in the sunroom and began reading. Once again, she was delighted by the weight of his young body as he snuggled into her lap.

This is love, she thought, as she began to read.

When she finished the story, she got apple juice for Joshua and invitated them for dinner.

"How is she?" Emma asked Frank.

"The same," he said. "You know her."

"Fine, but I never hear about Joshua and his problem. She tells me nothing."

"I didn't realize," said Frank. "That's terrible; I'll talk to her. They have put him on medication that they think will deal with the infection. We'll wait and see."

"Well, that's something," she said. "Thank you, my dear."

Frank lifted Joshua from the sofa and carried him upstairs to the television room.

"Carolyn is a firecracker; she doesn't shake her emotions easily," he said as he returned. "I decided to come today because she has no right to cut you off from Joshua."

"Did she know you were coming here?"

"I told her. She walked out and slammed the door."

"My God," said Emma, shaking her head.

"Don't worry, Emma. She'll get over it. I'll make sure of that. Your birthday's in August, isn't it?"

"August the twenty-fifth."

"I'm going to try and have her at the party, either at home or here. She's not really mean, but she can go off her head sometimes. She wants her mother to be a respectable granny."

At that moment the front door opened, and she heard Stefan enter. She looked at Frank.

"That will be Stefan, the object of Carolyn's concern."

She called Stefan and he entered the sunroom. Emma introduced the two men. Stefan was startled and slightly nervous, but Frank shook his hand with a jovial smile.

"Wonderful to meet you, Stefan," said Frank.

"I am also happy to meet you, sir," said Stefan, bowing.

Emma offered drinks.

"No thanks. We've got to hit the road. Let me get Josh."

"Your daughter knows about you and me?" asked Stefan when they were alone. She nodded. "And is okay?"

"It's okay. No problem."

Frank returned and introduced Stefan to Joshua, making the boy shake hands.

Stefan smiled happily.

"How old are you, my boy?" he said.

"I am three," said Joshua. "Next year I am four."

Stefan laughed and tousled the boy's hair. Frank said his goodbyes.

"What means 'hit the road', Emma?" Stefan asked after the two had left. "Makes no sense."

She laughed and explained. He laughed.

"Also, Mama phoned today. Is not cancer. Is some lump they take out, not cancerous."

"Wonderful. I'm happy for you both."

She gave him the ballet magazine and he began to read, tracing each line with his finger. They ate and gave each other accounts of their day. After dinner he watched wrestling, then a police show. The lovemaking was tender and cheerful. She went to sleep dreaming, drifting back into her timeless flow.

Chapter 33

Emma buzzed Archer Brown's condo from his lobby. A matronly-sounding woman's voice answered and asked her to wait. The voice returned and invited her to enter. Archer's housekeeper opened the door.

"He doesn't remember your name," she whispered. "Should he know you?"

Emma explained that Archer had agreed that she could come to look for the Digital Communication documents. The woman smiled and led her into a large living room. Archer was sitting in an armchair by a window with a rug over his lap, staring at the cityscape to the south. His room was in the style of a previous century, with horsehair armchairs and sofas, Tiffany lamps and Persian carpets. One wall was hung with what appeared to be family photos: a Victorian couple, unsmiling, others possibly of his parents and siblings or cousins, all in black and white.

"Mr. Brown, Emma is here to see you."

The old man turned his head, stared at Emma and smiled.

"I know you. We've met before. What did you say your name was?"

"Emma. I worked for you at Eberhart Williams."

"Oh, that place. I'm well out of there."

"I'm happy you're doing well."

"I'm getting by. So kind of you to visit." He paused and adjusted his glasses, then stared at her with a birdlike curiosity. "I do know you. I hired you to replace what's-her-name."

"Donna."

"Exactly. I can't tell you how kind you are to come. None of the rest of them bother, you know. Once they've wrung the last ounce of blood out of you, they throw you on the scrap heap. Merciless." He rose to his feet. "Come, my dear, let me show you my pictures. Alice will get us tea. Alice, the lapsang oolong with those biscuits I like."

Alice nodded as he led Emma to the wall of photos. He identified his parents, his brother who had died at the D-Day landing on Juno Beach, his two sisters and several cousins. He had anecdotes and memories for each photo, which made their progress slow. Alice wheeled a tea-wagon into the room.

"Mr. Brown, the tea has steeped and it's the way you like it. Why don't you and your guest come and sit."

"Of course." He turned away from the pictures. "Come, my dear. Nothing worse than cold tea. What did you say your name was?"

"Emma. We worked on the Digital Connections file."

"If you say so. Now Emma, one little thing. When you come again, I would appreciate it if you let us know. Gives us time to prepare."

"Of course. Now Archer, I was hoping that I could look through your Digital files."

"Oh, why is that?"

His glance was curious but not hostile.

"We can't find some documents and emails they say they've sent, and I wondered if you might have anything."

"I see. Well, you're welcome to take a look; it's all in my study.

Alice will show you. I don't remember a thing. My record-keeping isn't what it was."

"I understand."

They chatted mostly about Italy. He was eager to tell her about his last visit to Venice. There was no mention of the gondoliers and no picture of one. Apparently, when he was home he reverted to being a church elder. Alice led Emma into the study, where files in boxes were piled on a refectory table. Fortunately, the boxes were labelled, and Emma had no difficulty locating the Digital files. She soon found a group of emails and accompanying documents dated the last year of Archer's practice which she had never seen. She took them to the living room.

"Archer, these would help us," she said. "With your permission I'd like to take them to the office, copy them and return them to you."

"Do what you like with them." He waved his hand. "They're of no earthly use to me." He glanced at his watch. "Oh, my heavens, it's my nap time. I'm sorry, my dear, but you'll have to go. I get beastly if I miss my nap, don't I, Alice?"

Alice nodded. Without another word, Archer rose and shuffled away to his bedroom. Alice put the documents in a shopping bag and showed Emma to the door.

Extraordinary, she thought. Just a trip to Venice every few years. Did he love his gondoliers? Can you live without love at all?

Don Elton was satisfied; Emma's haul contained the missing New York correspondence. While they were sorting through the material, he told a joke that was actually funny. He laughed heartily, and she smiled. When they finished it was time for her to meet Alec Runciman, this time in his office. Emma was unsure about why they were meeting. When she arrived, Dora Lassinger waved her through with a non-committal smile. Emma's uncertainty increased when the director's hug was peremptory, his expression tense.

"Sit, my dear," he said. "How have you been?"

"Very well, thank you."

She sat waiting.

"I said I invited you to discuss Eckhardt's situation, but that was a sham, a cover-up."

"I guessed that."

"I wondered if you might. I must say that I hate subtlety and indirection. So, Emma, we are friends and I owe it to you to be frank. I am getting pressure from several board members over my decision to advance Stefan without apprenticeship. More than that, I have told the board that I have decided to let Stefan dance Romeo opposite Tatyana's Juliet — I will make the public announcement tomorrow — and I am being questioned about that. The lead critic is a new member, a lawyer named Stuart Blenkinsop, very bright, very articulate."

"Yes, I know him. He does commercial litigation for one of our competitors."

"So, you understand what I'm dealing with." She nodded. "No one is disputing my right to make the decision. But they have made it clear to me that all eyes will be on Stefan when he dances. To complicate matters, your relationship with Stefan is common knowledge, as is your friendship with me. You can see what nasty minds will make of this."

"That I used our friendship to persuade you to let my lover dance Romeo before he was ready."

"Yes. The irony is, you would never do such a thing. It was Tatyana who demanded him as her partner."

"I wondered about that, about how the decision came to be made. It wasn't Stefan's idea?"

"Not at all. It was my decision." He stroked his hair. "She came in here and…." He paused, shaking his head. "Tatyana Vasilievskaya is a brilliant dancer, everyone knew that. However, she has a formidable personality and everyone, including me, knew that also before she left Russia. We got her because the Bolshoi was relieved to be rid of her and most other companies would not accept the risk, given the price that she demanded. Not only did we have to buy out her contract with the Bolshoi, we had to pay off her boyfriend, an oil and gas billionaire. We couldn't have done it without Bill Shrubb and his cheque book. He had seen her dance in Moscow."

"Obviously, you thought she was worth the price," said Emma.

"I did. When Dora told me she had made an appointment, she warned me that Tatyana seemed in an aggressive mood. I was mystified. I had given her Juliet — she is renowned for her Juliet — and her Romeo was to be Ralph Lyndhurst, our leading male dancer. But she came in, sat where you're sitting, hitched up her skirt and demanded Stefan for her Romeo. She insisted that Stefan was our best. And she actually threatened me that if I didn't give her Stefan, she would develop an illness and miss the show altogether."

"That's blackmail," exclaimed Emma. "Surely you didn't…"

"God, no. What do you take me for? She has a contract and she knows she can't break it. If she did, she'd be finished with us. She can't go back to Russia and no one else would have her. She lost control with her threat, but she wants to dance Juliet and she knows the final decision is mine. The decision is complex. I don't know of another female dancer with the combination of native talent and Bolshoi experience that she has. All eyes will be on the performance, to see if she was worth the money, and if Stefan was the right Romeo. I need her to be brilliant, and to be brilliant she needs to be happy."

"So, you gave her Stefan to make her happy."

He shook his head.

"Stefan is good, better than any man of his age that I have seen. I put him with Jeanne Masset as Juliet, and I was confident that he would do well. Tatyana and Ralph were to be our opening night team to make the evening a smash. I told her I would think about it. She was furious. I was supposed to give her what she wanted on the spot. She ran out and slammed the door. I bet they heard it in the parking lot." He chuckled. "I did think about it for a day or so and decided that if the chemistry worked, Stefan and Tatyana could be exceptional."

"You know, Alec, most of us don't think of the ballet in terms of risk and danger."

"I know; just girls in tutus and gorgeous music." He frowned.

"Now I have to worry about Ralph. He will likely see this as himself being usurped by Stefan, which is in fact true, but I need him to be happy. Fortunately, Ralph's a reasonable guy and I may be able to explain the circumstances to him. And I can give him a solo in this Elvis Presley piece Sokolovski is doing." He paused and smiled at her. "That brings me to you."

She frowned. "And whether my relationship with Stefan will make him tense and hurt his dancing."

"Exactly. I was trying to reach him all last week, but he wasn't answering his phone. Was he with you?"

"Yes, he was. We spent a week at my cottage on Bear Lake."

"I see." He frowned. "How was he?"

"He was fine. He was upset by a message from his mother saying that she might have cancer, but yesterday she phoned to tell him that the lump was not malignant. They're going to cut it out."

"You see, that's the sort of thing I need to know," he fretted. "Other than that, he seemed in good spirits?"

"He had a great time. I taught him to water-ski."

"Water-ski?" His face flashed anger. "How could you do that? What if he hurt his leg, twisted his ankle?"

"Alec, he is a healthy, confident young man. He got up in three tries. There was no danger."

"As it turned out. So he comes back happy and healthy."

"You needn't worry. We ended up having lots of fun. One of the last nights he tried to make me his ballerina on the dock. He lifted me, lost his balance and we both fell into the lake."

"How very bizarre."

"It was bizarre. I didn't want to do it, but he insisted."

"He was drunk!" Runciman's eyes widened.

"Yes, he was," she admitted.

"Emma, he is only twenty-two. He normally doesn't touch alcohol; he is so focussed on his dancing. Yet he spends a week with you, drinks too much and.... I don't know what to say to you."

"You don't need to say anything. He has been back for two days and hasn't touched a drop. He is looking forward to the fall and dancing Romeo. It's all he thinks about. You seem to think that I am some aging trollop seducing and corrupting him."

"I don't know what you are right now, Emma, but I don't think you understand what you're doing. I will be keeping a close watch over our young friend, and if I see any problems whatsoever, emotional or physical, he won't be dancing Romeo."

"All I can tell you is that I want him to have as great a success as you do. My reason is different from yours, of course. Stefan and I are happy together and that should be good for him and for you. I know he will dance well."

Runciman sighed as he rose from his chair.

"Love is such a bugger, Emma. Please be careful. You know I wish the best for you, my dear friend, but I wish the best for Stefan, the show and the company even more."

"I understand."

She arrived home early, fixed herself a drink and sat staring at the garden. Hollyhocks and daisies had replaced the peonies, and the trees were just past their June brilliance. She felt betrayed. Runciman had failed to understand what was happening to her. His phrase, "love is such a bugger", was still on her mind. She had loved her daughters, but had there been a choice? Hormones, the sense of family responsibility had dictated the years of work and care for them. And then Joshua. She loved him absolutely, she thought, but he was Carolyn's child. Loving him was so easy, and yet was it not essentially selfish? The front door closed, and she heard Stefan's tread in the hall.

Delight surged through her and she lost all sense of time in the flow of her absolute love.

Chapter 34

They met this time on a bench in the park two blocks from the company's rehearsal building. Tatyana had asked him to dance with her for one hour, so they might learn each other's styles. She had the music for the Bluebird pas de deux and the pas de deux with the Sugar Plum Fairy in *The Nutcracker*, since he had danced both in performance. They ran through each one. To his surprise, she knew the steps and intuitively anticipated his every move. He was impressed. They finished, pleased with each other. She told him she wanted to talk to him privately. He nodded and she excused herself. When she returned, she had made herself up: long eyelashes, violet eyeshadow and lipstick and rouge on her cheeks. He looked at her suspiciously. If this is for me, she looked better dancing, no paint on her face, he thought.

"So, Stefan, I know you are a very good dancer, but that dancing was not nearly as good as when you danced on stage."

"What do you mean? What was wrong with my dancing?"

"You danced savage. You swung me and threw me with your muscles, not your heart. On stage, you danced with love and sensitivity. Today you threw me around like a Russian bitch."

She looked at him with an amused smile. He struggled for words.

"I danced like a man," he said, and fell silent.

He knew she was right. Although he had agreed to dance with her, he had been in a turmoil when he arrived for their session.

"This cannot be," she said. "If Alec sees this, it's goodbye Charlie."

"I know," he said. "I will fix."

"I don't think you can fix. You are not dancing with me, the girl you love. You are thinking of your beautiful patron, Emma Peters, taking her to bed. It is impossible for you to fix your dancing; you are in love with her."

"Not your business," he said angrily. "I can dance, you will see."

"Maybe. But there is one way necessary to fix this problem." She hesitated.

"Is no problem," he said angrily. He looked at her and took a deep breath. "Okay. What is that?"

"I tell you later. I must think."

He rose without a word and strode away from their bench.

*

Runciman was on the phone with the artistic director of Ballet Manhattan when Dora Lassinger entered. He waved her to sit. He was trying to arrange a gig for Ralph Lyndhurst to dance James in *La Sylphide* three seasons away. He was smiling when he hung up.

"They'll get back to me in a week, but Ralph looks good for *La Sylphide* two seasons after this one."

"Good, boss," said Dora. "I'm sure Ralph's gonna like it, dancin' in Manhattan and all." She paused. "Tatyana is outside."

"What does she want?"

"She wouldn't say exactly. She wants to talk to you about *Romeo and Juliet*. But she looks tense; something's on her mind."

"Damnation, I thought we had settled that." Dora noticed him stroking his ponytail, the only indication he ever gave that he was nervous. "You know, Dora, we hire Tatyana, arguably the best interpreter of classic romantic roles at the moment, and then we move Stefan directly into the company from school, recognizing his unusual talent. Then, brilliantly, I agree to match them in *Romeo and Juliet*." He spoke with a self-deprecating nuance to his tone. "What if I'm wrong?"

"Too soon to be thinking that way, boss."

"You're right," he sighed. "Send her in."

The director stopped stroking his hair, exhaled and smiled genially as Tatyana entered. In contrast to their previous meeting, she seemed subdued, perhaps nervous.

"Thank you for seeing me, Alec." She smiled gratefully; he nodded and waited cautiously.

"There is a problem with Stefan and me," she said.

He sat up straight in his chair and stared.

"What problem?" His voice was tense.

"We have been dancing together. I am trying to show him what I know, how he should be. He does not listen to me. He is not dancing like the way he danced the Bluebird. He throws me around like a bag of turnips. He is not dancing Romeo."

"I'm sorry to hear that," he said. "Do you have any idea what the problem is?"

"Sure. Is Emma Peters. He sleeps with her and dances with me. Doesn't work."

I'd better get somebody, fast, he thought. Put Ralph back with her and get another guy for Jeanne.

"That is a problem. Leave it with me, let me think. It looks like you'll be dancing with Ralph after all."

"Maybe," she said. "Maybe not. I have better idea."

"What is it?" His voice was flat. The thought of the rearranging, the uproar and the politics he was facing was overwhelming.

"He sleeps with me and dances with me."

His expression froze.

"What on earth do you mean?"

"You know what we would do in Russia, Alec."

He stared and didn't answer.

"It is expected that when a man and a woman dance romantic together, they must make love. They are stage lovers, only for months or maybe a season. In this way they develop a passion that you cannot pretend on the stage. Sometimes they fall in love, but not usually. The dancing that results from the sex is fantastic. The audience goes crazy for it. My Russian boyfriend, Leonid, fell for me because he saw me dance Juliet with André Pleshnikov as Romeo. André and I lived together for three months before the show and we were hot on stage. Then we broke up." She shrugged.

He couldn't stop staring at her. At the same time, he was calculating rapidly. Could it work? Was it possible that it could, and he would escape the mess that would occur if he had to change Stefan's casting?

"Interesting," he said finally. "I have heard of this kind of arrangement before, with you and André even. We haven't done that here. Perceptions are different in Canada." He rose from his chair and stared out the window before he turned back to her. "Tatyana, I must think about this, but I am interested. Do you think he would he do it?"

"We make him do it. I make him do it. If he wants a career."

"Okay, I'll get back to you tomorrow."

As soon as she closed the door, he knew that he would agree. The alternative was too horrible to think about. He would have to talk to Stefan — a difficult conversation. He sat in his chair and was beginning to relax, when the impact this would have on Emma came to him.

*

"We can't continue with you like this, Stefan. You are not dancing Romeo. We cannot go on stage. Alec will not allow it."

They had agreed to meet in the canteen next morning. Stefan was subdued. During the night he had admitted to himself that his dancing had suffered, but he did not want to consider why.

"You say you know how to fix things. What is that?"

"You must sleep with me."

He gaped at her. "Don't be ridiculous," he snarled.

"Is not ridiculous. In Russia we do this. A man and woman who dance romantic sleep together to develop feeling that will show on the stage. They will dance like lovers on stage. We need this, Stefan. You think of her and you cannot be my Romeo."

He sat for a minute, his elbows on his knees, staring at the floor. "I cannot do this," he said eventually. "I cannot hurt her."

"You must, Stefan, if you want to dance like a man. You can have a magnificent career, but you must give everything you have for it. You must sleep with me. I can take you to a place you can't imagine if you will let me. You will dance like you never have before. And do not worry about Emma. She has a good life and she has no right to keep you for herself and damage your career."

"It's easy for you. You leave your man for me and it means nothing to you."

"I don't love Billy and he knows that. I won't love you, but I will enjoy it. You will enjoy it. And when we dance before the audience, you will understand."

He stood up and drained his coffee.

"I must think. I don't know."

"You don't know," she said. "But you must learn, for your life, for your dancing."

He walked slowly away, shaking his head.

*

"I thank you so much, Alec, for agreeing to see me. I know you are very busy."

"Never too busy to chat with you, Stefan. What can I do for you?"

Stefan hesitated. He grabbed his left wrist with his right hand. Runciman could see white on his knuckles.

"I have problem. You will think I am foolish. I don't know if I should ask you."

"Ask. I'm here to answer your questions."

"But this question…. I don't know. I think maybe you never hear this question before."

"That would surprise me. There aren't many situations or problems I haven't had to deal with. Out with it, my boy."

The paternal affection he heard in the director's voice calmed Stefan. Runciman noticed the relief in his face. My God, he's young, he thought.

"Here is problem," said Stefan, summoning his courage. "Tatyana and I dance together for first time, in rehearsal room. She says we need to know how we dance together."

"Excellent," said the director. "How did it go?"

"Not so good. She danced very good, but she says I am stiff and throw her around too much. Am not sensitive or romantic."

Runciman smiled.

"Stefan. I have seen you dance the Bluebird pas de deux and the pas de deux in the last act of *Nutcracker*, and you did a beautiful job both times. That is why we gave you Romeo. But it is natural and quite common for a young man to be nervous when first dancing with a star like Tatyana. I'm sure you will soon relax and dance well with her."

Stefan twisted in his chair and clenched his fists.

"Is true. But she says I treat her like Russian bitch." He hesitated. "She says we have to sleep together so I will not treat her like bitch. She says they do this in Russia, to make men and women dance more romantic. She has done this before. She says if I sleep with her, then we will dance better than anyone." He fell silent.

The director sat upright in his chair and started to stroke his hair.

"I know some companies encourage that, especially in Russia," said Runciman. "However, we never have here." He thought immediately of Emma. "I know you are already in a relationship with Emma Peters."

"Is true. Vasilievskaya say that is preventing me from dancing good with her."

"I see."

The director looked at Stefan, considered his youth and his naiveté and decided that the Russian was right. She would give the boy an experience that would emphasize his manhood and make him her match in the dance. Emma, however, would be devastated. His head began to throb.

"Stefan, it is not my job to tell you what you can or cannot do. I can see you are unsure about this choice, but I cannot make it for you. My only concern must be that when you step on stage as Romeo you must be at your peak, physically and emotionally. If you dance as well as I know you can, you will find yourself at the beginning of a great career. Nothing should stand in the way of that."

"That is what I want," said Stefan, excitement in his voice. "So you are not telling me it is wrong, what Tatyana says."

"I can't tell you that."

"Thank you," said Stefan, rising from the chair. "Thank you so much for listening to me. Is very big help."

Runciman sank into his chair. It was clear what Stefan would do. He would have done the same thing at that age had the circumstance arisen. He refused to believe that he was betraying Emma, although he understood the pain she would suffer. She had been warned of the risk and was apparently accepting it.

Dora entered the office. "So, what was that about? He left with a smile on his face."

He summarized the discussion he had just had with Stefan. Her jaw dropped when he explained Tatyana's proposal.

"So, you think that's what he'll do?" When Runciman nodded, she asked, "And Emma Peters is history?"

"Will be," he said.

"You look worried, boss, but it's not your problem. She should have known this would happen. She's too goddamned old for him."

"I know that." He shook his head. "The last thing I want is to give love advice to ballet dancers. Am I supposed to write a lonely-hearts column in the newsletter?"

Dora snorted.

He smiled. "All I want is the best dancing possible when this company takes to the stage. Always."

"You'll get it, boss," she said. "I know you will."

Chapter 35

Emma and Julie met at Café Vert in the late afternoon. It was still warm enough to sit on the patio, and there were kids throwing frisbees in the park, but the tree leaves were showing the faded green of late summer.

"I hate this time of year," said Julie. "It's still warm, but the nights come sooner and they're cool."

"I'm sorry I couldn't meet earlier. It's been crazy at work. I've been back and forth to New York, selling a client to an American buyer."

Emma told Julie about rescuing files from Archer Brown.

Julie laughed. "So, you've been busy. Tell me."

Emma paused. She wondered if Julie was sceptical about her relationship with Stefan because she was jealous.

"Things have been good." Emma's tone of voice was matter-of-fact. "Stefan and I spent a week at the cottage in June." She started her account with the quarrel over the cushion colours. Julie frowned. But when Emma continued with a description of the water-skiing, she smiled.

"I can picture it," she said. "That gorgeous body upright on the skis, laughing in the sun. Beautiful. Emma, you're a lucky girl."

Julie was enjoying her account of their week at Bear Lake, so Emma decided not to hide her pleasure. She described the golf club dance and Stefan's attentiveness to her and the solitary ladies.

"A gentleman of the old school," said Julie.

Emma continued with the pas de deux on the dock and the collapse into the water.

"I don't believe it," exclaimed Julie. "You got him drunk. What fun!"

"Alec doesn't think so. He thinks the water-skiing risked injuring his Romeo, and that I've been corrupting him with wine and sex."

Julie waved a hand dismissively. "He's an old mother hen when it comes to his dancers," she said. "But you can't blame him. He has all these kids at their physical prime, looking for excitement on stage and off."

"Stefan is now twenty-two." Emma's tone was defensive. "And he hasn't been drinking since we've been back. Alec also told me that some board members have been asking him about his promoting Stefan to the company directly without the apprenticeship period and letting him dance Romeo. They suspect that I'm using my influence with Alec to get special treatment for my friend."

"What crap! That's Stuart Blenkinsop. He's a lawyer, new on the board."

"I know him," said Emma.

"Then you know he's bright but really pompous. As often happens with new board members, he wants to make an impression and show how brilliant he is. But men like him know little about running a ballet company no matter how successful they are. As if Alec were stupid enough to play favourites so obviously. He'd never survive."

"Of course. But Alec is still is worried that something — maybe me — will rattle Stefan and affect his performance."

"Paranoia, but natural," said Julie. "He's got a lot on the line. Keep that boy happy."

"I try. And it seems to be working." Emma paused. "Alec says that he can find a stand-in for Stefan if he has to. Apparently, the Russian demanded Stefan to dance her Romeo and threatened to fake illness and skip the show if she didn't get him."

"Ridiculous. If Stefan doesn't do well, Tatyana herself will want to be rid of him. She wants what Alec wants."

"That's what Alec says," said Emma. "He can find a replacement, but he won't need one. Stefan is brilliant. He will be superb."

Julie smiled. There was light in Emma's eyes.

"Of course he will." She paused, then grinned. "I have some good news."

"Tell me."

"Good old Vern has made some of his money back. In fact, he's made a lot of his money back."

Emma tensed. She suspected that Julie was introducing good old Vern's success to make him look good in comparison with Stefan.

"Wonderful," said Emma. "You must be so relieved. How did he do it?"

"He did talk to Bill Shrubb, to my surprise. He showed Bill the information he had been given that convinced him to buy certain shares last April and Bill said it was incomplete and inadequate. The promoters downplayed the risk involved by not revealing some contingencies in their projections. The contingencies never materialized and that caused the collapse. Vern's lawyer threatened to sue and they settled, not for the entire loss but for half. And Bill advised Vern to buy a couple of companies in his artificial intelligence area. The shares shot up in the last month and Vern made some money."

"I'm happy to hear that." Emma glanced at her watch. "Goodness, I've got to go." She stood. "I promised Stefan that I'd fix him some Bulgarian cherry soup with sour cream."

"Ugh," said Julie. "But before you go, your birthday's coming up on the twenty-fifth. Sit for a minute." Emma sat. "I want the party to be at our house. No, don't argue. I've made up my mind. So, who's coming?"

The invitation shamed Emma. I must be paranoid, she thought. Julie's a generous friend.

She mentioned Runciman and a few other friends and colleagues, but she wasn't sure about Carolyn.

"I know Anne's in Halifax, but what about Carolyn's family?"

"I don't know. She's still not speaking to me."

"You're kidding!" Emma shook her head. "I'll phone her myself with the invitation and if she doesn't accept, I'll let her have it."

"Phone her, but don't give her trouble. That never works with Carolyn. It would only drive her further away."

"Lord," said Julie. "Surely she loves her mother."

"I think she does, ultimately. But who knows what love means to her?"

*

She set the cherry soup in front of Stefan. He tasted it and nodded. "Is good, Emma. My mother does not make it better."

She watched him finish the soup and was happy. For the rest of the meal, she served a lasagna and some raspberry pie. When they finished, he helped her load the dishwasher.

"Emma," he said. "I must tell you that in September rehearsals are starting and my schedule is different. I will work late and sleep at my apartment more. Is necessary."

Her nerves tensed and her face flushed.

"I suppose you must," she said. "Our summer was so beautiful. I wish we could go back to the lake."

He shook his head.

"Was beautiful, your lake, but was not real life. Was dream for me. But now I wake up; I dance. You must understand this."

He calls it a dream, she thought. It was reality for me.

"Of course," she said. "You must dance."

He read his newspaper; he watched television; they made love. Soon there will be fewer of these nights, she thought.

Chapter 36

Over the next week Stefan became tense and sombre. He had agreed with Tatyana on the night she would move in, two nights before Emma's birthday. He had wanted to do it after the birthday, but decided that it would be easier to leave Emma with a celebration. Tatyana was pleased — the date had been fixed — and told him she would prepare the meal on their first night together.

When the night arrived, he told Emma that he would be rehearsing late and would sleep at his flat. I lie, he said to himself. Is terrible lie. Tatyana was already in the flat when he returned from his workout. He had given her a key. He noticed that she was wearing no makeup and was dressed in an embroidered Russian peasant blouse and a knee-length skirt. He froze when she kissed him.

She pushed him away.

"So what, my Romeo? You are thinking of poor Emma and not your Russian bitch?"

"Be quiet, please. Is difficult."

He walked past her quickly to change from his workout clothes. She went to the kitchen. He could smell the aroma of her cooking. He had to remind himself that he had agreed to this new life. When he returned, she emerged from the kitchen with a bottle of champagne and two glasses.

"No, Tatyana, I don't drink during the week, for my dancing."

She set the glasses and bottle on a table and turned to him with her hands on her hips.

"Really? You say we will sleep together and I can move in. I leave Billy and come to you, but you don't kiss, and you don't drink my champagne? So how can we fuck?"

He stood, unsure of what to say to her. Then the absurdity of the situation hit him and he smiled.

"So, you smile." She tossed her head. "So, I can stay? Or do you want to leave me here and go to your Emma?"

"No, of course you stay. But give me time, Tatyana. I need time. Give me glass of champagne."

She poured two glasses; they clinked together. He sipped.

"Is not so bad?" she asked. He nodded and smiled.

"Meal is ready," she said as she finished her champagne. "Go and sit at table."

She served first a yoghurt soup with cucumber and dill.

"Is good," he said. "Is Bulgarian soup."

"No, is Russian."

The main course was marinated lamb, grilled with rice, flavoured with onions and peppers.

"My mother can make this," he said. "How you can know this?"

"My mother made this," she said.

He grunted and gobbled the meat and rice. "More champagne, please," he said.

Dessert was an apple strudel with cinnamon and sour cream. When the meal was finished, he looked at her with a curious smile. Why did she do this, he asked himself. She is different person. She cooks for me like Mama.

"So, your Russian bitch can cook," she said.

"Yah, you can cook. Why you do this?"

She picked up the bottle of champagne. "Come with me to bedroom. I'll tell you there." She rose.

He hesitated. "I must tell you. Friday is her birthday. I must go."

She walked to stand by his chair and glared down at him. "Then you take me with you." Her tone was angry.

He shook his head. "How I can do that?"

"Because I tell you. You pick up the phone, call her and say we rehearse late and you will bring me."

He sat for a moment, then nodded. She smiled briefly as she took him by the hand, led him to the bedroom and sat him on the bed. Then she poured them each the rest of the champagne.

"If we will make love and dance together, I need to change your head. To you I am a slut, a bitch. But tonight, I cook for you like your mama, yes?" He nodded. "So tonight, I am not bitch, Stefan?" He smiled and sipped his champagne; he was feeling a pleasant lightness. "But still you aren't sure, I have to pull you into the bedroom."

"I said is difficult. I said give me time."

"Is difficult maybe, but we don't have time. Listen to me. Who is Juliet? A fourteen-year-old girl. I can be that young girl like I can be your mama. Is easy for me. You are twenty-two, perfect for Romeo, but to be Romeo you must love your Juliet. For tonight, for the season, you must love me."

There was sadness in her voice. He stared at her.

"So, I must change your mind. I must become your Juliet. Then you will be my Romeo."

"I don't know." He was shaken. "I will try, Tatyana."

"Good. Then let us try." She stood before him, hands at her sides. "Undress me."

He removed her blouse and her skirt. She stood still, smiling modestly, innocently. Trance-like, he removed her underwear, then stood and removed his clothes. He embraced her. She kissed him gently, tenderly. He lifted her to the bed and laid beside her.

"Who am I, Stefan?" she asked as he rolled on top of her.

"Juliet," he murmured. "You are Juliet."

Chapter 37

Emma arrived at the Fredericks' house at six on August twenty-fifth, the night of her birthday. Darkness was falling and the house was brightly lit inside and out. Spotlights illuminated flowers and bushes in the garden, casting their shadows on the house. In the front hall, between the opposite staircases curving to the second floor, a young man in a dark jacket and olive-green slacks was playing a Chopin étude on the grand piano, moved to the hall for the occasion. Emma and Julie embraced.

"The house looks fabulous," said Emma.

"Thanks, Emma. You look fabulous. Sexy and elegant."

Emma had dressed to make an impression. Her teal cocktail dress, cut to emphasize but not reveal her figure, was offset by russet pumps that matched the colour of her hair. She had painted her lips a dull rose, matched by stones in her earrings, necklace and bracelet. She felt good.

"I'm here to have a ball," she said, laughter in her eyes.

"That's the idea. Where's Stefan?"

"Rehearsing. He'll be here soon."

"Get a drink and go in. You'll find your friends there."

Emma took a glass of champagne from a waiter and walked in to cheers and applause. She bowed and began to circle, greeting everyone with hugs and kisses. From the ballet were several board members, including Bill Shrubb, Rhoda Marks, ladies whom she had met at the ballet school when she first saw Stefan, and Alec Runciman. Several of her neighbours were there: Bob and Cindy from next door and Janet somebody from the other side, both of whom had accepted Stefan on the street with a smile and a nod. Don Elton and Donna di Carlo were both there without their spouses. Freom the corner of her eye, Emma saw them inching through the crowd towards her. She surveyed the room quickly and saw that Carolyn was not present; she repressed a momentary pang. Two waiters were circulating with trays of canapés, and Julie kept reminding people there was a buffet in the dining room.

"Emma, wow," said Donna. "I had no idea you were sponsoring a ballet dancer. Is he … with somebody?"

She was staring at Emma, who calculated her response.

"He's only twenty-two, Donna."

"I see." Donna's curiosity was not satisfied.

"The firm didn't know you were so involved with the ballet world," said Elton. "We like to publicize our partners' charitable work."

Runciman came and stood with her. She introduced her partners.

"Delighted to meet you, sir," said Elton, shaking hands with his usual intense smile. "Emma's been telling us about her involvement with the ballet."

"Has she? Emma contributes in so many ways."

Emma heard the irony in the director's tone. She changed the topic to the coming season. After several minutes of discussion — Runciman explaining and Elton enthusing — the two lawyers drifted away.

"Emma, you do look smashing. Your beauty is ageless," Alec said. "When I look at you tonight, I understand you and Stefan. You fit with him."

"Thank you, Alec. It would be awkward if you…"

"Disapproved?"

"Yes."

"I don't disapprove. I worry, but I don't disapprove."

Julie came up to her, smiling uneasily. "Stefan has just arrived, and he's brought Tatyana with him."

"He phoned and said they'd be rehearsing late and could he bring her," said Emma. "No problem."

Emma followed Julie to the front hall where Stefan and Tatyana were standing awkwardly.

"Welcome, Tatyana," she said, extending her hand.

"Thank you, Emma," said Tatyana. "You are so very kind." The Russian smiled coolly. She was wearing a violet workout sweatshirt and pants with an orange scarf over her shoulders matching her orange hair and lipstick.

She looks old, thought Emma. She's had a facelift, but they didn't fix her neck.

"Lovely to see you," said Emma. "Get a drink and come on in."

Stefan walked beside Emma as they entered the living room. Bill Shrubb glanced at Tatyana and walked to her quickly. They embraced briefly. Emma noticed the tension in Shrubb's face. She turned to the guests and waited for silence.

As she concluded her remarks, she added, "For the non-ballet people here tonight, I want to introduce my protégé and friend, Stefan Grigoriev, who will be dancing Romeo in *Romeo and Juliet* this November." The guests clapped enthusiastically. "And with him is Tatyana Vasilievskaya, who will dance Juliet." More applause.

After bowing in acknowledgement, Tatyana wandered to where Runciman was standing. Stefan approached Emma and revealed a package he had been holding behind his back.

"Emma, I have present for you."

She took the package from him.

"I can't open it here. Come."

She led him into the sitting room at the rear of the house and opened the package. She held up a piece of silk with an image woven into its fabric. She spread the piece out on the floor and saw a young knight sitting beside a pond surrounded by flowers, his sword on the ground, while a young woman played a lute and looked adoringly up at her knight. The colours were soft greens, reds, mauves and gold. What will I do with it, she wondered. I'll have to hang it somewhere.

"Stefan," she exclaimed, "It is absolutely beautiful. Look at the colours — so romantic. I love it. Where did you get it?"

"Mama made it," he said with pride.

"How perfect. Your mother! Oh, my darling!"

She embraced him. He kissed her tenderly. She felt tears in her eyes. At that moment, Julie led Frank Thomas and Joshua into the sunroom.

"Someone to see you," said Julie.

Josh rushed to her, hugged her and handed her a package. She opened it and saw it was a book.

"Happy birthday, Grandma. Can we read it?"

Emma laughed.

"Not tonight, my dear. I have to look after my friends."

"Josh, you come with me," said Julie, taking him by the hand. "There's a boy next door. His name is Charlie. He's your age and he's very nice. You guys can play together."

Emma turned to Stefan.

"Sweetheart, would you mind leaving Frank and me alone for a while. I need to talk to him about family stuff."

Stefan smiled and left. She turned to Frank.

"What happened with Carolyn?"

"Nothing good. She told me last week about Julie's invitation and said she wouldn't come. I argued with her, but she wouldn't budge. I told her tonight that I was taking Josh. She walked out and took the car for an hour."

"I thought we might be okay tonight."

"So did I. She's behaving really poorly."

Emma sighed and sat on the sofa.

"Let me be for a minute, Frank. I need to … you know."

"Sure."

She sat all alone, her stomach in a knot. The pianist was playing up-tempo tunes — Broadway and jazz — and the house was filled with the buzz of conversation and laughter. The party was at its height. She looked at Josh's book and Stefan's mother's wall-hanging or tapestry or whatever it was, and smiled weakly.

"Excuse me, madam."

Tatyana was standing in the doorway.

"I must leave now." The voice came from deep in her throat. "Stefan has called a taxi. Thank you for your hospitality."

"A pleasure," said Emma.

The pale-blue eyes revealed nothing. Emma sensed the woman's sensual power. It emanated from her husky voice, her bittersweet smile and the aggressive, hip-accentuated posture.

"Glad you were able to come."

"That little boy,. Is your grandson?" Emma nodded. "Very handsome boy. His mother is here?"

Emma shook her head. "She couldn't be here tonight," she said, wondering where the conversation was going.

"Is too bad. You have one daughter?"

"Two. Anne is studying in Halifax."

"You are lucky woman," said Tatyana. "Nice family. And beautiful. Enjoy."

The Russian turned abruptly and walked away. Emma, mystified, hesitated for half a minute, then left the sunroom. Tatyana was gone and the party was beginning to calm. The catering staff were picking up glasses and plates and mopping up wine spills. Julie came up to her, a frown on her face.

"I just phoned Carolyn and gave her shit. I told her she was an ungrateful little bitch to treat her mother so badly."

"You said that to her?"

"Not in so many words, but she got the message." Julie shrugged. "She hung up on me."

"Of course. You cannot confront Carolyn. It never works."

"Maybe not, but I feel better."

Frank went next door and picked up Joshua for the drive home. Emma went to the hall and saw that Stefan had left without saying goodbye. She grimaced but attended to her guests as they left. Soon only Shrubb and Runciman were left. Emma noticed Shrubb hovering and sensed that he wanted a conversation. She realized that he was not with Tatyana. She didn't want to talk to him and managed to avoid getting drawn in to conversation with him. Eventually he left, looking disgruntled. Runciman waited only to thank Julie and chat briefly with Emma, wanting to leave her reassured. Emma hugged Julie, who walked with her to her car. She returned to her house comforted that Stefan had brought her a present.

Chapter 38

The beginning of the next week was trying for Emma. The Digital Connections sale was about to go through, but the purchasers' financing was held up because of questions about some contingencies in the projected cash flow. Emma had to meet with the accountants in Toronto who had prepared the cash flow: they removed several of their estimates and described the two remaining more clearly in their notes. She was also filling in the gaps in documentation for the New York lawyers that Archer Brown had missed. She was working late most evenings and would have been unable to be home for dinners with Stefan. It was almost a relief for her that he was rehearsing late and spending nights at his flat.

Then Don Elton told her that the lawyers in New York wanted to discuss some loose ends in their deal, mainly the cash flow and its effect on the value of the company. She left for New York on Thursday morning and was back home by midnight of the same day. The next morning, she had to meet with Elton and report that the purchasers were now satisfied. They had accepted the cash flow and agreed on a price. She and Elton then had to prepare a memorandum of understanding for the New Yorkers to sign off on. By mid-afternoon they were done; Elton thanked her and told her to go home.

During that week she thought often of Stefan. Although she missed him, she considered his absence a reasonable sacrifice, given the demands of their separate careers. When she arrived home at four-thirty she poured herself a gin and tonic, put her feet up, and worried. She had found no sign of him in the house, but told herself that they would get together over the weekend. She thought of phoning him but didn't. She found the fabric he had given her and walked around the house looking for somewhere to hang it. Finding no other place suitable she decided it would have to go in the bedroom. That would be a romantic solution that he would like. She poured another drink and sat staring at her September garden. She had set out red chrysanthemums, the sole remaining colour in the fading green. Emma felt lonely. She microwaved some frozen ravioli, drank some red wine, watched the late television news and went to bed exhausted. Tomorrow would be a better day.

However, it was not. Stefan phoned mid-morning to say that they were rehearsing late over the weekend and he would be sleeping at his flat again. She bit her tongue and told him she understood. She suggested they have coffee Sunday morning. She heard him pause, then agree with apparent enthusiasm. She spent the rest of the morning in the garden, weeding and putting tools away in the shed. She ate some leftover ravioli for lunch, then phoned Anne in Halifax. She described her New York trip to Anne, who then updated her mother on her progress with her courses.

As they rang off, Emma heard her doorbell. She walked to the door in good spirits from her chat with Anne. She opened the door to find Bill Shrubb standing there, looking tentatively at her.

"Sorry to show up like this, but I saw your car in the drive."

"So, you just happened to be in the neighbourhood and thought you'd drop in and say hello?"

He flashed a hint of his boyish grin.

"You got me, lawyer. It was planned. You and me gotta talk. Will you let me come in? It won't take long."

She was annoyed but held the door wide open, motioned him in. He refused her offer of a drink.

"This must be serious," she said. "You're not wearing a tee-shirt."

He didn't smile.

"It is serious. Tatyana has left me."

Emma sat nodding silently for several seconds.

"I'm sorry, but I'm not available," she said.

He grimaced.

"Jesus Christ, woman, be human. I'm not heartbroken, but I'm not dancing for joy either."

"You're right," she said. "That was a bitchy thing to say. What happened? Did she say why?"

"She said she was moving to new heights in her career and she thought she needed to be alone, blah, blah, blah. She thanked me for my support. What she really meant was that she had only been with me as payment of a debt she felt she owed me for getting her out of Russia. I knew that, and I knew this day would come eventually. So, it's sad but I'm not heartbroken."

"Where will she go?"

"No mention. That's why I'm here."

"I don't understand."

"Stefan. Is he living here?"

Her heart sank.

"Yes, of course, although he's been staying at his flat this week. I've been in New York and he's been rehearsing late."

He nodded. "Call it coincidence, but Tatyana has been sleeping out this week."

She froze. "What are you saying?" Her voice was barely audible.

"Christ, Emma, do I have to draw you a diagram?"

"You're saying they are together at his flat. Do you have evidence of this?"

"I haven't hired detectives."

"Then how can you possibly know where she has gone?" Her voice was angry. "How dare you come here and insult Stefan and me with your little suspicions."

He rose from his chair. "Emma, you're not being fair. I'm sorry to upset you, but I thought it would help you to find out this way."

"Fuck being fair. You have no proof. I want you to leave. Get out!"

"I hope you survive this," he said when he reached the door.

"Get out!" she screamed.

She returned to the sunroom infuriated. She sat down and tried to calm herself, thinking of the week on Bear Lake, of Stefan's birthday present and his words of love. Shrubb had no evidence. She thought that since he was interested in her, Shrubb was probably jealous of Stefan. That was it, he was trying to weaken her love for Stefan.

Without thinking, she reached for her phone and called Julie.

Emma said hello and poured out a jumbled account of her conversation with Shrubb without waiting for Julie to say a word.

"I don't believe him," Emma said as she finished. "He has no proof, and I know Stefan. He is honourable. He wouldn't do that to me."

Julie was silent.

"What, Jules?" Emma exclaimed. "What are you thinking?"

"I'm thinking I don't know what to think."

"You mean you think he could be right about Stefan?" Emma's tone was shrill.

"Of course, he could be right. That doesn't mean he is. Listen Em, I know how hard this must be for you. Are you seeing Stefan tonight?"

"No. He's been rehearsing late and sleeping at his apartment. He's coming here tomorrow morning for coffee."

"So, Emma, you have to tell him exactly what Shrubb thinks is happening and see what he says. I know how difficult that will be, but it's the only advice I have. At least that way you'll know."

"I'm not sure I want to know," said Emma.

"I understand that. Listen, my love, should I come over?"

"No, thank you. I'm better off alone right now. I'll call you."

For the rest of the day she couldn't remember what she had just been doing even a minute earlier. She drank a lot and watched at least three films on television. She was once again obsessed with the difference in their ages, but refused to believe he no longer loved her. It could not be over; there was no reason for it to end.

She slept little that night. She read, watched television and fussed around the house, tidying and re-arranging things. When the sun rose, she was sitting staring at the garden.

Chapter 39

Stefan had slept with two women in the space of a few weeks. The simple fact that he had chosen to make love to both surprised him, but he refused to have regrets. Nor was he filled with triumphant pride; they were not conquests. He had genuinely loved Emma. He dreaded telling her of Tatyana and had no idea how he would do it. The question of loving Tatyana was complicated. It was necessary that he make love to her, and that made leaving Emma necessary. He had made that decision for the dance. He loved ballet, which meant more to him than any woman; he was beginning to understand that about himself. He also understood that the love Emma had given him was something he would never have again. These thoughts had caused him many changes in mood during the week since Emma's birthday.

The dancing with Tatyana, inspired by their nights together, was exploding. When they rehearsed their pas de deux he lifted her with care and affection, he set her down as if she were a precious child and when he left her to dance solo, his leaps, powered by his desire, hung in the air so that they awed those watching. And he sensed the response in her, her total trust in him and her passion when she danced alone. When they left the hall, they walked several blocks before they held hands. She was happy.

The idyllic time faded, however, when he told Tatyana that he had agreed to have coffee with Emma.

"I see," she said, her expression alert. "Did you invite?"

He shook his head. It was Saturday morning and they were finishing their coffee before leaving for the rehearsal hall.

"So, she invited you and you go like a good puppy?"

"I cannot be cruel to her, Tatyana. She is a good woman."

"Good woman, bullshit," she screamed. "She's an ordinary person who is sucking your talent away. I do not trust you, Stefan. You are too weak, too soft. I must ask Alec to find another Romeo."

She was shaking with anger.

"How can you say that? I only have coffee with her."

"Hah. You give her that shawl your mother made and you don't tell me. Why? Because you are afraid to tell me. All week I wait for you to come to me and say you have broken with her, but it does not happen. Why? Because you are weak and afraid. And now you run to her. Why? To tell her she is finished? No. You will have coffee, kiss her and come back to me. No! It will not be."

"You are jealous," he said contemptuously. "I have no time for this. You are jealous and crazy."

"I'm not crazy!" she yelled. "But I am not Juliet. Now I am Russian bitch and Russian bitch will not rehearse with you today."

She went to the bedroom and slammed the door. He decided he would have to find another place for the night.

Chapter 40

Stefan arrived at Emma's house at ten the next morning and rang the bell, for the first time in ages. He was nervous and exhausted. He had slept in the flat he had shared when he was a student.

"You don't have to ring, you have a key," she said.

"Yah, Emma, I have, but I didn't want to wake you if you are sleeping."

He embraced her affectionately. She went to the kitchen and brought a pot of coffee and two mugs. He was sitting stiffly on the sofa as if he were a guest in an unfamiliar house.

"You've taken all your things from our bedroom and the bathroom," she said. She spoke quietly. She was determined to keep her emotions and her voice under control; she would not scream at Stefan.

"I will be sleeping in my apartment until after the performance in November, Emma. I am sorry but is necessary."

"Is lying to me necessary?"

His smile disappeared.

"What you mean lying to you? I said no lie."

"Who else will be sleeping in your apartment. Who *has* been sleeping in your apartment?"

She saw alarm in his face.

"So, you know," he said quietly.

"Yes, I know," she said. "It seems you have left me. Thrown me away like an old rag."

His face reddened.

"No, Emma, don't say such a thing. Is not like that."

"So tell me how it is, Stefan. You said you loved me when you were fucking that Russian at the same time. Tell me how it is."

"Was not at same time. I never do that."

He forced himself to look at her directly and face the anguish in her eyes.

"I do not love her, I swear to God. Is for the ballet, she says. We will dance better."

"Better than you and me, I'm sure. You couldn't keep me out of the water."

The reference to Bear Lake shook him. He wiped away a tear.

"My God, is a mess. Maybe I make a mess."

"Maybe? So, you thought you would sleep with your Russian until your performance. And then what?"

She saw the confusion in his expression as he tried to find words. She knew how inarticulate he was. Not only was English a second language, she had always thought him dyslexic, a person whose skill was movement and rhythm rather than speech. She was a lawyer. She could humiliate him.

"I don't know, Emma," he muttered. "I don't know what I think."

"Do you plan on staying with her? Or would you come back to me? Or would there be someone else you could try for a couple of months?"

"You are not fair to me."

"Were you fair to me?"

She saw his expression change as he got up from the sofa.

"Maybe no. I thought we could be friends. Maybe I'm wrong."

"I loved you," she exclaimed, no longer able to control her voice. "I gave you everything I had. Everything you wanted. And now I'm a piece of garbage."

His eyes were angry.

"You sponsor me, and I am grateful. But you think you buy me. You think because of money you own me. Is not true, madam. I am free and I want to dance. That is all that is important for me."

"So, you leave me when you no longer need me. Rhoda Marks or somebody will take you on and you can fuck them. You make me sick."

"Madam, you have children, grandchildren, nice house, everything. And me, I have only dancing. Like Tatyana has only dancing. She says we help each other to dance great. I believe her. That is everything for me. But I do not love her."

"Did you love me, when you said those words?"

He hesitated. "Yah, I think so."

"I think it's time for you to go, Stefan," she said quietly.

He began walking to the door.

"I understand you are hurt, Emma. I wish you were not."

"Go now," she said.

She began to cry as soon as the door closed. She walked to the kitchen and poured herself a double gin and tonic. By the time she was sitting in the sunroom, tears were streaming down her cheeks and she was trembling. She grabbed the arms of the chair and squeezed, but the shaking continued. She stood up and walked into the kitchen and back; the walking relaxed her nerves and the trembling stopped. She didn't know what to do. She was afraid that if she sat down, she would start to tremble again. Suddenly the message, 'Call Julie', flashed from her cerebral cortex. She had no idea where her phone was. She went again to the kitchen, but it wasn't there. She returned to the sunroom and found it in plain view on the sofa.

"You've been crying," said Julie as soon as she heard Emma's voice. She immediately added, "I'm coming over."

Julie was at the door in twenty minutes. She embraced Emma and wiped her runny nose.

"I come with tissues," she said. "Always be prepared. Emma, you look a mess. Did you sleep last night?"

"No, I didn't. I'm a wreck. And a stupid wreck. You know what,

Jules? I listened to him and I even sympathized. He thinks screwing the Russian will make their performance better. What was I thinking? What did I expect?"

"You weren't stupid, you were in love. And love makes us stupid sometimes."

Emma started to laugh, but the laugh had a hysterical quality and she began to tremble again. Julie took her by the arm.

"Come with me."

She led Emma upstairs to her bedroom and laid her on her bed. She lay down beside Emma and put her arms around her.

"You need to be held right now, my dear," she said. "Have someone's arms around you."

Emma sighed and snuggled into Julie who held her for several minutes until she fell asleep.

Chapter 41

Stefan walked slowly from Emma's house back towards his flat. He kept debating with himself, repressing feelings of guilt. What he had done was necessary. It took him forty-five minutes to reach home. When he entered, she was not there. He went to the bedroom and checked the closet. Her clothes were still there.

He sat, feeling some relief — at least the breakup with Emma was over. He could not get the image of her anguished face out of his mind, so he turned on the television to his wrestling channel. This kept him preoccupied for half an hour until he heard her key turn in the lock.

"So, my hero, my Romeo is back," she sneered. "Wrestling is good for you. Maybe you learn something from that. Maybe that is your career."

"I told her." It wasn't exactly the truth, but close enough.

Her face glowed and her mouth broadened into a wide smile.

"You tell me true? You do not lie to me?"

"I do not lie," he said.

She turned off the television, came and threw herself on his lap and kissed him.

"So, we can do it, my Romeo. We will dance like lovers."

Chapter 42

Emma's descent began later in the afternoon when she woke with her head throbbing. Darkness was falling outside, and her window was misted over. She called Julie, but there was no answer. She knew that anguish, in the figure of Stefan, hovered at the edge of her mind, but she refused to acknowledge it. She would keep herself busy. She heard the static from the television room, walked in and turned it off. The room was littered with newspapers and magazines. She gathered them up and walked downstairs to the garbage bin. Tea, she thought; that's what I need. She put the kettle on. Soon she was sitting at the kitchen table sipping her tea, thinking how badly the cabinets looked. They needed either to be replaced or painted. Suddenly her stomach began to heave. She ran to the bathroom toilet and just managed to get her head over the bowl when she vomited. There was short relief from painful nausea, but it soon returned, and she vomited again. She continued to vomit for several minutes until the heaves were dry.

Nothing left, she thought. I must relax.

She went to the liquor cupboard. There was no tonic for the gin, so she poured herself half a tumbler of whiskey and added ice. She sat looking at the twilight silhouettes of bushes in the garden outside, tryng to focus.

This is not a good idea, she thought, looking at her glass. She drank some of the whiskey, and after a minute it seemed to have calmed her stomach. She drained the glass and lay back. Her nerves stopped vibrating and her head felt lighter. Not such a bad idea, she muttered.

When she shut her eyes, however, the image of Stefan on water-skis, smiling and sun-drenched, came to her.

She began to cry. The reality of her loss overwhelmed her; she could not bear the memory of him. She went to the cupboard and poured herself another drink. When she returned to her seat his image was gone and her fear and longing had given way to anger. He was a cheat and a liar. How long had he been deceiving her, while saying that he loved her? As her anger focussed it became hatred, revulsion at the memory of his face.

No!

She began to pace. It was wrong to hate him. The poison of her emotion would harm her, madden her. It was not his fault. How could she have expected to hold him, this magnificent dancer, this beautiful young man? She thought of her body and felt a sudden revulsion. Her breasts sagged and her belly was no longer flat. Wrinkles defiled her. How could he have wanted her? Had it been her money after all?

No! She knew that wasn't true. He had loved her.

It's the goddamned booze, she muttered. It depresses me.

Her phone rang. She saw Julie's number and put the phone down. She did not want to talk to Julie or see her. She felt enclosed in her house, as if she were in a subterranean cave. Her pain was private and not even Julie should intrude. She must heal herself. She let the phone ring until she saw the message light. She walked to the front hall, set the phone on a side table, and locked the door. Then she got her glass from the sunroom, went to the kitchen and filled it again. She felt safe in her cave with her whiskey.

During the dark hours between midnight and daybreak she lay stiff as a board in her bed, going over every hour she could remember of her time with Stefan, wondering when it had started to come apart or whether she had caused it by something she had done. There were mild bouts of nausea during the night, but she didn't vomit. Next morning, Monday, having slept very little, she phoned the receptionist and asked her to tell Don Elton she was ill and wouldn't be coming to work. She had vomited up a poached egg. She had wanted to go to work, thinking it would be a distraction, but the vomiting kept her at home, her mind churning. She continued to think of Stefan in every light, from every angle, and her feeling about him continued to rage and revolve. She did this in front of the television, ignoring the series of shows on dressmaking and the soap operas that were morning television.

Elton phoned about eleven. He hoped her illness was minor. The Digital Connections deal had closed, and the purchasers were throwing a celebration in New York at the Pierre on Wednesday of the next week — cocktails and dinner. She had to be there; she had made an impression in New York. Emma stared at the phone. The idea of lawyers and New York was not appealing.

"Sounds great," she said quietly. "Look, Don, if I can't go, take Donna."

"Can't do it. She quit this morning."

"My God, why?"

"She got a job with the family business. Corporate counsel. Suits her. You know she wasn't brilliant on Digital."

"Right. Okay. Don, I'll keep you posted."

Digital Connections doesn't matter, she thought. What people do to each other matters.

Julie phoned a few minutes later. She told Julie that she wasn't desperate and wanted to be alone. Julie could come the next day.

"That's not good, Emma. At a time like this it's dangerous to be alone."

"Why? I'm not suicidal. See you tomorrow."

She hung up too abruptly; her patience was wearing thin, even with Julie.

She prepared a lunch of consommé, dry toast and ice cream. She managed to keep them down; so, she celebrated with another glass of whiskey. She vowed it would be her last of the day.

Somehow the afternoon passed. Later in the afternoon, she heard a key turn in the front door lock.

"Hi, Mum." It was Anne's voice. She stood in the entrance to the sunroom staring at her mother. "Jesus, you look bad. It's all black under your eyes, and they're bloodshot. Are you okay?"

"I'm okay."

"Are you sleeping?"

"No. Who told you?"

"Julie. She phoned me yesterday."

"And Carolyn?"

"Julie asked me to phone her."

"And?"

"She didn't say much. I'll phone her later if we don't hear from her." She sat beside Emma and put her arm around her. "How's my mum? Rough times?"

"I feel like such an idiot. Everybody told me, everybody warned me." Tears moistened her eyes.

"Forget idiot, Mum. Really, if there's one thing you're not, it's stupid. Better to have loved and lost, you know. And was he ever cute. What else could you do?"

Emma stared at her daughter, surprised, then began to laugh.

"So, you're saying, if I fell for a boy-toy at least he was a good boy-toy?"

"Good? He was devastating. You had to."

Now Emma was giggling. "Oh, my Anne. You're good for my soul."

They heard the front door open. Carolyn strode into the sunroom. She removed her sunglasses and stared at her mother. "Mum, you look like shit."

"I know. I don't feel very well."

"So, he did it to you, the bastard." Carolyn looked around the room. "This place is a mess. What are all these glasses?" She sniffed one. "Whiskey. So, what have you been doing? Why didn't you put your glasses away?"

"I forgot."

"Jesus." She picked up the glasses and took them into the kitchen. "Holy shit. There are three more here." She returned to the sunroom. "I don't believe this. You're too pissed to clean up after yourself."

173

"Carolyn, please don't lecture me," said Emma, tears in her eyes. "I can't take it right now."

Emma began to sob. Anne put her arm around her mother's shoulder. Carolyn stared at her mother, dumbfounded. Then her face reddened with anger.

"That goddamned dancer did to this to you," she exclaimed. "I want to kill him. He doesn't deserve to live." She looked at her mother and her expression softened.

"Forget about him," Emma sobbed. "What about my grandson? You tell me nothing."

After a moment of stunned silence, Carolyn burst into tears and stood looking helpless. Anne rose from the sofa, took her by the hand and sat her beside her mother. Carolyn put her arms around her mother's neck, laid her head on her shoulder and sobbed. Emma stroked her hair.

"He's better," Carolyn blubbered. "The medication seems to be working."

"Thank God," said Emma.

"Our father did it to you and now this asshole," said Carolyn, wiping her eyes. "It's men."

"Not all men," said Anne. "Frank's okay."

"Says you." Carolyn's eyes flashed. "You should see him playing cute with the women he flies."

"He's very good-looking," said Anne. "And you got Josh with him."

"If God created the world, why did he invent this stupid system, men, women and sex?" said Carolyn. "Nothing but trouble."

"But fun sometimes," said Anne. "Sorry, Mum."

Emma smiled. "I'm going to see if Julie would like to come over and have pizza with us. Anne, please phone Julie and then order for us. Da Maria delivers and their pizza is good. None for me, please."

"Mum, you know you have to eat," said Carolyn. "You can't survive on whiskey."

"I've been vomiting," said Emma. "I'll try one slice."

"Vomiting," said Carolyn. "The bastard."

Julie came and opened a bottle of chianti. Carolyn warned Emma not to drink too much. The conversation turned to Josh's school and Anne's PhD thesis. There was laughter. Emma found herself barely thinking of Stefan. The pizza arrived, she ate a slice and enjoyed it.

Chapter 43

Emma's physical problems had mostly disappeared by the weekend. Anne returned to Halifax on Friday, Julie and her husband went to Montreal, and Carolyn and Frank took Josh to Frank's brother's cottage for the weekend. Loneliness fell on Emma like the grey autumn rain. She kept imagining the sounds of her front door opening and his tread in the hall. When seconds later she heard the silence of emptiness, she would fall into despair. She went to work Monday morning, with little to do.

Over the next couple of days, she kept to herself in her office and turned down suggestions for lunch. She spent her afternoons going to movies and shopping without buying. She had several drinks before bed, thinking they would help her sleep. When she looked in the mirror next morning, she saw bags under her eyes and creases in her skin that she couldn't remember seeing two months before. And, most upsetting, she was aware of a diminished sense of herself. She wasn't sure who she was anymore.

Was she a wealthy, self-centred person who had used Stefan for her own pleasure, or was she the victim of his deception and betrayal? Was she being punished in some Presbyterian way for the life she had led or was she just unfortunate, a random person who had experienced random harm? Had she chosen him or was she driven by needs and forces beyond her control, a feather in the wind? Was she a good lawyer? Did anybody care? Was her love for ballet genuine or the fantasy of a depressed person who needed entertainment? What did she want for the rest of her life and what should she do tomorrow?

She looked forward to the distraction of the trip to New York. They left Wednesday morning. The flight down with Don Elton was enjoyable. He told one of his jokes — she managed a chuckle — then they revelled in the great success of the Digital deal and gossiped about their partners. The dinner was even better. She was placed beside Miranda, the lawyer who had worked with her on the deal, and who had given her and Donna baseball tickets. They chatted easily; it was a relief for Emma to talk with an articulate, attractive person who knew nothing about her troubles. Moreover, the meal was excellent, featuring a filet of beef encrusted with foie gras and mushrooms, and a superb claret.

Speeches, however, accompanied the dessert and coffee. The president of the purchasing company — a communications firm located in Dallas — welcomed them all and thanked "our Toronto friends" for their good work. He complimented his New York lawyers on their choice of the fine red wine and then began to extol their deal as a contribution to the prosperity of the United States and the entire civilized world. He showed no sign of letting up until one of his colleagues whispered in his ear and pulled him down. One of the lawyers, not as drunk but no less verbose, replied, complimenting the Texans on their business acumen and 'get up and go'. The American lawyers were Miranda and five men who looked to be in their fifties, products of many hours on exercise machines. Emma was bored and wanted to leave. She glanced at Elton who was regaling one of the lawyers with a joke. How do I get out of here, she wondered.

"Emma?" She turned to Miranda. "You look glum all of a sudden. Is something the matter?"

Miranda was looking at her with concern. She was a beautiful woman with dark eyes and hair and full lips. Emma guessed that she must be Italian.

"Nothing serious," she said. "Although I have to say, speeches are not my thing."

"Not mine, either," said Miranda. "The boys sure do go on. But Emma, you look really unhappy. Are you sure you're okay?"

Emma had drunk her share of the claret. She looked at Miranda's sympathetic smile and shrugged.

What the hell, she thought. What the hell.

"My boyfriend dumped me," she said. "It hasn't been fun."

"You poor thing." Miranda rested a hand on her arm. "What kind of jerk would lose a woman like you? Tell me."

Emma smiled shyly and began an abbreviated account of her relationship with Stefan. Her friend's smile was warm and sympathetic.

"So, there it is," Emma concluded. "I should have known better. I feel so stupid."

Miranda squeezed her arm.

"Emma, you are a brilliant lawyer and a beautiful woman. You feel stupid right now because that dancer humiliated you. I have an idea." She removed her hand from Emma's arm. "Why don't you come to my place and sleep over? You could use some sympathetic company."

Emma looked into the dark eyes and the warm smile.

Why not, she thought. I hate being alone.

"What about your friend, the baseball player?"

"He's gone, disappeared into the mists of time, or something. There'll be just the two of us."

"What a sweet idea. Let me go and talk to my boss."

She rounded the table. Elton had just completed a story and the men were roaring with laughter.

"Don, I'm beat. I'm going to get a cab to our hotel."

"Okay, honey." He finished his glass of wine. "I'll be along in a little while."

She returned to Miranda. "Miranda, I really appreciate your offer, but the boss says we have an early morning flight. I'll have to go back to our hotel and get some sleep."

The woman's eyes narrowed.

"What a shame. Maybe next time."

"Maybe."

Emma hurried to the door, trying to avoid running.

*

What was I thinking? She was staring at her flushed face in the bathroom mirror. *I would have gone with her. I almost did. It would have been fine, just a friendly cuddle. But I didn't want it.*

By the time she was ready for bed, she understood that it was Stefan's arms she wanted to cuddle her. But there would be no Stefan. and tonight she had chosen to be alone. Was she stupid, really? She lay awake, tormented and angry in her loneliness.

*

They arrived back Thursday afternoon about three. Elton was seriously hungover and slept for most of the flight, snoring peacefully. She took a cab to the office; Don went directly home. She checked her messages and found she had a text from Miranda.

"Yes, I was disappointed, but you know what's best for you. I know you will conquer your sorrow. If you ever need a friend, I'm here. Affectionately, Miranda."

Why hadn't she gone? Was it some latent Presbyterian taboo in her, or was it street smarts of some kind? Or, horrible thought, was she being loyal to Stefan?

She went home eventually, fixed herself an omelette and started to drink gin and watch the television news. Loneliness seized her and bit at her heart. It was unbearable; she decided she couldn't live through another night alone. She picked up her phone and called Ryan Connell.

"It's Emma," she said when he answered. "Would you like to come over tonight?"

There was a brief silence.

"I thought we were through, Emma."

"Forget that. Would you like to come over tonight?"

"No hard feelings, is that it?"

"Right."

"Good. Listen, I'm tied up 'til Sunday night. Your place?"

"My place."

"Geez Emma, like old times. See you Sunday."

She put aside her phone and sat amazed. She had acted on instinct, phoned without thinking, but she quickly put aside her doubts. She had made a decision and acted on it and as a result was feeling less helpless. She had been his lover for years and the prospect eased her despair. At least she would not be alone.

*

He arrived with a bottle of champagne. They drank a glass, talked uncomfortably and briefly, and then she led him to the bedroom. Ryan was still effective; the sex was good. They finished the champagne in bed, without saying much. Ryan got dressed as soon as he could and made an awkward exit. She was not sorry to see him go, but the lovemaking and the champagne had blurred her loneliness. She managed to fall asleep easily.

When she woke Monday morning, however, the house was empty, and she was alone again. The despair returned. The memory of rutting with Ryan Connell made her sick. She loathed herself.

Chapter 44

Stefan and Tatyana stood facing each other. Brent Sokolovski was standing beside them, telling them what he wanted. They nodded, he withdrew and signalled the pianist, who struck a chord. The couple took their dance positions, she began to play, and they began the balcony pas de deux from *Romeo and Juliet*. Dancers and staff had gathered in the hall to watch.

"They're beautiful," murmured Dora. "Boss, you've done it. They're sensational." She was sitting with Alec Runciman in chairs arranged for them, to one side of the hall. The director didn't respond, but kept his eyes fixed on the dancers.

"It's not bad," he said finally. "They still have a way to go."

"Gosh, I think they're unbelievable. What's wrong with them?"

"It's all about them at this point. They aren't the star-crossed lovers Romeo and Juliet, they're Stefan and Tatyana, dancing like stars who are really pleased with themselves."

"I know you see that," she said. "To me, they're wonderful."

"Look at Tatyana. She's smiling at him as if she were a mature woman who wants to take him to bed, not a shy teenager in love for the first time. And he's revelling in it. He needs to be a little more star-struck."

"It's really sexy, though."

"It's blatantly sexy and that's the problem. We need less lust and more the tenderness of young love. I know Tatyana can do it, and Stefan should have learned by now."

"So, they're living together? Is that the problem?"

"Shouldn't be. The theory is that having sex together makes them more sensitive to each other. I'll have to talk to Sokolovski."

"I feel sorry for Emma. Have you seen her?"

"No, I haven't. I had assumed she was devastated, and didn't want to intrude until she was over the worst part. I'm not good at consoling the heartsick, you know. But I phoned her yesterday and I'm going to her house after I leave here."

"I'm sure she'll be happy to see you."

"I don't know. She sounded subdued on the phone."

*

As he rang Emma's doorbell, the director felt guilty that he had not been in touch earlier. He kept reminding himself that he had a ballet company to run. He was not paid to listen to donors with emotional problems.

"Alec, thank you for coming." Her voice was barely audible.

He looked at her and was shocked. Since he had last seen her she had lost weight, her cheeks were hollow, her eyes lifeless and she walked with her head down in a shuffle.

My God, he thought, I've had a hand in this.

As he followed her in, he realized that her beauty had been

important to him from the beginning, not in a romantic way but as a complement to the beauty of ballet, the music, the sets and the movement of the dancers' bodies. She belonged in his world. When she counselled him, her physical presence was delightful; it reassured him. But this survivor, this victim, belonged in some other place. He noticed an empty glass on the coffee table; books and magazines were strewn on the sofa and the floor. He took a seat and began stroking his ponytail. He was nervous.

"How are you, Emma?"

"All right, I guess. Would you like a drink?"

"A whiskey, please."

She went to the kitchen and returned with his whiskey and a glass of a clear liquid. He knew she drank gin.

"How am I, you ask?" she said. "He dumped me. You warned me about that."

"Yes, I did." He said. "I'm very sorry about how things turned out."

"Why are you sorry? You did what you could. But you didn't understand what was happening and that meant your advice couldn't help me. I was not some horny old broad looking for a boy-toy, which everybody thought, including you."

"That's absolute nonsense! You have no idea what I thought."

"Now I don't care what you thought." Her voice was harsh and her eyes were angry. "What none of you understand is that Stefan really loved me. His tenderness and his passion were real. No one can behave that way as a performance. I know this. I was there. You people were not."

He thought there was a hint of paranoia in her use of the words, "you people".

"Emma, you are my friend, and I believe what you tell me. I believe that he loved you. But how did he love you? He loved you the way a dancer loves."

Her eyes flashed. "What the fuck does that mean?" she demanded angrily. "Is he not human? Am I not human? Are ballet people special? Do they live by different rules? Do they love in different ways? Is that what you did, love them and leave them?"

He sighed. "My dear, if we are going to talk you must calm down and listen to me. And my experience is not something we need to talk about. Understood?"

She nodded.

"Now as I said, I don't doubt that Stefan loved you; he is an honourable man."

She snorted.

"Listen to me. Stefan loves dance and he loves it more than anything. Do you understand the hours of practice he has put in every day, almost, since he was eleven or so? And do you understand that he could not have worked that hard for so long unless he were driven by a passion that most people never experience?"

She nodded again.

"Good. So, you arrive on the scene, you admire him, and you sponsor him. What does that mean to him? It does not concern the money, which is only a means to an end. It means that you have become part of the ballet of his life, if I may put it that way. You have joined his dance, and of course he loves you for it. To complete the analogy, he loved you the way he would have loved a ballerina who was his partner."

She remembered the night on the dock when her drunken Stefan lifted her. "My ballerina," he had said, before they toppled into the water. She remembered how they looked, surfacing in the water, and how they laughed on the dock. She winced.

"So, you are saying that the show is over for me; he needs a new ballerina, it's time to move on. And I am some kind of collateral damage."

"In a way that is what I am saying. As far as being collateral damage, that's up to you."

She got to her feet, her gin in her hand.

"Are you people all like that? Is that how you lived your life?"

"I didn't come here to answer your questions about my life, and I will not. What I will say to you is that for all of my adult life, as a dancer and now as the company's artistic director, the show is the thing. Nothing else matters."

She set her gin down. There were tears in her eyes. The director stared at her apprehensively.

"I'm so sorry, Alec. I should never intrude that way. As you can see, I'm a mess right now and I make poor judgements." She wiped her eyes. "Please, tell me one thing. Do you think he misses me?"

"Don't know. How could I know?"

She started to cry. The director had a moment of panic, imagining her clinging to him, crying on his shoulder.

"If you're going to blubber, I'll have to go."

She stopped crying and forced a smile.

"I wish I could help you, but I'm not good in emotional situations, especially when they get heavy. What I'm good at is putting ballets together."

"Please don't go," she said. "I'm going to get another drink. Do you want one?"

He shook his head. She returned from the kitchen with another gin.

"I'll have to be going soon," he said. "I have a meeting with Sokolovski at six. The show really must go on. My dear, you really must put all of this behind you. Is there no one else?"

She sipped her drink; she hesitated. "Okay," she said finally. "Here goes."

She told him of her experience with Miranda at the dinner in New York. At the end of the story he was smiling at her sympathetically, but said nothing. She then told him of her evening with Ryan Connell; as she concluded, his distaste was clear from his expression.

"Any port in a storm, I guess. Must be a common reaction in your situation, but not a solution. Neither is alcohol, by the way."

She held firm to her glass. "I know, but it's all I've got right now."

He shrugged. "Tell me something." He paused. "It seems to me you fell for him like a teenager, head over heels. Nothing wrong with that. It happens here all the time with the students and younger dancers. I have to keep an eye on these passions to make sure they don't become disruptive." He looked at her. "Didn't you get this out of your system when you were seventeen?"

The question surprised her. She remembered her attraction to Neil in high school.

"No, I didn't. I was still a faithful Presbyterian when I got married. I knew my duty, but there was nothing…."

"Nothing like Stefan?"

"Nothing like Stefan. When the marriage broke up I had two girls to raise, so I wasn't looking for romance. When they were older I hooked up with Ryan, but that was purely sexual."

"So, you never had a young person's first love?"

She agreed.

He hesitated and looked at her tentatively. "May I make an observation?"

"Okay."

"In my experience, personal and otherwise, youthful passions are ecstatic. Your first love is like no other experience and while it lasts, you are transported to some other place. The ecstasy is short-lived, however. Sometimes it ends in heartbreak, but sometimes the relationship continues, and in that case, it transforms itself into a more mundane routine as reality sets in. Children arrive, careers are started, and the lovers' bliss is replaced by worries about money, success and all that. All right so far?"

She nodded.

"So, you were in love with Stefan, but he was not in love with you that way. He is in love with dancing. When his reality does set in for him, it will be about building his career, dancing all over the world, hiring an accountant, managing fatigue, handling failure and so on. It will never be for him again as it is right now, in his pure joy of the dance. And you understand, my dear, that you cannot be a part of that, unless you want to give up your career and follow him around, managing his travel arrangements and getting his clothes cleaned."

"I do see that," she said with a smile.

"And for you, the bliss is over and reality returns, but it's not a new reality. It will be the one you have had: your law practice, your family and friends and, I hope, your priceless support of me."

"Not so bad, I hear you saying."

"Not so bad."

"I accept that." She frowned. "But you have been lucky in your life, Alec. There is far more romance in directing a ballet company than there is in the practice of law."

He laughed.

"I cheated. I fell in love with ballet when I was a teenager, but when I became too old to dance, I managed to move into ballet administration. I've never lost my commitment to dance. I love it to this day."

He got up to leave.

"Time to meet Sokolovski." He turned to her. "Emma, you will get out of this adolescent misery. You were blindsided, hit by a truck, but the Emma I know will survive and return to the adult world. I look forward to that."

"Adolescent," she exclaimed with a wry smile. "What an insult!"

"Only if you think it is. Give me a hug, Emma, provided you don't get tears on my jacket. It's silk, from a tailor in Shanghai."

*

"How is Emma?" asked Brent Sokolovski.

"She'll live," said the director. "These things take time."

They were meeting in Runciman's office to discuss Tatyana and Stefan and their dancing. Runciman outlined his concern: the egotism and lack of sensitivity to their characters. Sokolovski agreed.

"That's exactly right," he said. "I've been trying to get the message through, but they aren't listening. Stefan especially seems off in a cloud. And she just keeps looking at him and smiling. She's a pro; she should know better than that."

There was a knock on the door.

"Here they are," said the director. "Let me have a go. I'm in the mood for some straight talk."

Sokolovski opened the door and Tatyana and Stefan entered. Stefan looked surprised, while Tatyana smiled in a casual, unconcerned way. Runciman motioned them to their chairs.

"Brent and I wanted to give you an update on how we think the show is going," he said.

The two nodded and smiled.

"We are not happy at all." The two looked at each other and their faces fell. "We don't think you have entered into the characters you are playing, two teenagers in the thrill of first love. You are dancing like adults who've been around. You are not convincing us."

There was silence in the room. Stefan stared, dumbfounded.

"Please be more specific," Tatyana said. "I don't know what you mean."

"No, Tatyana," Stefan exclaimed suddenly, his face red. "We are dancing great. Everybody in hall is liking us, applauding us."

Runciman looked at Sokolovski and rolled his eyes. Stefan was protecting his woman.

"Shut up, Stefan," she snapped. "You do not know what is correct. Alec knows. Please continue, Alec."

Stefan slouched in his chair. The director began to elaborate, citing what he had seen over several weeks. He was specific. When the music was doing this, they should be doing that. When the mood of the music changed, their dancing must change to reflect it.

"Tatyana, you have danced the role before, you know you are a young girl in love. Then stop looking at him as if you want him. And Stefan, when you do your solos, remember you are young and innocent. Now you are leaping around the floor like a rutting stag."

"What means rutting stag?" asked Stefan, still flustered.

Sokolovski explained. A sly smile crossed Stefan's face as he glanced at Tatyana.

"Maybe you have to keep away from me, Stefan," she said, arching a brow. "Maybe I corrupt you."

"Corrupt? What is that?"

"Never mind that," said the director. "Tatyana, you do know what it is that we're talking about?"

"I do," she said. "I was not thinking right. Is new relationship."

"And you, sir," Runciman said to Stefan. "Do you understand what I am saying?"

"Maybe," said Stefan, now subdued.

"Tatyana will explain some things to do. And Brent will tell you exactly what he wants from you, because that is what I want from you. If we don't get what we want, I can find someone in New York who will make us happy. I hope you won't make me do that. Okay?"

They both nodded.

"Now you may leave. The ballet master and I have other matters to discuss."

The pair left. Tatyana was smiling, but Stefan was staring at the floor, still in shock.

"Aren't you glad you're not twenty-two, Alec?" said Sokolovski when they were alone again.

"Of course. And so will Stefan be when he looks back at the year he and Tatyana Vasilievskaya danced *Romeo and Juliet.*"

Chapter 45

It wasn't until Emma had pulled herself out of her black hole of isolation and depression that she understood how far she had fallen. Partly as a result of her conversation with Alec Runciman, she hauled herself up into a kind of emotional false dawn, where light was scarce, shapes were hard to discern, but there were indications of sunlight on the horizon. She had cut back her intake of gin and was sleeping better, although she felt tired during her days. One afternoon she fell asleep at her desk and woke to a phone call informing her she was twenty minutes late for a meeting with Don Elton.

Through Bill Shrubb she had brought a new client to the firm, a company that manufactured the hardware that Shrubb used in his artificial intelligence projects. The company, only recently incorporated, was essentially five engineers and some assembly specialists. They were not satisfied with the inexpensive lawyer who had incorporated the business, so Shrubb had put them in touch with Emma. Because of her experience on the Digital Connections project, she was given the file. She threw herself into the work with relief, dealing with patent issues, employment and remuneration issues, financing and tax issues. As a result, she was less often reminded of Stefan Grigoriev, and when she did think of him, she was able to put him out of her mind with a grim smile.

She stayed away from the ballet company's premises. She rationalized this by saying to herself that Runciman had not called and apparently had no need of her help. However, when she phoned Julie to tell her that she would not be going to *Romeo and Juliet,* she had to admit to herself that she would not be able to sit beside her friend and watch Stefan dance with Tatyana Vasilievskaya.

At their Friday meeting at Café Vert, Julie was sympathetic.

"Of course," Julie said. "You've been to hell and back."

"I just can't bear to watch him dance close with that tired old Russian. Give the ticket to someone else."

"So, stay home. Vern's sister will be here, and I'll take her." She paused. "What about the sponsorship? I assume you'll drop it."

"I told Alec I would maintain it."

"Really, that's amazing. Can you do it? I mean, would you be able to stand the involvement with him?"

"I don't know. I think so. It's an ego thing. If I drop him, people will see it as evidence of the impact of the breakup on me, a sign of my humiliation. I think it's better if I appear carrying on as if there were no huge problem."

"Emma hangs tough," said Julie.

"Not really. But I don't like the victim role."

"Bravo," said Julie.

*

Emma attended Josh's birthday party late in October. Frank picked her up after work and drove her to their house. Carolyn opened the door to an uproar from the boys who were drinking soda, eating hot dogs and cake, and yelling at one another. Carolyn hugged her and made all the boys shake hands with her. Emma watched Josh open her two presents, an age-appropriate picture book about Jacques Cartier's voyage to America and a new tee-shirt with a cute puppy design. The boys whooped and hollered as each gift was opened. Then Frank led her to a living room, away from the bedlam, and poured her a drink. They chatted about her new client for forty-five minutes, and then parents arrived to take their boys home. Josh came into the room with his book.

"Read to me, Grandma," he said.

She held out her arms and he climbed onto her lap. She read for half an hour, holding him close. She was suddenly happy, kissing him lightly on the top of his head as she read. Carolyn entered the room, hugged her mother, and took Josh off to bed.

"Drive Mum home, Frank," she said. "She must be exhausted."

They didn't speak for the first ten minutes of the drive.

"You're great with Josh," Frank said. "You're a terrific grandma."

"He's easy to love, Frank. He takes after you."

"Thanks," he said. "Emma, you look in fairly good shape. Carolyn told me things have been pretty rough for you."

"They were, but I'm surviving. And Josh's birthday! I can't tell you how good that makes me feel."

*

Days later she received a mid-morning call from Bill Shrubb. She hesitated before picking up.

"So, did it take you two minutes to decide if you would talk to me, or were you in the washroom?" The familiar cheeky tone made her smile.

"It wouldn't take me ten seconds to make up my mind about you, Bill Shrubb. I was busy then, but I have a moment now. Consider yourself lucky. What's this all about?"

He suggested that she come to his premises to see Algorhythmics' progress in their hologram project and then join him for lunch. She paused before answering.

"And why would I do that?"

"Because the project is interesting. Some of the smartest people you'll ever meet are working on it, including me, and we're running into problems."

"Why do I want to see your problems?"

"Because they're problems at a level most of the world couldn't understand, but you're smart and you could. What's the matter, are you afraid of failure or something?"

Her laugh was bitter. "Are you serious?"

"Right, you could call the Bulgarian a failure, but I don't see it that way. But I asked you over here partly because we've shared the same fate, so to speak. We'll eat and we'll talk."

Again, she hesitated.

"Don't worry Emma, I won't come on to you. I've had enough romance for now, and I assume you have also. I like you, you're fun to talk to and I'm lonesome."

The word lonesome moved her.

"I'm coming," she said. "What time?"

She entered the Algorhythmics building at 220 Colby Lane just after noon and stood in the lobby. "Welcome, Emma," said Humphrey Bogart's voice. "Proceed to the second floor and President Shrubb will welcome you."

She climbed the stairs and found Shrubb waiting for her, a broad smile on his face.

"Since when are you 'President' Shrubb?" she asked, before he could open his mouth.

"I am the president of our board here. And not feeling great for the last month, I thought it would cheer me up, raise my self-esteem. Why? You don't like it? You think it's pretentious? What?"

She laughed. "You could never be pretentious, Bill."

He was wearing a tee-shirt that hung to his knees, with the words, "THIS IS NOT A TEE-SHIRT" on the chest.

"So, it's not a tee-shirt," she said. "What is it?"

"First of all, it's not a tee-shirt because it's too long and I know you don't like tee-shirts. Secondly...."

He turned around. On the back was lettered, "THIS IS HOW I COVER MY ASS."

"Brilliant," she said, "and definitely not pretentious. And it does lend you a presidential quality. I'll have to get used to it."

"Take your time. It'll be worth it."

With a smirk he led her to an area in the far corner of the floor where two chairs faced the centre of the room. Shrubb waved to a youth with acne and long blond hair standing in front of a machine, focussing its lens.

Shrubb gestured to him.

"This is Danny," said Shrubb, and Danny smiled. "He's going to operate the hologram projector. Hit it, Danny."

Danny flicked a switch and the image of a ballerina in her tutu appeared in the centre of the room. She began to move but disjointedly, with her body motion in a spasmodic series. They watched her move slowly back and forth in this way for about five minutes.

"This is so impressive, Bill," she said enthusiastically. "I can see you have some kinks to smooth out, but still. It looks like those early nineteenth-century movies, with the jerky movements."

"That's exactly what this is," he said. "Moving pictures. The problem is we can only move one hologram image every quarter of a second, so we can't get continuous motion. But we're working on it."

"So, you're still a distance from producing a holographic ballet."

"We are. Wouldn't it be a benefit to us all if we could replace these human dancers with holograms?"

"How boring," she exclaimed. "You really must be fed up with romance."

"For the moment," he said as he rose from his chair. "Let's go and have some lunch."

They ate in an unlicensed vegetarian café that advertised gourmet vegetarian food.

"I like it here," he said. "The food is good, and there's no booze, which I also like. I got drinking hard hanging out with Tatyana. Got to get back to my old self."

"I guess that's the trick," she said. "Remembering who you are. You mentioned you were lonesome."

"Yeah. With all her craziness, Tatyana was full of energy. There was always something happening, and her emotions were always electric. It was exciting, and I became used to it. Now I'm living the way I always have, and it seems dull and quiet. I miss her."

"I believe you," she said. "I'm probably less lonely, I think. I have my daughters and a grandson, and a good friend."

"So, you don't miss Stefan?"

"At first I did, but not so much now."

"Really? So, you're going to sit in your seat and watch the two of them dance as lovers without hating them?"

"No, I'm not going," she blurted out. "And I'm not going to hate anybody."

"And why aren't you going?"

She fell silent and stared at her plate.

Shrubb went on, "Because it hurts too much, Emma. It's obvious you miss him. Tell me I'm wrong."

She shook her head and wiped her eyes to prevent tears.

"So, here's some advice. Take it or leave it. You must attend the ballet. No matter how much it hurts, you cannot let it defeat you and become a pathetic little victim afraid to leave the house. If it hurts, go home, be sad and keep going. Never ever let what happened to you make you afraid. You belong in the audience on opening night."

She smiled briefly.

"I sometimes think that way. I actually agree with you, in theory." She glared at him. "But doing would be so goddamned hard!"

He held up his hands. "I know. I'm not going to love watching the bitch dance with Stefan, but I'm going. Why don't you come with me? We can prop each other up."

She shook her head. "If I go, I want to be alone. I'm sorry." She saw a flicker of sadness in his eyes. "Look Bill, I do like you, I think you know that. But not in that way. All I need is another boy-toy; I'm too old for you. And right now, I just don't want a social life. But sometime, next year perhaps, I would go to the ballet or have lunch with you, just as friends."

"That doesn't sound bad," he said. "Could I wear my tee-shirt?"

She smiled, he flashed his impish grin and they both began to laugh.

Chapter 46

After days of wavering, Emma Peters decided that she would attend the opening night of *Romeo and Juliet*. The prospect frightened her. She was not sure what pain the night would cause, but she could not bear the thought of being the woman scorned, the victim. She did not tell Julie or anyone else that she was going. She found a seat much higher than her usual subscription seat. She wanted to be away from her friends, and on the aisle so she could leave any time during the performance if she had to.

She arrived five minutes before the curtain rose, wearing a simple black dress.

Emma sat and watched the men and women taking their seats below. The orchestra members were tuning and practising their riffs. She could barely see; she was so fearful of what she was about to watch. She felt a sudden urge to leave before the curtain rose — there was still time — but she could not. She reached into her handbag for painkillers; her head was already throbbing. The conductor entered the pit and bowed to the applause. The lights dimmed and Prokofiev's overture began; the rich, sweeping chords sounded harsh to her ears. The curtain rose and her fists tightened.

I must do this to be free, she thought. Romeo appeared in the first scene, leading the young Montagues in a fight against the Capulets in the town square. Stefan was superb. He took her breath away — his strength and virility dominated the stage. She found herself almost wishing he would be killed in the brawl so that she wouldn't have to endure what was coming. Juliet appeared in the second scene, chatting playfully with her nurse. Emma trained her opera-glasses on Tatyana and was amazed; she looked like a pretty teenage girl. Makeup, she muttered to herself, and lowered her glasses, overcome with hatred. In the third scene, when the masked Romeo slipped into the Capulet ball, saw Juliet and fell in love, Emma took another painkiller.

The last scene of the first act began. Juliet emerged on her balcony and gazed at the moon, dreaming of Romeo. Emma studied her face and saw, through her glasses, the rapture of first love.

Look at her. She's a little girl; he cannot want her.

Romeo entered. He leapt around the stage in delirious joy and then stared up at Juliet in wonder.

Look at him, foolish for that slip of a thing.

Emma sat transfixed as Juliet descended the balcony stairs to Romeo, who waited for her, his arm outstretched. And, as Juliet drew nearer, Emma saw the elegant curve of her body, and the beauty of her features.

She is young and beautiful. She *is* Juliet. My God!

As Juliet approached Romeo, her steps and movements at one with the music and the love in her eyes, Emma was riveted. She leaned forward in her seat, her gaze on the stage, where Romeo — not Stefan, but Romeo — was waiting for Juliet. And when Romeo threw his body into a magnificent male mating dance, circling the stage with stunning leaps and spins, at one with the music, she watched his legs, his buttocks, his arms and his noble face, in awe. The music entered Emma; it sang in her bloodstream. She was both male and female, she was in the dance and the dance was in her — in her muscles, in her nerves and in her heart. And when they embraced and kissed, Emma knew that it was right, and felt joy. When Juliet, committed in love, ascended to her balcony, leaving Romeo below, also committed in love, his arm outstretched, Emma sat there, enchanted.

She understood, as the applause mounted, that what she had seen was a perfection that could never exist except on the stage. Although its beauty had overwhelmed her, it had nothing to do with her. As the scene ended, her anger and hatred had been washed away.

She watched the remaining two acts barely aware of what was happening on stage: the deaths of Tybalt and Mercutio, the banishing of Romeo and the business with Friar Lawrence. In her state of bliss, these petty actions could not register. And when the two star-crossed lovers killed themselves, she felt sympathy but no sadness; perfect love cannot survive in the world of swords and poison. Moreover, she understood that her imperfect love for Stefan was over. The dance was his and she had never been part of it. When the curtain fell, she rose to her feet, applauding. When Stefan and Tatyana took their bows at centre stage, she blew kisses to them and yelled her bravos.

She left the auditorium barely able to find her way. Her head was spinning, and her eyes were dim with tears. Emma had found in those hours a place of music, beauty and love that would never leave her. She smiled at the thought that Stefan was of that world, and she was not. She wished him blessings. She hurried through the lobby and into the night, avoiding her friends. She stood on the sidewalk, waving for a cab, feeling whole and purified.

Chapter 47

In the several days that followed, Emma very much wanted to tell someone of her experience and reveal her transformation. However, there was no one except perhaps Alec Runciman who could understand what had happened to her. The director did phone her, simply to say that he had been surprised to see her at opening night since Julie Fredericks had told him she wouldn't be coming. She began to tell him how much she had liked the performance when he interrupted. He was in a rush and just wanted to touch base — they would meet later and go over everything.

She met Julie at Café Vert the next Friday. Julie admired her courage but assumed that the night had been painful for her. She then recounted how Vern had now restored their fortunes almost entirely, her face glowing with pride. Emma understood that Julie was not ready to hear of her rapture; she held her peace.

She considered phoning Bill Shrubb, but decided not to. She was not in the mood for his banter, given her profound impressions from the ballet, and she did not want him to misinterpret a call. Her need for some kind of discussion was satisfied in an unexpected way, however.

Returning from a forty-five-minute workout in her fitness club, she entered the firm's reception area to find Tatyana Vasilievskaya waiting for her. The woman rose to her feet and approached Emma with her hand outstretched. Emma noticed that her hair was orange again. She wore leather boots, tight blue jeans, a leather jacket and a mauve scarf.

"Forgive me for coming here, please. I know you hate me." Her expression was tense, her tone unsure.

"Please, come in," said Emma, shaking her hand.

Tatyana sat twisting the corner of her shawl. She was nervous. Her physical presence was electric, however; the room seemed to vibrate. Emma understood the impact this woman must have on Stefan.

Where is Juliet, Emma wondered. Where is that innocent girl?

"I was not sure it was a good idea to come here, but I wanted to speak with you." She smiled tentatively. "I understand what Stefan did to you and you know I was part of that. And I know you have suffered. I have suffered also in this way, and that is why I am here. We are both women and we have to deal with men. They are disgusting."

"Not Stefan," said Emma, with feeling. "He's not disgusting."

"So, you say that after what he did to you. He is still a boy. When he becomes a man, he will become disgusting." Pain flickered in her eyes. "I came here not to apologize, but to explain, if you will listen."

"I'm listening," said Emma.

"Stefan will go to Bulgaria after Christmas, to Varna with his mama. I have moved out from his apartment. He has left me as he has left you. He is his mama's now, not mine, not yours. But you are right, he is not a bad person and that is what I want to explain." She took a breath. "In Russia, men and women who dance romantic roles together often sleep together. We think it makes the dancing more natural, more beautiful, if you don't have to pretend the love. So that is what we did. He did not want to hurt you, but I convinced him. I know how to convince."

Emma smiled at these words; the Russian smiled briefly back.

"He said he loved me. He said he loved you. Both are true. But Stefan loves in the ballet way, as I do. What means 'ballet way'? It means you love for the dance, for the art, for the performance, and it ends when the final curtain falls. Stefan does not love me now. He did not ask me to come and meet his mama. And I do not love him. We are through. And if we dance together again … who knows."

"So, Stefan loves only the ballet."

"Yes. He is like me. I will not have what you have — home, children, grandchildren. I must work while I can, so that when dancing is finished I will have enough money so I don't live on the street."

Emma noticed the fierceness in the blue eyes, the absence of self-pity.

"I can do this, Emma. I am Russian and I know the ballet world. I will do what I have to do, and I will not end up on the street, believe me."

"I believe you," said Emma.

"But you are not of this world. Your love is not ballet, your love is the meaning of your life. I hope you will return to your real life, your family and not mourn Stefan. He is not for you."

"I know this now."

"Good. Now you must tell me if you enjoyed the performance."

She was watching Emma carefully, the question in her eyes.

"Yes, I did." Emma spoke passionately. "And I was amazed by you and Stefan. You were children in love. The pas de deux was the most romantic thing I have ever seen."

Tatyana stood, smiling.

"Wait. I want to say something else." Tatyana remained standing while Emma got up from her chair.

"I cannot hate you, certainly not Stefan." Emma paused, searching for the right words. "When I sat in that hall and watched the beauty that you created on the stage, I was overwhelmed with gratitude."

Tatyana's eyes were riveted on her face.

"I understood the years of your lives you have given to make that gift of beauty possible. The complete dedication of the dancers, the designers, Alec Runciman — everybody. This gift is like nothing else I have experienced. Love itself between two people is always partly selfish, but this!"

Tatyana was nodding emotionally.

"You give everything — your hearts, your minds and your bodies — to make for me and for everyone something that is beyond value. What you give is priceless, and in return you receive only money and applause. How can I hate you?"

"I am so glad you understand this, Emma." Tatyana's eyes were burning. "That is why we do it; that is why we live — Stefan, me, Alec, everybody. And if you can feel that ... after...."

She walked around the desk and embraced Emma, no longer able so speak. Emma inhaled the scent of sandalwood; they kissed. Tatyana turned away and walked quickly to the door.

Chapter 48

As the year wound down, the demands of law on Emma eased with the season. Clients were partying, away skiing and preparing for the holiday. She threw a cocktail party for major clients in the upstairs room of the Wellington, a chic midtown restaurant. It was a great success. She was in her element, charming her guests and sending them home smiling. She began to shop for Christmas, gifts for family, friends and clients. She was herself again, moving well in the world she knew. Her life was different now, though. Her regular life was interwoven with the beauty of the ballet world, which had transformed her imagination and illuminated her emotions. The delight that the performance of *Romeo and Juliet* had given her dwindled into the warm feeling of the gratitude she had expressed to Tatyana. It seemed to her, when she thought about it, that she had returned home from a trip to an enchanted land.

Her thoughts of Stefan were less frequent and only occasionally tinged with sadness; sadness, she had come to believe, was in the nature of things. She was content. Stefan was not dancing in *The Nutcracker* this season and was probably already with his mother in Varna. She told herself she was at peace with him. *Tout comprendre, c'est tout pardonner*, she would say to herself. She would throw herself into ballet regardless of Stefan. She looked forward to sharing the rest of her subscription with Julie.

The Christmas season brought the annual presentation of *The Nutcracker* and Emma went to the opening night with Julie. By the end of the first act, however, she was bored. She soon realized that she was comparing the performance with last year's; the excitement of waiting for Stefan to appear was missing. When Ralph Lyndhurst entered to dance the Sugar Plum Fairy's Chevalier, she was determined to give him her full attention. He was not Stefan, though, and she found herself looking forward to the end of the pas de deux.

*

Emma and Anne drove slowly to Carolyn's on a cold, snowy Christmas morning along icy roads that were obscured by blowing drifts. Anne was driving and Emma sat beside her, half dreaming she was going home. It always snows at Christmas in Isherton, she thought. Her father would never pay for a turkey. Instead, he would kill two of their chickens. Her presents were usually clothes that she needed, but one year they gave her a bicycle. They would attend the Christmas service at Knox Presbyterian in Isherwood.

When they pulled into Carolyn's drive, she half expected her parents to answer the door.

This is strange, she thought. I'm a big girl now.

The feeling of being home lasted throughout the day. They settled with the family around the tree and opened presents. Frank had prepared brunch: eggs benedict with smoked salmon and Irish coffee to follow. In the afternoon they watched the film *Love Actually*, which had replaced *A Christmas Carol* as the movie for Christmas Day. Then Anne, Emma and Josh built a snowman on the front lawn while Carolyn and Frank finished cooking the dinner.

The turkey was tender, the stuffing was fragrant and the wine was a spicy zinfandel. There had been no wine on the farm, she remembered with a smile.

As they were finishing the meal, Carolyn stood up and announced that they had received a call from the hospital yesterday with Josh's test results; the infection in his lungs had finally cleared. They applauded Josh who smiled happily, not sure what the excitement was about.

Emma was filled with pleasure as she considered her family one by one: the difficult, passionate Carolyn, Anne, brilliant but gentle, and her beloved Joshua. And Frank, her handsome son-in-law who could endure Carolyn's moods with a smile and keep it all going.

This is it, she thought. This is home.

They moved to the living room, sat in front of a log fire and drank Frank's eggnog as they chatted and laughed. Carolyn sat beside Emma with her head on her mother's shoulder; Emma stroked her hair.

"You can't drive home in this weather, Mum," she said. "You and Annie can sleep in the guest room; there's a king-size bed."

Before they fell asleep, Emma and Anne marvelled at Carolyn's warmth and attentiveness.

"The problem was Josh's lungs," said Anne. "He's well now and she's human again."

Chapter 49

The theme of the ballet company's New Year's ball this year was Hollywood in the twenties and thirties. Guests were asked to dress in the style of those times, possibly imitating a movie star of the era. Alec Runciman had invited her to attend the ball with him. She sensed an unusual nervousness in his tone over the phone. She declined. He was silent for several seconds. "I'm so sorry, Emma, for everything," he said before he hung up.

He's nervous, she thought; he feels guilty. Had Runciman betrayed her? He had not, by his standards, the standards of the dance. It took her five minutes before she decided to call him back.

They agreed to attend the ball together and stay for an hour. He thanked her profusely. In a surge of affection, she invited him to come to her house after the dancing and spend the evening.

"My dear, that would be splendid. How kind you are." He paused. "I don't know about this costume routine. I don't see myself as a twenties gangster. I've never even held a gun in my hand. And I don't see you as a ... as..."

"As a gangster's moll?" She laughed. "Certainly not yours, Alec."

She put down her phone, pleased with their arrangement. She did not want to be alone New Year's Eve. Anne had returned to Halifax, Carolyn and Frank were entertaining their friends on the last night of the year and the Fredericks were spending it at a resort in the Bahamas. Most importantly, she was fond of Alec and felt no bitterness towards him.

*

They stood by the bar watching the flappers and hoods dance by to the big band tunes of the era. She was wearing a simple green dress and he, a grey hemp dinner jacket. He led her onto the floor, and they danced to 'Begin the Beguine' and 'Tangerine'. When they walked to the side, Runciman excused himself. She saw him walk out of the hall. She turned and almost ran into Bill Shrubb, in a striped jacket and straw boater.

"Dancing with the boss, I see," he said. "You look sexy. Working your way to the top?"

"Maybe." She smiled. "And you? Who are you with?"

"Tatyana," he said. "But only for tonight."

Tatyana walked across the floor and put her arm around his neck. She wore white leather boots and ostrich feathers that covered only her midsection.

"Am stripper," she said. "At midnight I strip." Shrubb winced. "What's the matter Billy, you don't like my body?" To Emma she added, "He asked me and I come, but I make him nervous."

The director joined them. Tatyana jumped in front of him.

"You dance with me, boss?"

He looked her up and down. "As long as your feathers don't fall off."

"Don't worry, boss. That happens at midnight." They moved onto the dance floor.

"Don't ask," said Shrubb. "It's better than staying at home. She's crazy but she's fun. But believe me, it really is only for tonight."

"I believe you," she said, patting his arm.

Runciman returned with Tatyana and motioned to Emma. He took her by the arm and led her out of the hall. They stood in a hallway and he faced her.

"Stefan is not in Bulgaria, Emma. He is here."

His words jolted her.

"What do you mean he is here?"

"He was going yesterday but there has been a huge ice storm in Sofia. The outside airport workers won't work and so planes have not been able to land. He's flying out tomorrow."

She glared at him.

"Interesting, but why do I have to know this?"

"Because he is right here, in the treasurer's office down the hall."

She held her breath; he watched her expression.

"You set this up." Her tone was harsh and accusing; he nodded. She took a deep breath. "Obviously, you have spoken to him."

"Yes. At first, he wouldn't hear of it. He thinks you must hate him and would refuse to see him."

"And you said?"

"That you might refuse to see him, but you were not the kind of person who did much hating."

"So he agreed."

He nodded.

"All right Alec, I'll do it; I have no choice. Where do I go?"

He took her to the treasurer's office door, patted her shoulder and walked away. She stood looking at the door for a minute and then knocked. The door opened and there was Stefan, his face frozen in a tense smile. He didn't speak. She brushed past him into the office, took a chair by the coffee table and motioned him to the other. He sat. His dark eyes were moist.

"Hello, Stefan," she said.

"Hello, Emma." His voice was barely audible. "Emma, I can't speak. I don't know…."

"It's all right Stefan. We'll sit until we want to talk. It's good to see you."

She was moved by his obvious distress. At the same time, she was relieved that the passion she had felt for him had softened to sympathy.

"You think that? I thought you would hate me."

"I don't hate you."

"You don't hate me? I know you have suffered pain because of me and Tatyana."

"Yes. I suffered. I loved you, and you left. Of course I suffered."

Stefan wiped tears from his face. "Emma, believe me. I did love you. I try to explain."

"You loved me like a ballet dancer, Alec says."

"He said that?"

"Yes. And I have also talked to Tatyana."

"Jesus. Why you talk to her?"

"She came to me. But let me explain something to you. I came to watch you dance Romeo to her Juliet."

"I did not know you came, Emma. I was sure you would not." He shook his head. "I think maybe it was not good for you."

"You don't understand. You were superb, both of you. I came that night full of anger and fear, and left in tears, delighted. You created the love of Romeo and Juliet on that stage, the way you moved, the way you looked. You were not Stefan and Tatyana, for me you were Romeo and Juliet. You made me feel love."

He looked at her in wonder.

"That is what we do. You understand that?"

"I understand. And I know that the love you create on the stage exists only on the stage, never in the everyday world of men and women. And I know that you were not deceiving me when you said you loved me. You loved me as you would a ballerina. And I am not a ballerina, as we found out on the dock."

For the first time, he smiled.

"I tried," he said.

"Yes. And I love that you tried. But you must dance, Stefan. You will dance with many dancers and you will love them all. And I will watch you dance and admire you more than anyone in your audience, because I know you as no one else does."

"Emma, you break my heart."

"Good. You'll know how it feels." She got up to leave. "Just a joke. You'll get over it, I'm sure."

"Will I see you again?"

"Possibly. I will certainly continue to sponsor you. But no more dinners, at least for now."

"Okay, Emma."

She walked to him, hugged him, and walked quickly from the office. She found Runciman in the hall by the bar, talking to one of the donors, who smiled and walked away.

"Let's get out of here," she said, grabbing his arm.

"How did it go," he asked as she led him to the exit.

"Okay," she said. "He was crying, which made me think he was human. It's over now. Closure, for both of us. Let's go home and drink champagne."

*

By ten o'clock they were sitting in Emma's sunroom. Emma had changed into a blouse and jeans; Runciman took off his dinner jacket and put his stocking feet up on a bolster. Emma produced a bottle of champagne and two glasses.

"This is serious champagne, Alec, not the prosecco they were serving at the ball."

"Budget, my dear. It's always money."

"Thank you, Alec, for arranging the meeting."

"Don't thank me. I need your company tonight." He turned to her. "Do you miss him, Emma?"

"Not really. I thought he had gone to Bulgaria and had put him out of my mind. But obviously I hadn't, given what happened tonight. I think we both felt better about each other by the time I left."

"That's good. And you said you will continue to sponsor him."

"I will. After all, I claimed I was helping his career, not looking for love." She sighed. "I don't ever have to see him if it's difficult. Just write the cheques."

"That is generous, Emma. I hope things work out for you." He hesitated. "You know, he came to me and told me that she wanted him to sleep with her, that it would improve their dancing as lovers." He looked directly at her. "I didn't say no. In fact, I thought there might be something in it. And I think he was going to do it no matter what I said."

"I don't blame you. You were always clear with me that the dancing was your main concern. You warned me."

"Yes. But I could have at least told you. As a friend."

"I don't think that would have made any difference. Although I don't regret any of it, the affair was a mismatch. He was not in love with me in the way I wanted. I knew he would leave me, but I couldn't imagine it. So, he left me."

"But you have come out of it all well, " he said. "Despite everything you have a balanced and sympathetic view of dancers. I'm afraid sometimes I tend to think of them as only dancers, as inventory almost. Occasionally I see myself as a merchant dealing in human bodies." He shook his head. "Is there any more champagne?"

She emptied the last of the champagne into their glasses.

"Hold my hand, dear," he said. "I need your body heat."

His hand was cold. She could feel the bones in his fingers. They felt old. She looked at him and saw the grey in his hair. She felt a surge of affection for this complex, elegant man.

This has been some night, she thought. And here I am, finishing my champagne, with Alec half asleep, feeling strangely fond of him. What is it? Why do I like him, despite … everything?

At this point the director snorted, then lifted his head.

"Sorry, I dozed off," he said.

He yawned and looked at his watch.

"Good God, it's past twelve. We've missed midnight."

"I don't care," she said.

"Neither do I."

"Shall we go to bed? I've set out a night-shirt my son-in-law uses in the guest bedroom."

"How kind," he said. "But please, can we sit for a while? I did nod off a little, but I'm not ready for sleep."

She smiled and nodded. As he looked out the window, the clock in the hall struck the quarter hour.

It's as if we were dancers in our own ballet, she thought. Alec, Stefan, Bill, Tatyana and me, stumbling around, trying to find what we think we want. And how wonderful that, for a short time, I was part of the dance.

She looked at Runciman, at his fine profile.

"Look, Emma," he said looking out the window. "Isn't it just the most beautiful night."

She followed his gaze. A sprinkling of snow was falling from an invisible sky, settling lightly on the boughs of the black spruce at the bottom of her garden.

Acknowledgement

I want to acknowledge those whose talents helped improve this novel. Grateful thanks to Lindsay Fisher, Principal Ballet Master of the National Ballet of Canada, for reading the manuscript and ensuring that my descriptions of the ballet were both accurate and credible. My patient and imaginative editor, Jane Warren, and the meticulous team at Inglewood Press, together improved the book.

Brian Metcalfe

Made in the USA
Monee, IL
30 November 2020